Valentine's Fall

ALSO BY CARY FAGAN

FOR ADULTS

FICTION
The Mermaid of Paris
The Little Underworld of Edison Wiese
The Doctor's House and Other Fiction
Felix Roth
Sleeping Weather
The Animals' Waltz
The Little Black Dress
History Lessons

NON-FICTION
City Hall & Mrs. God: A Passionate Journey
Through a Changing Toronto

FOR CHILDREN

NOVELS
Jacob Two-Two on the High Seas
Mr. Karp's Last Glass
Ten Lessons for Kaspar Snit
Directed by Kaspar Snit
The Fortress of Kaspar Snit
Daughter of the Great Zandini

PICTURE BOOKS
Thing-Thing
My New Shirt
Ten Old Men and a Mouse
The Market Wedding
Gogol's Coat

BIOGRAPHY
Beyond the Dance: A Ballerina's Life (with Chan Hon Goh)

Valentine's Fall

A Novel by Cary Fagan

Cormorant Books

Copyright © Cary Fagan 2009
This edition copyright © 2009 Cormorant Books Inc.
This is a first edition.

No part of this publication may be reproduced, stored in a retrieval system or transmitted, in any form or by any means, without the prior written consent of the publisher or a licence from The Canadian Copyright Licensing Agency (Access Copyright). For an Access Copyright licence, visit www.accesscopyright.ca or call toll free 1.800.893.5777.

Canada Council for the Arts / Conseil des Arts du Canada

ONTARIO ARTS COUNCIL
CONSEIL DES ARTS DE L'ONTARIO

The publisher gratefully acknowledges the support of the
Canada Council for the Arts and the Ontario Arts Council
for its publishing program. We acknowledge the financial support
of the Government of Canada through the Book Publishing
Industry Development Program (BPIDP) for our publishing activities.

Printed and bound in Canada

LIBRARY AND ARCHIVES CANADA CATALOGUING IN PUBLICATION

Fagan, Cary
Valentine's fall / Cary Fagan.

ISBN 978-1-897151-45-7

1. Title.

PS8561.A375V34 2009   C813'.54   C2009-903837-4

Cover illustration and design: Nick Craine
Text design: Tannice Goddard, Soul Oasis Networking
Printer: Friesens

CORMORANT BOOKS INC.
215 SPADINA AVENUE, STUDIO 230, TORONTO, ONTARIO, CANADA M5T 2C7
www.cormorantbooks.com

To my father, Maurice Fagan,
for his example

1
Ridiculous

ONCE UPON A TIME THERE was a young man — a boy, really — who was handsome, rich, easy to like, and stupid. A boy who was crazy in love with his high-school sweetheart. The sweetheart was a raven-haired beauty, not quite so rich, but a good deal smarter, if less easy to like.

One day, as so often happens, the sweetheart dumped the young man for another. The young man was stricken. To win her back, and with the unwitting help of a friend, he stole something old and valuable. But in trying so desperately, the young man died. The girlfriend grieved, the friend grieved, and the memory of the young man turned to legend.

I can see this isn't going to work. It isn't a fairy tale. It is pathetic and even laughable — a bathetic tragedy, if I remember the word properly from high-school English. From the sublime to the ridiculous. That's what I would say of somebody who stole a suit of armour from a museum, fell off the school roof, and died.

But that was only the end of the story for him.

2

Get Up, John

THERE IS A LIVE RECORDING of Bill Monroe playing his instrumental tune "Get Up, John" at the Fincastle Bluegrass Festival, near Roanoke, Virginia, in 1965, the first bluegrass festival ever held. Naturally, it does not have the benefit of perfect recording conditions or overdubs or other improvements that can be made in the mix. It isn't his most famous composition — that would be "Blue Moon of Kentucky." It isn't even his most famous instrumental, which might be "Bluegrass Breakdown" or "Rawhide" or "Jerusalem Ridge." Monroe's mandolin is backed only by Peter Rowan on guitar. His playing is very fast but not blistering, a cascade of vibrating rhythm, of changing doublestops and open drone strings, of the sound both delicate and rough that he could draw from his 1924 Gibson Lloyd Loar mandolin. He plays a series of variations, making the rhythm surge here, hang back there, suddenly thrashing his pick in successive downstrokes, touching the high harmonic note like a bell. It's just the most alive, most human sound I have ever heard. You can feel the energy pouring from his hands into that small instrument. It's as if he could go on for ever or might begin to falter, but he does neither, he makes the music rise like a wave, hold there, and then, in a touching anticlimax, quit. It would be like Glenn Gould's *Goldberg Variations* or Pablo Casals's *Cello Suites* if they had written what they were playing.

The thing about music is that you can trust it. It's emotionally reliable. Playing or listening, it gives you what you need, when you need it. A lot of the time, that has seemed like enough to me. But it isn't enough. That's what I have sometimes failed to remember.

3
I Do Not Have a Dog

I HAD AN AISLE SEAT because I don't like to feel trapped. And although, unlike so many musicians, I don't drink to excess, and only smoke a little weed to calm down after the occasional gig, I ordered a Scotch from the airline stewardess. The screen above the seats was showing a documentary on the beer industry in Czech with English subtitles, and while I was half-watching, not even using the earphones, I started to have trouble breathing. My heart was beating too rapidly and my chest hurt. I didn't know what was wrong. I was forty-two years old, too young to have a heart attack. I clutched the armrests hard.

And then I felt a small, warm hand on my own. "You will be all right," said a sweet voice next to me in accented English. I looked at the girl; she must have been ten or twelve. Reddish hair in braids and a big handful of freckles tossed across her nose. She held in her lap a magazine with pictures of American pop singers on the cover. They were vaguely familiar looking, but I couldn't have said their names.

"Last year was my first time flying," she said. "It gets more easy. You are just having a, what is it called? A fright moment."

Jesus, she was right. I was having a panic attack. Just the knowledge of what it was made my heart subside a little. I wanted to say something reassuring to her. After all, I was supposed to be the adult.

"Do you like music?"

"I like rap. In my school we all do. You are going to London too?"

"No, I have to change planes. I'm going back home to Canada. Thank you for talking to me. It's very good of you. The funny thing is, I'm not afraid of flying."

"Then maybe you are afraid of going home."

The stewardess arrived with the girl's Coke and my Scotch. I paid with Czech korunas. Now that I knew the girl, I was sorry for what I had ordered and just let it sit on my tray, the ice melting.

"Are you?" she persisted.

"Am I what?"

"Afraid of going home?"

"I don't know. It isn't really my home anymore, I've been away so long. Is somebody meeting you in London?"

"My grandparents. They have promised to do anything I want. Who is picking you up?"

"Nobody. I'm going to see my mother, but I'm kind of surprising her."

"But then she can't have a present for you."

"I hadn't thought of that."

Whether it was a good idea to surprise my mother I was no longer so sure. The girl turned the page of her magazine. "I do not have a dog," she said.

"Pardon me?"

"My father is allergic. Do you have a dog?"

"No. I know an old tune called 'Pretty Little Dog.' But it doesn't have any words."

"I would love a dog so much. I think all the time of it."

She said this so sadly yet resignedly that if I could have, I would have bought her a cocker spaniel or a retriever or whatever she wanted. I wished suddenly that I could give every kid a dog, that I could give one to Maggie and Birdy.

4
The Dive

THE FIRST TIME I EVER spoke to Valentine Schwartz, he was preparing to do something so remarkably lacking in sense that I thought he must be joking. The school swimming pool was being drained, which meant that we could not have our first instruction class of the year. This was no loss in my opinion, but Mr. Tanhauser, our gym teacher, had made us change into our bathing suits anyway and gather on the deck for a lesson in personal hygiene, a subject that was still taught as if it were the 1950s.

A short man with a powerful upper body, Mr. Tanhauser wore a little gigolo moustache and was rumoured to own a Nazi SS uniform of his uncle's that he liked to parade around in for his girlfriend while she lay naked on his bed. As far as I could tell, being new to the school, the only reason for the rumour was Mr. Tanhauser's German surname and the way he barked orders like a drill sergeant. Teacher's nicknames, rumours of weird sexual preferences, who the prominent students were — these basic workings of Arthur Meighen Collegiate I was just starting to figure out. Where Valentine Schwartz fit was not so easy to say. On this first Wednesday in September, he was among the twenty or more boys standing on the cement deck shivering with their arms around their chests. The pool was in a concrete-block bunker with a few narrow windows that faced the rutted playing field. The chlorine fumes — someone had dumped in a bucket of chemicals — made our eyes sting and irritated our lungs.

Not a single other student knew my name yet, but I already knew who Valentine Schwartz was. He was the kind of person you know about without anyone needing to tell you. In Valentine's case, it wasn't because he was the quarterback (which turned out not to matter at Arthur Meighen), or always got the lead in the school play, or was some *Reach for the Top* genius. Valentine Schwartz was none of these things, but other than being the son of a rich father among other rich kids, I didn't understand yet what had made him known, I didn't get it.

While we stood with our teeth chattering, Mr. Tanhauser was in the pool office chatting up the girl's gym teacher, Miss Mickelberry. To me this was preferable to listening to a lecture on social diseases, but Valentine Schwartz apparently required some diversion because he stepped onto the diving board.

"This is too goddamn boring," Valentine said. "I think I'll go for a little dip."

Five or six others standing near him laughed. They were the athletic guys who, inconceivable though it seemed, actually looked forward to gym. But Valentine didn't laugh. He stepped to the end of the board and looked down into the water, which had sunk three or four feet below its proper level, exposing the tiles along the sides like rows of stained teeth. "No, really," he said. "I am absolutely sincere about this. I don't need it any deeper to dive. I've practised in the shallow end at home. I could be in the goddamn Guinness book for shallow diving. I'll bet anyone five bucks that I can do a perfect dive and not even touch bottom."

"You're on, Val," said a boy on the other side of the pool. He was curly-headed and pale and his white belly hung over his bathing suit. "Five bucks. But I get to call whether you touched bottom or not."

"No way. We need an impartial witness. This guy here."

And without even looking, he pointed at me. No words came out of my mouth. I had thought it best not to be noticed in the first week of school, to keep my mouth shut. But now every boy around the pool registered my existence. I looked at the water, which appeared to have sunk another inch. No matter whose side I came down on, I was bound to make somebody dislike me. It was only the third day of school.

"Somebody keep an eye out for Adolf," Valentine said, setting his toes against the end of the board.

"What happens when he asks you why you're all wet?" another boy asked. I knew him only as the driver of a beat-up Chevrolet with a faulty exhaust. I myself didn't have a driver's licence yet. I'd seen Valentine in a glossy new Toyota Celica, a present when he'd got his licence.

"Shit. I didn't think of that."

"You can say you lost your balance and fell in." This from a skinny kid near the wall. Felix something.

Valentine nodded. He stretched out his arms. He was a couple of inches less than six feet, with naturally bronzed skin and a beautifully proportioned body, like some statue by Praxiteles. Come to think of it, he had a rather Greek head too; close, curly hair, full lips, a prominent — well, too prominent — nose.

VALENTINE'S FALL

I'd heard a couple of jokes already about Valentine's nose and had wondered whether it was for his nose alone that he was famous. Personally, I thought it gave him some distinction.

Now, I was no expert in the velocity of falling bodies or water resistance or whatever, but I had more than my share of common sense and that water did not look deep enough to dive into. Valentine was slowly raising his hands until they touched over his head in prayer fashion. One of the kids, the same one who asked how Valentine would explain being wet, began chanting Kaddish, the Jewish prayer for the dead. "*Yisgodal va yisgodesh, shmai rabo.*" The kid's voice petered out and we all watched Valentine with intense concentration as his muscles became taut and he bent his knees as if to spring.

That was when I broke my rule about not speaking. I said, in the mildest voice possible, "Perhaps you shouldn't do it."

Valentine looked up. For the first time his eyes caught mine and he smiled. It was a thoroughly winning smile and he won me over with it. Then he lowered his head again and his feet lifted off the edge.

5
It's Not Cute

"WHAT DO YOU MEAN 'LOST'?" I was doing a poor job of controlling my voice. "How can it be lost? It can't be lost. You don't mean lost."

"I trust it's insured, Mr. Rosen. How much is it worth exactly?" said the woman behind the airline counter. She was looking at me through heart-shaped glasses as she dryly licked the corner of her mouth. How much was my mandolin worth? I didn't know. I'd never intended to sell my partner of the last eighteen years, my livelihood, my challenge, my comfort. Charlie Joyce hadn't been a well-known builder outside of East Tennessee, and he only built about fifty before he died. Mine had the usual wear of a professional instrument, tiny scratches and nicks, the varnish rubbed away on the treble side. It also had an almost invisible repair in the scroll from the time that Marta threw a screwdriver at me. She hadn't meant to hit me; she wanted me to repair the kitchen cupboard. The screwdriver blade chipped the scroll and then tore a gouge out of my thigh. I was bleeding all over the floor, but all I could do was look at the scroll in shock. Marta felt terrible, but more about my leg than the mandolin. She should never have thrown it — she had really lousy aim. Luckily the children had been watching the Czech version of *Sesame Street* in the next room.

"Maybe eight, nine thousand dollars," I said, tripling my guess. "But I don't have insurance. I can't afford insurance, never mind a new instrument. I wanted to take it with me on the plane but they said there was too much carry-on luggage. They assured me that it would be marked 'fragile' and given special care. I've got to have it."

I should never have handed it over, and as soon as I had, a bad feeling had come over me. I was too acquiescent, even now eager not to cause a fuss. The woman licked the corner of her mouth again; I didn't know how her loved ones could stand it. "All we can do at this point, sir, is fill out a form."

She slid a sheet of paper across the counter. I noticed her nails were bitten down. A uniformed airport worker came up, pulling a handcart of luggage. A stocky man with a closely trimmed moustache, Filipino perhaps. A lot of the airport workers looked Filipino or South American or Jamaican. I remembered Toronto as being a homogeneously pasty-faced city, but a lot must have changed in two decades.

"What is he looking for?" the uniformed man asked, avoiding me.

"A guitar."

"I already said it isn't a guitar."

"This is too small to be a guitar. A violin maybe, but it's a funny shape," the man said, hauling a couple of suitcases from the cart. From underneath he pulled out a beat-up hard-shell case — *my* case. I took it from him, lay it on the floor, undid the latches, and opened it. And there it was, resting in its fitted velvet bed. The deep varnish finish. The gently rising arch top, the beautiful scroll, the narrow ebony fingerboard, and the name, "Joyce," in mother-of-pearl across the headstock.

"It's cute," the man said.

"It's a mandolin," I said. "And it's not cute."

"What kind of music do you play with that?"

"Bluegrass." I closed the case again and picked it up. The woman looked at me from behind her heart glasses and — please no, don't — licked the corner of her mouth again.

"I don't like country music," she said.

6
High Lonesome

- BLUEGRASS ISN'T REALLY COUNTRY MUSIC in the same way that humans and apes aren't really cousins. We might have a common ancestor, but we separated into different branches a long time ago. Bluegrass music has no twangy electric guitar, no drums, no rhinestones. The instruments are all string acoustic — mandolin, banjo, guitar, fiddle, bass. Occasionally a Dobro or resonator guitar, although not in my band. Its roots are in old-time Appalachian mountain music, which itself is descended from English and Scots–Irish tunes brought over by immigrants to America. Most of the standard modern tunes were written in the thirties, forties, and fifties by people like the Stanley Brothers, Lester Flatt and Earl Scruggs, and especially Bill Monroe and the members of the Blue Grass Boys, his band, who gave the music its name. The early musicians travelled in crowded cars, instruments strapped to the roof, wearing their hats because there was nowhere else to put them. They drove across the country to play in barns, schools, fields, halls, and tents. They also played live on the radio, on stations with names like WBT in Charlotte and WSM in Nashville, home of the Grand Ole Opry. The listeners were mostly rural southerners who had migrated to the cities looking for jobs. They sang in a style called "high lonesome," sometimes in a keening harmony. The instrumentals, some originally dance tunes — hornpipes, reels, and the like — were played at a galloping tempo, too fast for any dancers, and each of the players not only had to keep up but throw musical sparks when it was his turn to take a "break," or solo, improvising like a jazz musician. There are breaks played on the songs too, but here the player had to be able to draw deep, elemental emotions, as if he was playing the blues.

Bluegrass music was not in my upbringing or my heritage. My mother's favourite singer was Barbra Streisand, who was, in her words, "Not just the greatest living Jewish singer but the greatest singer period." She owned *Funny Girl, On a Clear Day You Can See Forever*, and all her other records. My father, on the other hand, couldn't tolerate Barbra Streisand's voice or her material. He was from Chicago and devoted to the blues. He was a record collector and owned hundreds of 78s that he'd found in thrift shops, old record bins, and garage sales before people started paying a lot of money for them. That was one of the things he didn't like about Toronto; the city had no history of the blues.

There's a lot of blues in bluegrass, so I suppose that there's some of my father's music in my own. As a teenager, Bill Monroe himself was influenced by a black blues-guitar player named Arnold Schultz who worked in the mines around Rosine, Kentucky. Still, my father didn't listen to bluegrass; I, a northern Jewish kid, had to discover it for myself. I knew more about the South and its music than most southerners. I made a study of it, first while attending university in Tennessee, and then on my own. In my early playing days, I'd take a break on a tune like "Footprints in the Snow" and play it note-for-note the way

Monroe did, and later it was Sam Bush, Ricky Skaggs, Doyle Lawson. A desperate attempt to sound authentic. Of course knowing something is not the same thing as *being* it. I remember a parking-lot jam session at a bluegrass festival in Ohio, where I was playing with some real old-timers. There was this washtub bass player, a fellow with shifting dentures and hair growing out of his ears, who could get an amazingly deep sound out of that rope. After a tune, he said to me, not so anyone else could hear, "You play good, son, but too much like you made a study of it. You got to let go some."

My father once told me that a bluesman could pick up his guitar, place his slide — some old, broken bottle neck or piece of metal tubing — on his finger and sing his troubles out. Just listen and you can hear the voice of his mourning. But the blues aren't all sad, my father said. If you listen closely you can hear the laughing too. And just playing it, or listening to it, makes you feel better, lifts the woes from the chest. Well, I think bluegrass does the same thing. Blues for white folk, as somebody once said. Of course the woes settle back down again, but it's a relief to have them gone for a while.

As for my own troubles, I suppose that I was running away from them for a little while. The anniversary of Valentine Schwartz's death gave me the excuse. That and my mother. Now with the world changed so much and so many terrible things having happened and likely about to happen, Valentine's story was as quaint and musty as a tale by de Maupassant. I had told only a couple of people about it in the intervening years. Charlie Joyce, while he was using a finger plane to get just the right curve as he was thinning the top plate of the mandolin he was building for me. He didn't comment much, but his single caterpillar eyebrow went up. And after him nobody until Marta, who said a great deal, voicing her astonishment, laughing, and then hugging me with her thin arms and saying in her Czech English, "Poor, poor Huddie, to know once in your living such a remarkable, crazy friend." That was when she still loved me, when she used to wake me in the middle of the night with tears in her eyes and say, "Don't ever leave."

7
Nussbaum Knows the Neighbourhood

THE TAXI GLIDED THROUGH THE late morning traffic on the 401, past the factory outlets and big-box stores. Someone had left a *Globe and Mail* on the back seat and I stared at it, remembering that my father used to read the paper each morning. "What kind of a self-respecting city doesn't have a professional baseball team?" I said aloud to myself, remembering my father's voice every morning. He missed the Cubs.

"But we have a team now," the turbaned taxi driver said. "The Blue Jays. 1992 and '93 World Champions. Downhill ever since."

"I guess I'm out of touch," I said. The green exit signs slipped by. Islington, Jane, Keele.

"You are coming home or visiting?"

"Visiting. I grew up here but now I live in Europe. I don't think it will feel like home."

"Canada is the best country. You should come back here. But if you do, you must vote against the Liberals in the next election. We must defeat the bloody Liberals. They are remaining in power too long."

"When I was here, Trudeau was in power."

"Trudeau was a skirt chaser. Very bad morals. But he was good to immigrant people. Trudeau let me into this country. But now Chrétien and the Liberals are corrupt. Sweep them out, I say."

I was impressed by how the man had made the country his own. In Prague, Marta's friends had smoked endless cigarettes and drank bottles of Staropramen beer as they argued about the Slovak separation, or the dangers of joining the European Union, or some local corruption scandal, while I struggled to follow with my lousy Czech. Even when they switched to English I felt like a bystander, a strange and dismaying feeling. We'd exited the highway and came to the intersection of Yonge Street and York Mills Road, one of the crossroads in our part of the suburbs. There was the strip plaza where we had walked at lunch to buy chips or a drink and, across from it, the indoor skating rink. Houses receding into the distance, their windows glinting in the late May sun. As the taxi thrummed at the light I noticed a telephone booth and a cement bench. On the back of the bench was an advertisement for a real estate agent. It showed a man in a gold suit holding a miniature house in his cupped hands like a protective giant. Underneath it said:

> BUYING OR SELLING A HOUSE?
> YOU CAN TRUST LARRY NUSSBAUM REALTY
> NUSSBAUM KNOWS THE NEIGHBOURHOOD!

"Jesus," I said under my breath, and then to the driver, "Can you let me off here?"

"Are you sure? It is a fifteen minute walk to the address you gave me."

"This will do fine, thanks."

The driver shrugged and took the bills from my hand. He came around to open the trunk and I pulled out the mandolin case and my small suitcase. The cab pulled into the flow of Subarus and Camrys, so long and sleek next to the small, beat-up European cars clogging the narrow streets of Prague. I turned to look more closely at the photograph of Larry Nussbaum. He was a little bulkier, and hollowed under the eyes, and he'd lost most of his hair, but it was definitely him. The adult version of the kid who had asked Valentine Schwartz, standing by the swimming pool, how he was going to explain being wet. The eyes themselves hadn't changed. He still looked as if he was about to tell a dirty joke that he'd read in one of his dad's *Playboy* magazines.

I opened the folding door of the telephone booth, fished out my one Canadian quarter, and dialled the number on the sign. Maybe because I wasn't ready to see my mother, who thought I was coming in a few days. Maybe because I remembered Larry fondly. Maybe because, after twenty-five years, I still hadn't got back at him for hijacking me in his first car, a ten-year-old Chevrolet. Instead of giving me a lift home, he had driven to an office building at Sheppard Avenue where I had waited almost an hour while his orthodontist adjusted his braces.

The phone picked up after half a ring. "Nussbaum here."

"Hello, Mr. Nussbaum. My name is ... Jeffrey Rosenberg. I'm interested in purchasing a house near Arthur Meighen Collegiate. I'm from out of town and thought you could help me."

"You have come to the right man," Larry said. I could hear background noise; he was on a cell. "Have you got some time? Usually my Saturdays are packed but a client cancelled on me so I'm free for the next hour. And I have some fantastic properties to show. Are you thinking of a pool? A sauna? A billiards room? If you want to see the most amazing ensuite bath —"

"As it happens I'm standing at the corner of York Mills and Yonge. And yes, I've got an hour."

"Let me just make this U-turn. I'll be there in three minutes. Prick! Like the guy couldn't see what I was doing. Look for a blue Mercedes, Jeffrey. You won't be sorry you called me."

8
I Think I'm Becoming My Father

LARRY NUSSBAUM WAS DRIVING A blue Mercedes all right, only it was at least a dozen years old. It had a front headlight held in place by duct tape, and the right passenger door had been replaced by one painted with rust-proof. I threw my suitcase and mandolin into the trunk, onto the junk that was already there — tennis rackets, Rollerblades, textbooks on real estate marketing, bundles of flyers, a transistor radio with the back missing. I couldn't get into the front seat until Larry shovelled aside more debris: old copies of *Sports Illustrated*, a portable CD player, dress shirts needing to go to the laundry, a screwdriver set. It was exactly like Larry's car in high school; whenever you needed something, say a high-powered flashlight or a pair of binoculars or a ping-pong paddle, all you had to do was ask and it was probably somewhere in Larry's car.

He pulled away from the curb. "Glad to meet you, ah, Mr. Rosenberg. It's a good thing you called me. In this neighbourhood you have to be especially careful. There are a lot of dishonest agents out there. A-holes, if you'll pardon the expression. They want to sell you the most expensive piece of dreck on the market. And there are a lot of sinkholes around here.

Sure they look good — tennis court, fancy entrance, three fireplaces. But some of them were put up fast when the boom was on. Poor insulation, bad plastering, shortcuts on the wiring. Don't buy anything built after seventy-nine, that's my opinion. A solid roof over your head. You're lucky you called me and not one of the girls."

"The girls?"

"That's what I call them. The Jewish women in their fifties who got into real estate like it might be a nice hobby. Pin money. Me, I've got three kids to clothe. One of those women, she brings you homemade strudel, makes a fuss over the kids, lets the wife cry on her shoulder. But all the time she's zeroing in on the kill. Ten years ago it was worse, now they're starting to retire to Florida. It gives me heartburn just to think about those days. They were the Dark Ages."

"So you've got three kids of your own."

"Boys. Twelve, nine, and seven. They drive me crazy but they're beautiful kids. Look like their mother, I'm glad to say. With a little luck they won't have inherited the classic Jewish-male balding pattern. Actually," he said, glancing at his watch, "I've got to pick them up after school. Soccer practice. So tell me what you're looking for."

"Something grand. A showpiece. I don't care about when it was built. But it's got to impress people."

"You serious?"

"With a pool, tennis court, games room. The works."

"It's your money. I've got the perfect house. Hold on —"

He made a couple of quick turns, getting honked at, and we were on Upper Highland. I remembered that a couple of kids at Arthur Meighen had lived here, one of the more modest streets in the neighbourhood. Two minutes later he was pulling into a circular drive. The house before us was so huge that it dwarfed the homes on either side and cast a deep shadow over one. Cartoon Italianate, with arched windows, pale yellow stucco finish, wrought iron, a three-car garage. Its sheer size made it lumpy and brutish.

I whistled. "Maybe I could just live in the garage."

"That's all you're probably good for, Mr. Rosenberg."

"Pardon me?"

"Or should I say Mr. Rosen. Mr. *Huddie* Rosen." Larry put on a big grin.

"Shit, you recognized me."

"As if you've changed," he said, smacking me hard on the shoulder. "You look exactly the same, I'm disgusted to say. Maybe a few wrinkles around the edges. Besides, your voice on the phone sounded familiar. You want a Coke?" He turned around and fished in the back seat, coming back with two cans. I just shook my head, and as we opened them in unison, both of us swore when the spray came up.

"I guess they got a little shook up," Larry said. He took a long swig. "You know who built this mausoleum before us? Danny Gladstein and Robyn Mandel."

"I remember them. Danny's the guy who ran for high-school president and lost. Then he gave a party anyway. Filled his parents' house with hundreds of people. Pizza. Beer. Movies on a big screen. Disc jockey."

"Yeah, it was bigger than my bar mitzvah. He and Robyn got married during university. Danny took over his dad's development company. Two kids. Then he got fat and addicted to young secretaries, she got slim and developed a taste for yoga instructors, and so the blessed ruin their lives. Right now they're fighting over the division of spoils."

He said these last words bitterly, a tone that was uncharacteristic of him, or so I remembered. I was going to say something when he pointed out the window. "Do you remember who lived next door?" he said. "Andrea Wasserstein. She used to sunbathe naked in her backyard, at least that's what everybody said. I used to dream of Andrea turning over to bake her other side. She went to California and married some hot-shot film producer. They both got into cocaine and he was nabbed for trafficking. Last I heard they were producing shows for a porno channel on cable. Or cooking. Or some combination. So, *boychik*, I can't believe you're here. How long has it been? More than twenty years."

"Twenty-five, Larry."

"Of course. You're here for Valentine's unveiling."

"Not exactly. It's really a coincidence."

"Yeah, sure. You were Val's best friend. I should have known you'd come. What a *meshuggenah* idea, a statue for Valentine. It's like giving somebody an award for doing the stupidest thing in high school."

"Listen, can you drive me to my mother's house? I'm staying with her."

"On Finchley, right? I've got this weird memory for exactly where everybody lived, but don't ask me to conjugate *avoir* or tell you about the Krebs cycle. I can't remember a thing we studied in class."

It took ten minutes to cross Bayview, pass Arthur Meighen Collegiate, and reach my old street. He already seemed to know that my mother lived alone and that I was in Prague and never came to visit. "I don't know if I feel sorry for you or envy you, living somewhere else," he said. "I never did that. My house is nine blocks from where I grew up. My parents moved into a condo at Steeles and Yonge, and I take the kids for dinner every Friday night. Is that little suitcase all you brought?"

"I travel light."

"You mean you're not exactly rolling in it? I thought musicians were like movie stars."

"Not my kind."

"Well, you should see the size of my second mortgage. It isn't all paradise around here."

"It doesn't actually look like paradise."

We pulled up in front of my mother's house. I could hardly get myself to look at it through the window.

"Do you want to come in?" I asked.

"No chance. Go and see your mother, Huddie. Pretend to be a *mensch*."

"What's with the Yiddish?" I said, opening the car door.

"I don't know. I think I'm becoming my father. Hey, listen, Huddie. Tomorrow you'll come for dinner. We like having people over, though usually they don't come back."

"Sure, Larry, I'd be glad to come."

He nodded and reached out his hand for me to shake. The teenage Larry had always shaken hands goodbye, an affectation we'd found funny back then. He popped the trunk and I got out my stuff. As I watched him drive off it occurred to me that he never said who it was that *he* had married.

I turned towards the house just as the side door began to open.

9
O Baby

THE AMBULANCE TOOK VALENTINE TO the North York General Hospital. Three days later I decided to visit him after dinner. My bike was a French-made Tour de France racer with ten speeds and narrow tires, and I had bought it with money I'd earned myself. As I rolled it out of the garage, the sky over the houses looked drained of colour. A lone kid was taking shots on a basketball net in his drive.

The main road that fronted Arthur Meighen Collegiate and separated our cluster of streets from the bigger houses to the north got a lot of truck traffic because of its connection to the highway a few miles on. Every passing truck shook the frame of my bike and made my heart jump a little. I was glad to see the hospital smokestack and I turned into the entrance, gliding by the emergency doors and chaining my bike to a rack. Inside it was bright and new and the receptionist at the desk smiled as she looked up Valentine's name and told me the number of his room.

I had pictured walking into Valentine's hospital room and standing silently beside his bed while recognition dawned in his eyes. That I was the one who had said, "Perhaps you shouldn't do it." But as I came down the corridor I heard voices, louder than from any other room, and when I looked in I saw at least a dozen visitors, all crowding around the bed so that Valentine himself was all but screened from my view. I recognized most of them from school as they passed around a box of chocolates and made jokes and jostled one another and brandished the remote at the television bolted to the wall.

There was no way that I could approach Valentine, but I stood watching them for a moment. And then Valentine cried out, making a sort of yelp.

"Jesus! What are you doing, trying to kill me?"

The crowd backed up and I could see Valentine wincing with pain. A complicated looking brace held his chin in a metal cup and seemed to balance his head on his shoulders. He blinked his eyes rapidly.

"I'm really sorry, Val," one of the boys said.

"My shoulder just happens to be connected to my neck, you turd."

"I was just trying to reach —"

"Forget it. It's just that the rest of you can go home again and I'm stuck in this goddamn birdcage. I want to get out of here."

He bellowed these last words, pounding his fists on the bed so that he really did seem like an animal trapped. That was when a girl (I hadn't noticed her because she was on the far side) leaned forward and kissed him on the forehead, her hair falling forward. I recognized her as Marjorie Luckenbill, who was considered the most beautiful girl in school.

Valentine grasped her arm with his hand. "O baby, I couldn't even make it without you."

"You'll be all right," she cooed, stroking his cheek.

"No, I mean it, Marjorie."

"I think you'd better rest now."

It was just then that a nurse pushed abruptly passed me and went into the room.

"I already warned you about breaking the rules," the nurse said. "You have too many visitors. Everyone has to leave."

Valentine ignored everyone but Marjorie as they shuffled out. "Come back tomorrow, baby," I heard him say even as I turned to walk quickly down the corridor.

I probably wouldn't have gone back again if it hadn't been for a small incident that followed. Dinner at the Golden Wing Chinese Restaurant with Marshall Ornitz.

Marshall Ornitz had befriended me in the first week of school, mistakenly identifying me as a student who excelled. I still hardly knew him when he invited me to go to the Golden Wing on Bathurst Street and then come to his place to stay up and watch *Monty Python's Flying Circus*, which was appearing on Canadian television for the first time. Marshall would pick me up in his dad's Lincoln.

"What I want to know," Marshall said when we were seated at a round table big enough for twelve, "is what is the relationship between the Chinese won ton and the Jewish *kreplach*? My theory is that one of the lost tribes of Israel showed up in China and taught them how to stuff little pockets of dough. And then some Chinese waiter in the Ming dynasty accidentally dropped one in somebody's soup ..."

This was how the conversation went. Marshall ate quickly, his chopsticks moving rapidly between his plate and his mouth. The restaurant had red velvet wallpaper, a fish tank of sorry-looking carp, and a bored waiter folding napkins at the front counter. I imagined a year of Saturday nights just like this.

The waiter roused himself enough to bring our fortune cookies. "I've got a great idea," Marshall said. "Let's send a fortune cookie to Valentine Schwartz in the hospital. It can say" — here he mimicked a Chinese accent and showed his upper front teeth as if he were Bugs Bunny — "*He who searches for treasure in shallow pool find only headache.* Wait, wait, I've got a better one." He crossed his eyes and waggled his head from side to side. "*Man with small brain should not make big decisions.*"

"Come on, Marshall," I said. "The waiter will see you."

"You know, I hear Valentine is going to be in a wheelchair for life. He won't be able to play ride-the-horsey with Marjorie Luckenbill anymore. Then she'll dump him."

"You're wrong. He isn't going to be in a wheelchair. And Marjorie isn't going to leave him either."

I didn't know why I said these things, or even if they were true. Marshall looked at me as if to say, *What's wrong with this guy?* "The Chinese invented gunpowder and macaroni," he said. "For a long time they were way ahead of the West." He picked up his chopsticks and stuck the ends under his upper lip so they hung down like fangs. "Look at me! I'm the Chinese Dracula."

The next day I went back to the hospital.

10
Why Are You Roasting a Chicken?

MY MOTHER HAS WHITE HAIR. Those were the first words that came to me as I saw her open the side door, her thin face showing extreme emotions as she saw me, a terror of happiness. The last time I had seen her, fourteen months ago when she had last come to Prague bearing GapKids boxes, she was still colouring her hair. Not the "mousy" brown of her youth, as she'd called it, but a silvery blond common to Jewish women of a certain age. But at some time she must have let it go natural and I was shocked to see how white it was. She was just sixty-seven. I had thought of my mother as small but not especially fragile, yet here her face looked gaunt, her body a wisp, her wrists as delicate as twigs. She managed to get herself more or less under control and simply look glad as she reached me, her hands outstretched. I didn't know what expression I wore but it caused her to hesitate so that I had to reach out to make sure the hug actually took place.

"Oh, you're just awful," she said. "You don't even tell me what day you're coming."

"I'm sorry. I wasn't sure until the last minute."

"You mean you couldn't decide until the last minute. I was hoping ..." But she couldn't say any more and shuddered against my shoulder. But then she stepped away and pulled an ever-present tissue from inside her sleeve, wiped her eyes, and smiled at me as if everything was all right. "The point is you're here," she said. "Let's go inside before Rita Meyer spies us from her window and invites herself over."

"Rita Meyer? Does she still live across the road?"

"The only holdout besides me."

The house smelled delicious. Despite not knowing exactly when or if I'd arrive, she'd clearly been doing some preparatory cooking. There was a gloriously aromatic and still warm apple cake on the island countertop beside a plate of sugar- and cinnamon-sprinkled mandel bread. The kitchen itself looked unchanged from my time in the house: the lilac-wallpapered nook with the oval teak table and matching chairs, which we had brought with us from the old house, the little television on the shelf above the cookbooks, the old Mixmaster by the double sink. Only the coffee maker and the Cuisinart were new. It was hard for me to make out my own emotional response except for an almost choking sensation in my throat. I tried to take deep breaths as I put down my mandolin case and sat down on the stool by the island.

"You look thin, Howie," she said. I'd been about to say the same of her. I saw a large pot of soup simmering on the stove. She used a wooden spatula to push in some diced carrots from a cutting board. "I've got a brisket on order at the butcher's. We can have it tomorrow night."

"Actually, I ran into Larry Nussbaum. He asked me to come for dinner. Tomorrow."

She looked almost panicky, as if about to lose me. "You're already making plans to go out?"

"I can cancel. I should have thought about it."

"No, you go. I've got my book club tomorrow evening anyway. I read the book so I might as well not skip it. And it'll be nice for Larry, that poor man."

"What do you mean, 'poor man'?"

"You don't know?"

"He didn't say anything to me."

"You don't keep in touch?"

"Mom, I don't keep in touch with anybody."

"He lost his wife. Cancer."

"Oh, Jesus. There was something unspoken but I didn't pick it up. How long ago?"

"Two years. From what his mother tells me, he was crazy about her. A *happy* marriage." She didn't even pretend the remark wasn't meant as a reproach. "He was a mess the first year, could hardly take care of the kids. But then he pulled himself together. He's a wonderful father." Possibly another dig, harder to pass over. "He's been very brave."

She picked up the oven mitts, put them on, opened the oven door, and withdrew a broiling pan.

"Why are you roasting a chicken? You didn't know when I was coming." Without meaning to I said it in a mean-spirited, almost resentful tone.

She didn't look at me. "We can have it cold."

Already the walls felt as if they were moving in. Jesus, it was airless in here. Why didn't my mother ever open a window? The thought of my not knowing Larry's wife had died flushed me with shame. It was impossible that this could be the same

Larry Nussbaum I'd known in school as a deliberate goof, who had refused to study for tests, who had a complicated number system for rating girls, who knew a real bookie and spent his weekly allowance betting on American college football. All these years I'd assumed that Larry and everyone else I'd known — everyone except the dead Valentine Schwartz — had simply grown into older versions of their high-school selves.

My mother turned to me with false brightness. "You tell me your news, Howie. How are my darling granddaughters? Do you have any new pictures?"

I wondered if there was any way not to talk about this now. But my mother already read my face and I saw her eyes change and her mouth drop a little.

"I haven't seen the kids for a few days."

She remained still a moment before carefully hanging the oven mitts on a little hook by the stove.

"Marta and I have separated. For now. I was staying at Annet's. Marta and I agreed it might be a good idea if we had a little space for a bit. So here I am."

"Oh, Howie."

"It's all right, really. It'll work out somehow. The kids are doing okay."

She came around the counter and I thought she was going to hug me or put her hands on my shoulders. Instead she struck me with her small fists. Repeatedly her furious but harmless blows fell on my chest. I was too stunned to react for a minute. Finally I grabbed her hands, trying not to hurt her.

"How could you? How could you, Howie! They're my grandchildren!"

I felt tears sting my own eyes, but I was angry too. "Not

everything's my fault, you know. I didn't want this to happen. I want to be with the kids. Maybe a little time will help. We'll cool off and get some perspective. It'll be better soon. And you're really not helping me right now."

I let go of her wrists and her hands collapsed to her sides. She said, "You always pretend that it's okay, that there's never anything to worry about. But what if it's not okay? You don't think this will affect the kids? It always does, no matter how well you do it. It's terrible for them."

"I know," I said quietly. "Of course it is."

My mother slumped into a chair by the table. "I didn't want you to marry her," she said. "She lived so far away, she wasn't Jewish, I didn't know a thing about her. But that first time I came to visit, I saw what a lovely person Marta is. Such a generous nature. It's not just for the kids. I wouldn't like you to lose her either, Howie."

"Mom, I know you'd like to make everything better, but you can't. You just have to leave it to me. To us."

She gave herself a moment to calm down, closing her eyes. She opened them again and looked at me, neither smiling nor frowning. I said, "Let's leave it for now. Tell me what's going on with you. The big secret."

"I don't know what you mean."

"Yes you do. Those hints on the phone. That you were doing something for me. For me and the girls."

"Oh, that. Is that why you've finally come home? To find out what I'm doing for you? I thought you'd only come back when your father rose from his grave. I've been going to the cemetery for twenty-five years and he hasn't moved yet."

"I can't believe you said that."

"I'm sorry. I'm just upset."

"And I'm tired from the flight," I said, getting up. "I'm going to lie down."

She put her hand on my arm as I was passing her. "I am doing something for you. But I'll show you later. Just don't go down into the basement."

"All right." I grabbed my suitcase and headed for the stairs.

11
Third Fake Spanish

MY PARENTS MET AT CRYSTAL Beach, a cottage resort on the north shore of Lake Erie. Somewhere in the house is a decal-edged photograph of them that first summer of 1955, my mother in a one-piece bathing suit like Lana Turner, and my father in trunks, skinny and near hairless, with horn-rimmed glasses, his arm tentatively around her waist. She was from Toronto, the third daughter of a successful jeweller (who gave me my first watch just before he died), and lived in a pleasant house on Albany Avenue. She took piano and voice lessons, and her mother had a woman who came in every other day as well as a gardener. My mother's older sisters married a chartered accountant and a pharmacist, solid professionals. My father was from Chicago, born to labour activists in the garment industry and raised in a tough neighbourhood. When he was still a kid the Jews started to move out and blacks move in, but his own family stayed. While my father himself didn't feel himself to be a "political animal," as he put it, he'd been indoctrinated enough not to be able to stomach law or dentistry. Instead, after high school he chose "honest work" as an apprentice printer.

VALENTINE'S FALL

My father came into Toronto by train to visit my mother every second week for three months before he proposed. His permanent move to the city was a sacrifice made for her, and for the rest of his life he pined for his hometown. For him, Toronto meant no baseball team, no elevated train, and worst of all, no history of the blues. He'd learned to love the blues from the blacks who had moved in after the Jews had left, not the new electric blues, but the old-style country blues that he heard from the back porches. But here in Toronto there were no stories of black southerners riding the rails from the Delta to play their shitbox guitars on State Street for a few dollars and maybe getting asked into a nearby recording studio. Toronto had only a small black population back then, mostly from the Caribbean. So all he had were his records, which he had begun to collect as a teenager. Robert Johnson's "Sweet Home Chicago" was the song he played when he was feeling particularly melancholy. He built special shelves in the basement of the new house, created an elaborate catalogue system, owned the best hi-fi of anyone we knew, and an expensive reel-to-reel tape recorder so that he could preserve the original recordings.

When he arrived in Toronto, my father went to work for a small print shop that did a lot of union work. It got swallowed by a chain of printing houses that expanded the building to twice its size and put my father in charge of a new Heidelberg four-colour offset press. When I was in junior high the company was gulped by an even bigger fish, AmericaInk, the third-largest printing operation in North America. By then, my father was foreman and the job became even more demanding and stressful, with profit targets coming from head office. He still got ink on his hands and picked up a wrench from time to time, but he envied the guys who only had to worry about running the presses. Yet even though he'd already been promoted beyond the station he wanted, my mother pushed him to take night courses in management and accounting at the Ryerson Polytechnical Institute so that he could apply for plant manager. I used to hear her nagging him in the kitchen at night, telling him that he sold himself short, or that she didn't want to stay in our drab and narrow house forever, or that he had to set an example for his son, meaning me. And so he did apply for manager, and got it, and as far as I could tell he was never happy again. After a while he stopped complaining about the pressure from head office and just kept it to himself, but I could always tell when he was expecting a visit from his boss at head office, a man with the strange and sinister name of Elsdon Neebe.

It was the income from the new job that allowed us, just before my last year of high school, to move up to North York, or what my mother called the "near suburbs," so as to distinguish it from Markham or Thornhill or somewhere farther and less reputable. Until then I'd been a city boy, going to Harbord Collegiate like my mother before me, and knew the suburbs only from visits to the Flosses, my Uncle Norman and Aunt Min and their kids. My father didn't come with us most of the time; he resented Uncle Norman, who had never approved of him. Our house on Manning Avenue was cramped and had only one bathroom. The noise on College Street had gotten worse, and my mother was always cutting out newspaper articles about drugs for sale in the downtown schools. I still didn't expect my father ever to agree to move, but maybe he got tired of fighting the traffic, or thought that this, at last, would make my mother happy. Whatever the reason, he finally said yes.

Our house was in a new development called "Elysian Fields," a name that my father joked was entirely appropriate. The developer had divided the property into modest lots on winding lanes and cul-de-sacs, with the idea that people who couldn't afford the more established streets could still find a toehold in a desirable suburban neighbourhood with a high school that had a reputation, with so many Jewish kids, for high academic standards. Navigating the new streets in the first week or two, I lost my way several times, for it was almost impossible to tell the houses apart — a fake Tudor next to a fake Spanish next to a fake English cottage and then a fake Tudor again.

Our house was the third fake Spanish on a long crescent. My mother was thrilled to be in a brand-new, germ-free house. My father moved his record collection into the finished basement. My own bedroom was a small turreted space above the garage, like an inverted ice cream cone on top of a hatbox. It felt more like a very small castle or tree house than a real room.

I had the summer to get used to my new surroundings before the school year started. I tried to keep up my friendships with kids from the old neighbourhood, but it wasn't the same. One day I rode my bike to the library, to find out about Arthur Meighen, the man my new school was named after and who neither of my parents knew anything about. He turned out to be the ninth Canadian prime minister, a man hated by working people for having ended the Winnipeg General Strike. When I told my father, he just said, "That figures."

12
Glass of Milk

MY ROOM HAD CHANGED EVEN less than the kitchen. The same Mercury rocket-ship wallpaper, already childish when I moved in. The same pine desk with the blue knobs, the drawers crammed with essays. I had written them as quickly as possible, receiving respectable if not impressive marks while Valentine, usually working beside me, would struggle to form a coherent paragraph. There was the same imitation-patchwork cover on the bed, and on the dresser the Neapolitan-style, round-backed mandolin on which I'd picked out my first notes.

I unpacked the suitcase and threw myself on the bed, which didn't give at all. Perhaps my mother had replaced the mattress, or I'd been too light back then to make much of a dent in it. On this bed I'd spent countless hours staring up into the cone-like turret and dreaming about a girl named Annie Lynch. Annie of the dark hair and bangs. Annie of the braces and quick, piercing laugh. Annie of the deep brown eyes. Annie of the withering tongue. Annie who used to make fun of Valentine without him even realizing it. Annie who was my buddy and who I thought would never be more because I was too chicken, but who snuck me into her basement the night before I left Toronto and showed me how to love. Thinking of her in the years after, I would imagine her running a leper colony in northern India, or editor-in-chief of the *London Times*, or owning a restaurant on Crete.

I fell asleep. When I raised my groggy head again and looked at the ticking clock on the dresser, almost two hours had passed. The clock was the old windup kind, which meant that my mother had either started it again in anticipation of my arrival or had kept it going for the last twenty-five years. I made my way to the bathroom, stripped, and stepped into the shower. The hot and steaming pulse of the water was heaven next to the lukewarm dribble that came out of the shower in our apartment in Vinohrady. I came downstairs to find a note taped onto the pepper grinder on the kitchen counter.

Number One Son,
I have gone on my power walk. Slowpokes better stay out of my way! I have left you a sandwich and a glass of milk in the fridge. xxoo Mom.

The tone of forced cheer made me feel crappy. It had been years since I drank a glass of milk, and even longer since someone had poured one for me. But I ate the tuna-fish sandwich, made delicious by the chopped Valencia onion, and drank the milk, losing the battle not to feel twelve years old again. I wondered if my mother went for a walk every day and whether she had company. Although I spoke to her on the phone every couple of weeks, I really didn't know what her days were like — what her life was like. I rinsed the plate and the glass, put them in the empty dishwasher, and went to the case that I'd left in the kitchen, undid the clasps, and picked up my mandolin. It always calmed me when I felt uneasy or untethered. Sometimes people saw the word Joyce glinting in mother-of-pearl script on the headstock and thought that the mandolin was named for a woman, the way you might get a tattoo on your arm if you were drunk. But I always thought of the instrument, despite it being small and higher-pitched than a guitar, as masculine. I sat in a chair, drew the pick from under the strings, and started to tune. It settled against me where it belonged, and I looked down at the curved top, carved to a precise thinness and hand-varnished to a dark lustre. The spruce and maple Charlie used had been aging in his barn for eight or ten years. By now it looked like it had been played for a couple of decades, but all that use had sure opened up its voice. I put my hand for a moment on the scroll that curled from the top of the body and towards the neck, an almost classical adornment but also organic, an unfurling leaf. Charlie had taken a long time carving the scroll and had sworn something awful while performing the finicky task of fitting in the thin, ivory-toned edge-binding into the routered groove. I played a few warm-up arpeggios, loosening up my picking hand and pressing the strings to the ebony fretboard with the calloused fingertips of my left hand. It didn't have the rich sustain of the violin, its sister instrument, or the range and fullness of a guitar. Its sound was narrower and either harsher or sweeter, depending on how it was played. There was something more primitive in its voice, wilder. It had a faster heartbeat, like a small animal.

I leaned back in the chair and began to play "Wayfaring Stranger," using a forlorn tremolo. I didn't choose the song, it just came to my fingers, and as the introduction faded I sang the first verse and chorus under my breath.

VALENTINE'S FALL

> *I am a poor, wayfaring stranger*
> *travelling through this world of woe.*
> *But there's no sickness, toil, or danger*
> *in that bright world, to which I go.*
>
> *I'm going there to meet my father.*
> *I'm going there, no more to roam.*
> *I'm only going over Jacob.*
> *I'm only going over home.*

I played another instrumental break, emphasizing the minor key, and then sang the second verse. After that, with my hands getting warmed up and wanting to feel more lively, I strummed a quick intro and lit into "Pike County Breakdown." That got my own heart pumping and my spirits lifted, so I sang the fast tempo "Roll in my Sweet Baby's Arms" and then picked "Cattle in the Cane." I'd pretty much forgotten where I was, when I looked up and saw my uncle Norman standing in the doorway watching me.

He was thin and short like my mother but his seven extra years showed in his concave cheeks and mottled skin. A thin patina of hair lay across his irregular scalp. He stood in his khaki trousers hitched up with a belt, one foot slightly lifted, to compensate for his childhood polio, glasses so thick they had the distorting effect of a fishbowl. I stopped playing.

"For this," rasped Uncle Norman, "you gave up law school?"

13
Pastrami Killed Jack Melanovsky

MY UNCLE HAD COME TO take us to dinner. My mother had telephoned to tell him and Aunt Min of my arrival, but she hadn't expected them to show up (Aunt Min waited in the Caddy) and she was not pleased when she returned from her walk a few minutes after they had arrived. "I wanted you for myself just one night," she snapped at me as we climbed into Uncle Norman's car, where Aunt Min sat with the patient smile of Buddha and I had to lean in and kiss her powdered cheek. Uncle Norman slowly backed out of the drive. He had a good three feet on either side of the car but he managed to hit the curb of the drive anyway and thump down into the road.

"Are you sure Norman should still be driving?" I whispered in my mother's ear. The interior was so large I didn't think there was much chance of him or my aunt hearing me. "And look how slow he's going. If we actually survive, we won't get to the restaurant for days."

"Sshh," my mother said. "He's sensitive about it."

"What's that?" Norman said. "You want the air conditioning on?"

"No," I said quickly, "that's okay."

"Here it goes. It'll be like a fridge in here in no time."

"So, Norman," I said, "where are we going to eat?"

"What's with calling me Norman? What happened to *Uncle Norman*?"

"I'm forty-two years old. I thought we might address one another as adults."

"That's right, you're forty-two years old and still you have to be difficult."

"I don't mind if you call me Min," said my aunt.

"You do so mind. It shows a lack of respect."

My mother jabbed me in the ribs with her elbow. I said, "Uncle Norman, I'm happy to call you whatever you want. If you want, I'll call you Sir. I'll call you Doctor Floss. I'll call you the King of Discount Eyeglasses."

"Now that's funny," he said. "I like a good joke. You hear that, Min? I could use that in our next ad. And I'll call you the Jewish Bluegrass Boy. The only bluegrass musician who has had a bar mitzvah. The circumcised mandolinist ..."

"Please," said Aunt Min.

"Now that's funny," I said. "But I still don't know where we're eating."

Min turned around in her seat and smiled at me. She went to the hairdresser every Thursday and had a wash and a spray to keep it curled up at the ends. As a kid I used to touch her hair for the shivery thrill of feeling how stiff it was. She said, "Where else? The Pickle Barrel."

It wasn't really true that I gave up law school to play bluegrass. I'd been attending the University of Tennessee in Knoxville, where I had enrolled because we were all supposed to move down there at the end of August, only a year after we'd moved into Elysian Fields. For years my father had asked for a transfer to Chicago, a move my mother was only reluctantly willing to accept, and then suddenly Elsdon Neebe had complied, sending him to Knoxville instead but saying that if he went there first he could move to Chicago in three years. And then before we moved my dad collapsed on the shop floor from a brain aneurysm. It was the last place he would have wanted to die. This was only three months after Valentine had died. Valentine's death had been shocking and had left a peculiar hole in the world. My father's death had made the world collapse.

The only decision that I was capable of making after my father's death, although it made my mother's grief more desperate, was that I would go to the University of Tennessee anyway. Because I could not stay here. It had been Uncle Norman's idea that I should take the LSAT exam for entry into law school. He believed that if I got in I would give up the ridiculous ambition of becoming a musician, which had come to me during those three college years in Tennessee. I took the exam and got a mark not good enough for the University of Toronto, but sufficient for Western or Queens. Which I then refused to do. Norman told me that not going to law school — not returning to Canada — was an unspeakably cruel act towards my mother. Even at the time I thought that he might be right.

Someone was honking at us. We were going maybe twenty-five kilometres an hour in the left lane. A car pulled past us on the right side, the driver giving us the finger, but Norman didn't notice. He was busy fiddling with the radio, insisting that he got better reception in his car than most people did on their home stereos. He left it on a station where somebody was speaking in Cantonese. We drove up Leslie past more rows of suburban housing and a few doctor's buildings until we came to a strip plaza. Norman jerked the steering wheel, throwing us sideways, and I heard tires squeal behind us as we entered the parking lot. He slowed to a crawl. There were empty spaces around the perimeter but Norman insisted on waiting for a spot right in front of the restaurant, which meant idling in the car while we waited for some other old Jewish man to pull out. "What's taking him so long?" Norman said. "An *alter kocker* like that, they ought to take away his licence." Then he eased the Caddy in like it was the *Queen Mary* going into dry dock.

"Nice job, Norm," said Aunt Min. She leaned over the back seat and said to me in a conspiratorial whisper, "He was always a good parker."

There hadn't been many places to eat around here and the Pickle Barrel was still a hit, judging by the crowd inside and the lineup waiting to get in. I could hardly hear what my mother was saying over the noise of voices and the clash of cutlery. Norman winked at me and boomed, "You watch. I'm in like flint here." Then he sauntered up past the line to the hostess stand like he was Sinatra claiming his favourite table. Nevertheless, we had to wait twenty minutes to get in. Aunt Min, whose ankles were bad, sat on a chair. Finally, we got a table and the waitress immediately brought the menus, which were so gigantic I thought that I was going to have to ask the man at the next table to hold one end for me. A Czech restaurant meant pork, dumplings, and pickled cabbage, but here, besides deli food, there were stir fries, pastas, Thai, "healthy heart" specials. I was surprised to see my mother fussing indecisively over her choice, changing her mind three times before finally settling on the all-white omelette.

"Mom," I said. "You're too thin. You should eat something more."

"It's enough for me."

What was going on with her? One minute she was telling me off about my life, and the next she was trying to efface herself. Uncle Norman grabbed my arm and said, "Whatever you do, don't order the pastrami. Pastrami killed Jack Melanovsky."

I didn't want pastrami but I ordered it just to defy him, as if I had become a surly teenager again. I said, "It's just for a treat, Norman. They don't have Jewish food in Prague."

"That's because they don't have Jews in Prague anymore. Didn't you hear? There was a war in Europe. At least ask for it lean. Bessie," he said to the waitress, "give it to him lean."

"Bessie retired," the waitress said.

"She retired?"

"I don't want it lean," I said.

"All a person can do is try," Aunt Min sighed.

"You look well, Howie," my mother said, clinging to my arm. "Doesn't he look well, Min?"

"Very well. You have to see Brent and Beverly," she said. "I'm sure they'd love to show you their new house. The kids have their own bathrooms. You liked the house, didn't you, Fran?"

"Oh yes, I did," my mother said. "It's very nice. The kitchen's a little small."

"You don't know what you're talking about," said Norman. "That kitchen's big enough to cater a wedding. So where's our food? The service is slow today. This waitress is no Bessie."

"It's only been three minutes," I said.

"Howie, you have to come by the shop. When was the last time you had your eyes checked?"

"To be honest, I can't remember."

"I got a new young fellow working for me, Greenbaum, not

much over fifty. But I'll examine you myself. You'll come and see the changes we made. Everything's different, from top to bottom."

"I chose the decor," Aunt Min said, smiling.

The waitress arrived with a tray that must have weighed fifty pounds. She rattled down our enormous dishes heaped with food. "Did you put the dressing on the side?" Aunt Min said.

The waitress didn't bother to answer. I looked at the pastrami and felt my appetite disappear. Norman was right; I should have ordered something green.

"The chicken burger is too salty," Norman said.

The waitress was still putting down side plates of pickles and sliced bread. "You want to send it back?"

Norman took another bite. With his free hand he held up the salt shaker. "See, there's salt on the table. You can always add more salt but you can't take it away. And as for health ..."

"I'll take it back for you."

The waitress reached for the dish but Norman slapped her hand away. "No, I'll eat it. I don't like making a fuss. I just hope it isn't a bad sign. The place could be going downhill."

Through all this my mother said nothing. She didn't seem to be paying any attention, playing with her eggs more than eating them. Norman said, "There's Harry Plaskett. Used to be in the *shmatte* business, men's underwear. Had his shop at King and Spadina. Last year they turned the building into loft apartments. A half-million each and they sold like hotcakes. He ran a sweatshop and made a fortune and now he sells and makes another. So tell me, Howie, how is Europe these days? Do they really like that hillbilly music of yours?"

"Some people do."

"How's that president of yours? Havel. Min and I were thinking of going to Europe in June. But we decided against it, didn't we, Min?"

"Yes, Norman, we decided against it."

"Europe is against Israel. It's just anti-Semitism in disguise. Do they want us not to defend ourselves? If only they held the rest of the world up to the same standards. They'll just have to live without my tourist dollars."

"It is possible to criticize Israel and not be anti-Semitic," I said.

"It's possible but it's not the reality. It's a cover-up. It's the polite way of calling us kikes."

"My ears," Min said.

"You have to go back to pre-1948, even to the Balfour Declaration, and see how the other Arabs treated the Palestinians ..." And so my uncle began his dissertation on Israeli history and politics. He might have been picking up our conversation of three years ago, when they passed through Prague as part of a package tour. I should have known better than to argue back. Not only would my uncle refuse to hear the slightest criticism, but he was better equipped to argue. He read every new political book on Israel that came out, every biography of its leaders. He had a subscription to the *Jerusalem Post*. It wasn't just Israel, it was *his* Israel, the country he saw struggle into existence, whose early fighters he had supported with donations that, back then, he could not afford. The Israel he had visited a dozen times on tours led by his rabbi, when he had donned his tallis and prayed at the Wailing Wall, and felt the ancient grandeur of his faith, and looked with admiration at the beautiful young men and women in their combat fatigues, fearlessly protecting their people and their land.

Several times Min had to tug at Norman's sleeve and remind him to keep his voice down. I turned my attention to my mother, who had grown silent. When she did finally speak, it was to say that she was tired and wanted to go home. Norman picked up the tab and we got in the car again. He drove so slowly that I imagined I could get out of the car, walk around it, and get back in. At last we were back at Finchley Crescent. I thought that my mother might want to stay up and talk but she said that she was tired, kissed me on the cheek, and went into her own room. A short time later I heard the television on low. I stood outside her door and remembered standing here after waking up from a bad dream, listening to the sounds of my parents sleeping. I would return to bed without going in. Now I went back to that same room, got undressed, and lay on the bed.

In bluegrass songs, the dear childhood home was gone forever, lost to the bank or burned down or just abandoned. In a bluegrass song you couldn't lie down in your old bed again, with your mother down the hall watching the cooking channel.

14
Not so Terrible

I WAS ASLEEP FOR LESS than an hour when the telephone began to ring. There was an extension on the bedside table that hadn't been there when I lived here and it jangled loudly in my ear, scaring the shit out of me. I fumbled with the receiver, not even awake enough to wonder who it could be.

"Hello?" I mumbled

Silence at the other end.

"Listen, I used to make prank calls too, but not in the middle of the night. Have a little heart."

Not silence but an eerie, palpable presence.

"Marta?" I whispered. "Is that you?"

"Things were not always so terrible, you know."

"Is everything all right? Are the kids okay?"

"Do you remember when we used to go out for dinner, just the two of us. Annet used to stay with the girls. We would walk along the river and then go to that place on Rámová, that little cavern run by Afghani people. Cheerful and cheap, that's what you called it. The food was lovely, the warm flat bread, the wine nothing special but we didn't care."

"Yes, of course I remember," I said, sitting up now.

"Why did we stop going? I can't even remember when. And the other day, such horrible words we said to each other. I can't believe we said such things."

"We were angry. And hurt."

"I don't think words go away. Maybe they stay forever. Like things you try to throw away but never, you know, break down."

"Words are just words, Marta. Sometimes arguments take on a life of their own. They gather up this kind of dark energy. We have to forgive ourselves."

"I forgive you, Huddie. I don't know if I forgive me. It would be easier if it was one thing, one clear thing. If somebody cheated, if you cheated —"

"I wouldn't cheat."

"I know. You are too good for that. And you need to see yourself as good. This way, maybe, you don't have to see."

"I do see. Some of it, anyway. I don't think it's helped, being a musician. I've been away too much."

"I never was unhappy for your playing music. You know that."

"I know, I'm just saying. Maybe if we weren't still in that crummy apartment without hot water half the time and no washing machine. And if you didn't have to work so hard listening to fat men make jokes on your table —"

"I'm a massage therapist, Huddie. I help people. You know what I wish? I wish we had more friends in common."

"You're jumping around. I guess I am too."

"I know, my mind is all swirling tonight."

"You like some of my friends. You like Annet."

"I love Annet. But Lukáš? And don't get me started on Grisha."

"Well, what about yours? And these new friends? They're like twelve years old."

"Oh, stop it. So they're younger. They have energy. They're idealistic. They think they can make a difference."

"Pavel wants to make a difference, all right."

Marta laughed quietly. "That's just normal. He's young and I'm helping him so he gets a little thing in his head. I'm not interested and you know it. He's a sweet boy and he made a beautiful film."

"Sure, if you think a low-budget, pretentious, pseudo-erotic art film is beautiful."

"At least my friends are trying to tell the truth in their films. Not like your bluegrass songs. 'We've been drinking whiskey before breakfast. I'm here to get my baby out of jail.'"

"At least listening to bluegrass is fun. Nobody listens to bluegrass to be a pretentious jerk. I shouldn't have said that."

"I'm tired. I have to go back to bed. I can't remember why I called anyway. Maybe I didn't have a reason."

"Can I speak to the girls before you go?"

"They're sleeping."

"Right. I forgot the time. Then tell me what they look like. Can you take a peek and describe them for me?"

"All right. I'm so sorry, Huddie. They miss you. Just wait a minute."

She put down the phone. In my mind I could see the blue receiver and the end table that it was resting on, and the little bowl of dried-up chestnuts beside it. In less than a minute she was on the line again. "Margita is on her back with the covers pushed off. Her head is turned to the wall. She's wearing the little gold necklace with the heart you gave her. And Bela, even in sleep she won't stay still. She is hanging half off the bed. I really have to go, I'm so tired. Just tell me how your mother is."

"Thin. Sad. I don't know if something's going on with her or if it's just age."

"You should have brought us to Toronto to see her there. I thought maybe you were ashamed of me."

"Of course not. It was just me. I couldn't bear to come back."

"So now you have. My head hurts. What is that song of yours? 'Nine Pound Hammer.' Well, it's banging on my head. I have to crawl into bed while there's still a little time."

"I'll call the girls."

"Goodnight, Huddie."

The phone went dead. I heard something from the other side of my bedroom door. The faint shuffle of footsteps moving away.

15
Alpha-Bits

I DIDN'T SLEEP AGAIN FOR hours, and when I did it was a shallow, fitful sleep. In the morning the telephone woke me again, but this time I let it ring until my mother answered it. The sun streamed in through the east-facing window, just the way it had warmed me when I was seventeen. I willed myself to feel the skinnier, dreamier kid inside me, as if the last twenty-five years were a mere shell that could be peeled away. Downstairs would be my orange juice and bowl of Alpha-Bits and my father who would ruffle my hair before heading off to the plant, and my mother telling me not to forget my lunch.

But these forced memories couldn't mask the melancholy that lingered from the phone conversation with Marta. It had been Marta I'd been dreaming of just before waking, standing in my mother's kitchen where in real life she'd never been, speaking in a Czech that I couldn't understand.

A knock on the door and then my mother's voice. "Howie, there's a phone call for you. Do you want some breakfast? I bought a box of Alpha-Bits."

"You didn't really. Who is it?" I said.

"Marjorie somebody."

"I'll be down in a minute." I couldn't imagine who was calling. I didn't know anyone here anymore, and besides, I hadn't told a soul that I was coming. I pulled off the covers, swung my legs over the edge of the bed, and picked up the receiver. "Hello?" I said.

"Huddie, it's Marjorie Bluestein. You know, Marjorie Luckenbill from school."

"Marjorie! But how did you know I was here? I didn't answer the email."

"Larry Nussbaum told me. I phoned him last night about the memorial ceremony and he said that he saw you."

"This is really strange. I haven't heard your voice in twenty-five years."

"Would you mind meeting me this morning? I'd like to talk to you."

"What about?"

"Please."

That tone, how well I remembered it. Marjorie was a hard girl — woman — to refuse. "Of course," I said. "Where do you want to meet?"

"There's a Movenpick in the plaza at York Mills and Bayview. Can you meet in an hour?"

"Sure, I'll be there."

"Good. You can see how much I've changed."

16
Painting a Fence

I HAD SEEN MARJORIE LUCKENBILL several weeks before I actually met her. We had moved to the new house at the start of summer and almost immediately I had found myself a job. I'd been working weekend and summer jobs since I was fourteen, saving most of the money for college but using some to buy a new bike, a night at the movies, records. This summer, three mornings a week, I would stand outside our front door eating a roll and jam until Georgio Granatelli rolled by in his pickup and Georgio's grandson Al reached down a hand to haul me up.

Mr. Granatelli was almost seventy, but he was the strongest man I had ever met. His sons had all started their own businesses, so his grandson Alfonzo worked for him, but he still needed one more. In the first week of July I had seen him leaning on his truck and eating his lunch of Italian sausage and bread. He listened to me ask for a job and then eyed me skeptically. "You sure this is a thing for you? It's not easy. Your back, your arms, they are going to feel it. I don't keep on people who don't like to work." But I told him I wasn't a shirker and he agreed to give me a try. In that first week I almost cut off my toes with the lawnmower, dropped a rake from the side of the truck onto

Alfonzo's head, and severed the roots of a new rose bush, but Mr. Granatelli didn't fire me. "At least you work hard, eh? Maybe after a while you will learn not to kill the plants. Besides, I got nobody else."

It didn't take me long to understand why Mr. Granatelli had been suspicious of hiring a kid from the neighbourhood. Most of his service contracts were for the giant homes north of Arthur Meighen. They had long or circular drives, great expanses of lawn, groupings of tall spruce or shade-giving maple, rock gardens, and immense flower beds. I spent that summer cutting grass, fertilizing, planting, while the children of these families swam in their pools and walloped tennis balls in their courts. Or else the houses were shut up because the families were in Europe or at resorts or the kids were at summer camp.

Of the kids who were around, I would later recognize some of them when school started, but the only one who I thought might recognize me was Marjorie Luckenbill. I didn't know her name, or Valentine's either, the first time I saw them in August when Mr. Granatelli left me to paint the wrought-iron fence surrounding Valentine's immense backyard. There was a pool *and* a tennis court, separated by a stone walkway through an overgrown English-style garden. From the other side of the fence, sweating in the heat, I watched a couple of dozen kids my own age cavorting in the pool and on the deck. They drank cans of Coke and ate sandwiches and chips. They cannonballed into the deep end, tipped each other's air mattresses, whooped and splashed and hollered. Some girl's bikini top came off and, screaming, she covered herself with her hands while the boys tossed it over her head.

As I dabbed my brush into the curves and angles of the fence, the sun beat down and rivulets of sweat ran down my face and plastered my shirt and jeans to my skin. I couldn't help resenting those kids at the pool. One girl in particular I couldn't help but notice; her narrow, exquisite face and large dark eyes, her straight midnight hair. She was the only girl to wear a one-piece bathing suit, the effect of which was to draw my eye not to her breasts or hips but to her wonderful legs. I didn't know how it was she drew my attention — compared to the other girls who shrieked and waved she was almost still — but she was impossible not to look at. I could see that the party's host was also giving her all of his attention.

Although I didn't know it at the time, this was the start of Valentine and Marjorie's romance. He had staged the party for the sole purpose of inviting her. By the late afternoon, my back was aching and my head throbbed from the smell of paint. I was concentrating on working the brush into a tight curve when I heard a voice say, "I thought you might be thirsty." I looked up and saw the girl with the raven hair holding out a can of Coke.

Her voice wasn't what I would have expected; it was more flat and nasal. "Thanks," I said, standing up and wiping my hand on my jeans. I took the can from over the fence, careful not to touch Marjorie's fingers with my own, which were tacky with paint. She smiled — I could see she had pleased herself by this act of kindness — and hurried back across the grass to the pool. I pulled the tab of the can and took a cold swig and watched as the boy waited for her to return, swooped her up in his arms, and dumped her shrieking into the deep end.

So it was Marjorie who I thought might have known me that first week in school. But when we passed in the hall and I smiled at her, she gave no sign of recognition. Annie Lynch recognized me, though. She'd been at the party too, as she later told me, but I had failed to single her out among the other girls.

17

One of the Living

THE TULIPS WERE ALREADY DROPPING their petals, the birds mad in the trees, bees working the front gardens. I passed the houses, Tudor, Spanish, English cottage, plastic and aluminum garbage cans neatly lined up at the curb, abandoned tricycles on the drives. A mailman slipped envelopes into a rusty mailbox, the creaking of the lid surprisingly loud. Families had grown up, moved on, new families had arrived. I wondered if Mr. Granatelli was living in some nursing home or had he gone back to Sicily as he always said he would, to be buried in the little cemetery overlooking the Tyrrhenian Sea.

The Movenpick restaurant in the strip mall, it turned out, was a kind of Disney version of the Europe I lived in: café tables along a faux-exterior stucco wall with a fake balcony and a realistic-looking plane tree spreading its papery leaves over the customers' heads. Including, I saw immediately, the head of Marjorie Luckenbill. She wore chic, narrow reading glasses to see the small book in one hand, a latte in the other. A beautiful woman in her middle years: lace-like lines around the eyes and the corners of the mouth, skin still lovely, a few strands of silver in the raven hair. A mohair sweater showed the angular lines of her shoulders.

Despite having been my best friend's girl, Marjorie and I had never felt any real connection or understanding. I used to think that she never quite saw me in focus, that I was somewhere in her peripheral vision. But now she looked up at me with apparently genuine pleasure. She rose to put her arms lightly around me and kiss me near my ear. "Huddie, it's so good to see you. I can't believe it's really you, after all these years. You look just the same."

"And you too, Marjorie. Better."

She gave a slight smile, accepting without really caring about the compliment. "I can't tell you what it means to me that you've come for Val's memorial. All the way from Prague. It's — it's more than I can put into words."

She sounded so personal in her gratitude, as if she were the prime mourner, the high-school widow of the late Valentine Schwartz, and not the girlfriend who had dumped him a week before his death. I said, "How did you find me? I was pretty surprised to get that email invitation. I didn't recognize who it was from at first. Marjorie Bluestein. I still think of you as Luckenbill."

"Grant wanted me to change it. I kind of wish I hadn't now, just as an example for my daughter, and actually I've been calling myself Luckenbill again. It wasn't hard to find you. I just searched your name. It comes up in all kinds of languages. Schedules for festivals in Germany, France, Holland. And the website of that bar in Prague where you play. Your group has a funny name, but I can't remember it."

"The Don River Boys." In Prague they assumed it was some wild river cascading down the Blue Ridge Mountains. They didn't know it was a polluted stream running under a Toronto highway. "So you really did marry Grant Bluestein. And you have a daughter, you say?"

"And a son too. She's sixteen and completely impossible. I think she's trying to kill me with worry. My son's ten. A real sweetie."

She sighed at the thought of them. She didn't reciprocate by asking about me, so I said, "I have to admit that I'm amazed the school is putting up a statue for Valentine. All I remember is how shocked and mortified the school board was. They just wanted it to go away. I guess twenty-five years changes things."

"That and somebody who wouldn't take no for an answer."

She couldn't suppress a little smile of triumph. I said, "What does it look like? The statue, I mean."

She leaned closer to me from across the table, hunching up those narrow shoulders. "Believe it or not, I haven't seen it. The shop teacher and his class want to keep it a secret. I'm a little put out, to tell you the truth, considering that I've organized the entire memorial. The committee has basically rubber-stamped all my decisions. Well, it better be good. It's going to be the way the Arthur Meighen community remembers him."

I didn't know there was an Arthur Meighen community, but I let that pass too. "Have you been in touch with Valentine's parents?" I asked. "Do you know where his family went afterwards?"

"No idea. I tried to find them but I couldn't. You know, there were rumours that came out the next year, after you were gone, that his father was crooked. Mixed up in some kind of mafia or organized-crime business. That was why he left the country. At least that's what I heard, but nobody seems to know for sure."

"There did seem something shady about Val's father," I said. "I never liked him much. He had this fake joviality about him. I thought he was a blowhard and a bit of a bully to Val."

"He used to come on to me," Marjorie said. "When he'd had a few drinks. Put his hand on my arm or my leg. At the time I didn't quite register what it was about, or maybe I didn't let myself think about it, but it always made me feel ill."

"Prick. Explains Valentine, in some ways. That neediness of his."

She visibly shuddered. "Let's talk about something else."

"Actually, I wanted to ask you about the memorial. I think it's an extraordinarily thoughtful idea but, well, is it really a good idea? I don't mean remembering him, but having a statue. I mean, he didn't invent insulin. He fell off the roof of the school, which was either a desperate act or, well, just not very smart."

"But he did it for a genuine reason."

"You mean you?"

She shook her head in frustration. "He was idealistic. He believed in something. It was so — so pure. That's what I want to be remembered, not the specifics of why. I just know the statue is a good idea. It's just something I really had to do, Huddie. Memorials are for the living, not for the dead. Well, I'm one of the living, aren't I? At least I think I'm still alive." She gave a wry smile, a more complicated look than she'd been capable of all those years ago. "The truth is, Valentine's death has affected my whole life. *Decided* my whole life."

"How can that be?"

"I'm sure it's why I married Grant. He might have just been another high-school boyfriend. We probably would have broken off after we went to different universities. But I hung on to Grant. Valentine died because I left him for Grant. It had to mean something, right? It couldn't just be for nothing."

"Jesus, Marjorie. Well, I hope it turned out for the best."

She didn't answer. "Do you know that the kids who go to the school now think of Valentine Schwartz as a joke? They hear bits and pieces of the story and they laugh at it."

"We would have laughed too."

"They say that the school is haunted with his ghost, that you can hear him clanking around in his armour. I just think that's awful. It mocks the memory of him. The memorial will bring Val's death out into the open. So he can be remembered and celebrated for who he really was."

"You sound very sure," I said. "Well, I'm glad that I'll be here."

"You better be. It's a week Friday. Listen, Huddie, I called you because I want you to be part of the ceremony."

"Excuse me?"

"You were his best friend. You could say a few words."

"I hate making speeches, Marjorie. I'm no good at them."

"All right. We've got enough people talking anyway. You could play something. You could sing and play your ukulele."

"Mandolin."

"Something appropriate. You know, solemn but uplifting and beautiful."

"I guess so. Sure."

She leaned over the table and kissed me on the cheek. I felt foolishly flattered; after all these years, she still had that power. "You can play while the statue is being unveiled. It's the final touch we need. Oh, I'm ecstatic." She paused again, looking somewhere past me to the shelves of expensive jams and European chocolates. That had been her usual habit, to look just over your shoulder, as if there was something more interesting going on. But then she looked at me again. "My daughter, Grace, goes to Arthur Meighen."

"That must feel a little strange."

"It does when she bothers to show up for class. I'm worried she won't even make the year. She's having a tough time finding a reason to care. If I let her, she'd lie on the sofa all day and read trashy magazines. We have such different temperaments it's hard for me to understand her. I didn't have those problems. And lately I can hardly talk to her. Screaming at her — that I can do. But talking is another matter."

"It's a hard age. It must even be harder these days."

"Actually, Huddie, the one thing she seems to have any energy for is music. Not your kind, of course, but some awful heavy metal-punk revival thing, I really don't know. She plays guitar. She has an electric and the other kind."

"Acoustic."

"Right. I bought that one for her hoping she'd make less noise. It's a good one, the man in the store said, and it wasn't cheap. A Martin."

"Good enough."

"Mostly she plays the electric though. God, what a noise. You know, Huddie, she might like to meet a real working musician."

"Or she might have the opposite reaction. I don't have any great wisdom to impart."

"You've got one big advantage over me. You're not her mother."

"Of course I'll talk to her if you want me to."

"I'd be grateful."

She picked up the book on the table, as if she really was going to go. The dust jacket looked familiar to me and I realized that

I had seen it in Larry's back seat, floating among the junk. On the dust jacket was a sepia-toned photograph of an unmade bed on which a woman was sleeping, her hair fanned on the pillow, bare arm over the quilt, narrow foot peeking out. And beside her, visible only as a form beneath the quilt, another body. Except that from the bottom of the quilt curled a long, hairless tail. As Marjorie turned her hand, I could see the title on the cover, *Rattsmann*, but her hand was covering the author's name. She moved her fingers. *Felix Roth*.

"That's Felix's book?" I asked. "The guy who went to our school?"

"Uh-huh. His latest novel. Although I haven't actually read any of the others."

So he really had become an author. I had always liked Felix. He'd been quiet most of the time, and then he'd raise his hand and say something smart or funny or both. He was terrible at sports, even worse than I was.

"Is the book any good? What's it about?"

She sighed. "I don't really know. It's very strange. I feel kind of sick reading it but I can't quite put it down. It's hard not to think about Felix, you know, wondering if it has anything to do with his life. I hope not for his sake. He lives in New York. I haven't seen him for years. Of course, we weren't very friendly."

From a nearby table, people started singing "Happy Birthday." I turned and saw them standing around a very, very old woman. I couldn't remember seeing someone that ancient in a restaurant. Frail, almost skeletal, her eye sockets deep, the skin of her lips split, and with some sort of lesion on her neck. But her remaining strands of hair were arranged neatly beneath the brim of her hat, her dress was new and pretty, and her eyes were amazingly bright. When the song ended she leaned forward and just managed to blow out the candle on a piece of cake. Then as they all applauded and whooped, she smiled a little, as if pleased that she had made them feel good about themselves.

Marjorie glanced at the woman without expression. "I've got a million things to do today."

I felt as if I had been dismissed. Nevertheless, I asked Marjorie to give me a lift back to my mother's house. She looked a little miffed, but she recovered herself and became gracious, telling me as we got into her gold Lexus about the business she started five years ago, importing a high-end line of French fashion, which she presented to clients at private showings in their homes. The best thing about the work, even if it didn't break even yet, was that she got to go to France twice a year by herself. "Five days of heaven," she said.

As she pulled out of the lot, I noticed a group of teenagers by the side of the road. A couple of the boys had skateboards. "There's Grace," Marjorie said. "In the leather jacket."

She waved at her daughter, but Grace just stared at us as we went by, cigarette in hand. I could see hair dyed purple-black, army pants, boots, leather jacket with chains, dark rings painted around the eyes. And something glinting — a nose ring, maybe.

As if reading my thoughts, Marjorie said, "She's got a stud in her tongue too. In her tongue! You think she asked me before she had it done? This is what my beautiful baby does to herself. It makes me want to be sick when I look at her. She has a tattoo on her lower back. You can see it when her shirt rides up, letters in Chinese or Japanese, God knows what it says. You know what I think of when I see a tattoo? Concentration camps. I'm sure she did it to upset me. When we were kids, we didn't mutilate ourselves. We cared about our futures. We didn't hate our parents."

The car turned into Elysian Fields. "It could be worse," I said. "In Europe, she would have run away to live in some communal squat in an abandoned fire trap of a building."

"We had a chance to be innocent," she said.

"I'm not sure what that means. We made choices too."

She pulled the car over in front of my mother's house and smiled in an unhappy way.

"Get out of my car, Huddie. I have things to do."

18

Bugs Bunny or Road Runner

THE SECOND TIME I TRIED to visit Valentine Schwartz during his hospital stay was on a school morning. I skipped first-period English and rode my bike through light traffic to the North York General. I wasn't sure if visiting was allowed during the day, so I walked quickly past the receptionist's desk and went straight to Valentine's room. His door was open and I saw that he was alone. On the small television anchored to the ceiling Bugs Bunny and Daffy Duck were pushing Elmer Fudd's gun back and forth, saying, "*Duck* season," "*Rabbit* season." I couldn't tell if Valentine was watching or just staring at the television because he couldn't move. His breakfast tray lay on a table with wheels, but from the look of it, he hadn't eaten much.

Probably I should leave, I thought, but I tapped my fist on the door.

"Who's that? Marjorie?"

"No, sorry. It's Huddie Rosen." Sheepishly I moved into his line of vision, my hands shoved into my pocket. "I'm in your gym class."

"Oh, right. And history, too."

"Yeah, with Tillitson."

"That guy's already got it in for me. And the way he calls everybody by his last name. 'No, Mr. Schwartz. That's wrong, Mr. Schwartz.' What's with that? The guy teaches the most boring subject in the entire school, except maybe French, and he acts like he's the dean of Harvard or something. Okay, military history, or Napoleon maybe. But he teaches *Canadian* history. The rebellion of 1837. Building the railroad. Nobody can stay awake through that. What's your name again?"

"Huddie."

"I've never heard that one before."

"It's a nickname. Because I don't like my real name. Howard. *Howie.* I don't know what my parents were thinking. A couple of summers ago I was complaining to my dad about how much I hate my name and he came up with 'Huddie.' After Huddie Ledbetter, the American blues and folk singer."

"He was a Hebe?"

"No, he was black, from Louisiana. He did time in jail for killing a man but the governor let him out because he was such a good singer."

"That's some nickname," Valentine said. I thought he might say something about his own unusual name, but he didn't. Maybe he didn't realize there was anything weird about it. "So tell me, Huddie," he said as I sat down on a metal stool at the foot of the bed, "who do you think is smarter, Bugs Bunny or Road Runner?"

I looked over my shoulder and saw that a Road Runner cartoon had come on. The coyote was uncrating a box of Acme dynamite. "Let me see. I'd say it has to be Bugs Bunny. Because he has human characteristics. I mean, he can talk. The Road Runner is just a smart bird."

"But that's just my point." Valentine's voice rose in excitement at his idea. "Bugs Bunny isn't a real rabbit at all. He's not realistic. It's not actually a valid comparison. The Road Runner is as smart as a real bird could be. He's more — what's the word?"

"Plausible?"

"Yeah, that's it. He's more plausible. So really the Road Runner is the smarter one because Bugs is totally not believable. Do me a favour and turn off the goddamn TV."

I did so, having to reach over the end of the bed. Then I just stood there as Valentine stared at the blank screen.

"What time is it?" he said. "Marjorie is supposed to come at noon."

"It's not even ten."

"You ever meet Marjorie?"

"Not really."

"If I don't see her for a while, this thing happens to me. It's like I'm a drug addict in withdrawal. Once she was an hour late — her family was at a wedding or something — and I started to shake all over. It was bizarre even to me. And my heart hurts. All the time. You ever experience something like that?"

"I don't think so."

"I never told anyone about it. Man, I've got to get out of this hospital. There are people in here who are actually dying. Cancer, brain tumours — it's like a horror movie. Yesterday some guy wandered in, oxygen tubes in his nose, a line sticking in his arm. His skin was the colour of the sidewalk. Emphysema, he tells me. Maybe nine more months to live. Then he asks do I like Scrabble. No, I don't want to play Scrabble with a man who's going to be dead in nine months. Get the hell out of my room! Anyway, that's what I want to say. But instead I play Scrabble with him, and I hate Scrabble. I'm no good with words. The guy beat me ten zillion to one, and during the whole game he was like bragging and taunting me, telling how he was creaming my ass. I wanted the bastard to die right then, forget about nine months. I'll tell you, Huddie, this is not a place to lift the spirits."

"When can you leave?"

"Maybe a day or two."

"Will you be in a wheelchair?" I asked. That was what everybody in school had been saying.

"Nah. Just one of those collars for a while. And no sports for a few months. I even get out of gym."

"You mean you'll be able to walk?"

"I could walk now if they'd let me. My spine was bruised, that's all. Doctor said I was one lucky fuck. One foot less of water and I'd be on a wooden platform with wheels begging for change in the subway."

"So you're coming back to school."

"Not right away. My mother agrees that I ought to ease into things, you know?"

"Absolutely."

"I get tired."

"Of course."

We were silent again. "I guess I better go and let you rest," I said.

"You want to stick around and meet Marjorie?"

"I've got a class. If you want, I can make you a copy of my history notes."

"Listen, Huddie, don't tell anybody about how I feel about Marjorie. Getting the shakes and that. People don't get it."

"No, I wouldn't say anything. I'll see you, Valentine."

"I remember that you were the one, Huddie."

"The one?"

"Who told me not to dive. Pretty retarded of me, I guess."

"But impressive."

"Yeah, retarded *and* impressive. Next time you give me advice I think I'm going to take you up on it."

I moved to the door. "I'll bring you those history notes."

"I'm sincere about that," he said. "I'm nothing if not a sincere guy."

19
LittleOnlineMama

MY MOTHER WAS MAKING BREADED eggplant in the kitchen, the little television on the counter tuned to Oprah Winfrey. She would take a slice of eggplant that she had put between paper towels, cans on top as weights to squeeze out the water, then dip them in the breading before laying them on the frying pan to sizzle. The smell was exquisite. "It's one of Oprah's book shows," my mother said. "She picks a book and it's an instant bestseller. Millions of copies. If your old schoolmate Felix could get his book on Oprah's show, he'd be set for life."

"It's funny you mention him. I just saw Marjorie Luckenbill with Felix's new book."

"Oh, I've read them all. I reserve them at the library. It's a little thrill, having known the author when he was a teenager."

"How's the new one?" I picked up a fork and speared a slice of eggplant that looked ready. Really I was trying to decide whether to say something about Marta phoning in the night. I wanted to talk about it, but I felt bad enough without my mother tearing a strip off me. Even at the age of forty-two you could fear your mother's wrath.

"It's different. Usually they're funny and touching. Novels about middle-class Jewish family life and relationships. Like the one about the young woman who goes to Paris to meet her great aunt who was in the resistance. I cried at the end. Or else they're weird. A newspaper writer who invents bizarre facts to insert into the obituaries he has to write. Or the one that moves backwards in time, so that a wealthy, assimilated Jewish family ends up in the shtetl. But this book isn't just weird, it's also sick. Funny and touching too, somehow, but definitely sick. So how's the eggplant?"

"Incredible. You really don't have to cook for me all the time."

"Why, do you plan to stop eating? So I gather Marta phoned you last night."

"Yes, she did."

"How is she?"

"To tell you the truth, I'm not sure."

"I knew things weren't always great, but you've never said anything to me. What happened? Is it impossible to fix?"

"I don't know. But I don't feel like talking about it, Mom."

"You're just like your father. He kept things bottled up. He wouldn't tell me how miserable he was at work. He'd just go down into the basement and listen to his records."

"What was there to tell? It was obvious how much he hated being a manager."

"Forgive me, but I think there might have been more to say. You were just a boy, Howie. Perhaps you shouldn't be so quick to judge."

"I don't even want to judge."

"Yes, you do. You always have. And this is a very neat way of diverting the topic."

"You brought up Dad, not me."

"Don't split hairs. You know, she phones me once in a while."

"Who?"

"Marta."

"Marta phones you? When?"

"Every week or two, when she's got a free moment. I tell her to reverse the charges. We chat."

"She never told me that she phones you on her own. What do you talk about?"

"The kids mostly. My exercise. Her work. When it gets her down and she wishes she could quit and do something else."

"She's never said that to me."

"I don't think she wants to worry you."

"Does she talk about me?"

"My son the narcissist."

"I mean, does she talk about us?"

"Never. She didn't give me an inkling either. Of course she talks about you — what you're doing, how many concerts you're giving."

"They're not concerts, they're just gigs."

"Gig. Am I hip now? Sometimes she asks me things like what you were like as a child. Whether you were a moody teenager, whether you talked about things that bothered you. I guess she's trying to understand you better."

"I'm not hard to understand. I always think I'm see-through. It's everyone else who's hard. But it's nice that the two of you talk."

"Yes, it is. She always lifts my day a little. So look, Mr. Cellophane, you want to see what I'm doing in the basement?"

"I've already guessed. You've become like the old ladies in *Arsenic and Old Lace*. You're making friends with lonely old men and then poisoning them. They're buried in the basement."

"How dull. Actually, I'm selling your father's records."

"You're what? Oh shit —"

I spilled coffee over my hand. It was near-scalding hot, the way my mother liked it. "Come here," she said, turning the cold water on. I thrust my hand under the jet. "Is it bad? Will you still be able to play your mandolin?"

She'd never shown concern about that before. "It just stings a little. What do you mean, you're selling Dad's records?"

"They've been sitting in that basement for twenty-five years. For twenty-five years I've been emptying water out of the dehumidifier and checking the temperature, making sure they don't get damaged. Well, I'm tired of it. I've asked you to take them —"

"I can't take thousands of records to Prague. Just shipping them would cost a fortune. I'd have nowhere to put them."

"Exactly why I'm selling them. On eBay."

"You're selling them online? You don't even have a computer."

"I do so. I bought one and a nice man from the store set me up. He showed me how to use the digital camera to take a photograph of the record, how to download it, how to sign onto eBay and put the records up for sale. I've been doing it for over two months."

"This I've got to see."

"Come on down then."

I followed her down the hall to the basement entrance. She switched on the light and as we headed down I breathed in the smell that hadn't changed, musty and sour. I had a sudden image of myself coming down these stairs to find my father leaning back in the chair, eyes closed, a trance-like expression on his face as the stereo played Lonnie Johnson's bright guitar picking or Hammie Nixon's harmonica or the delicate drawl of Mississippi John Hurt. Dad's metal shelves still lined all the walls and ran down the length of the basement room in two rows, but about two-thirds of them were empty. On the desk where Dad had sat cataloguing his latest acquisitions stood a Dell computer. Beside it was a bridge table stacked with stiff mailing envelopes, labels, packaging tape.

My mother touched the computer and the screen flickered to life. "I've got high-speed," she said proudly, clicking on the Internet icon. The eBay home page came up on the screen with her seller's name at the top: LittleOnlineMama. She clicked again and I saw a list of her current items for sale: Tampa Red's "Gin Headed Woman" on the Bluebird label, Willy Trice's "One Dime Blues" on Trix, Blind Willie Johnson's "Take Your Burden to the Lord and Leave it There" on Columbia. Almost all of them had bids and some were up into the hundreds of dollars. Memphis Minnie and Kansas Joe's "My Mary Blues" on the Vocalion label was up to $397.50.

"At the beginning, I would try to describe the records," my mother said. "I'd use your father's history books on music to say why a record was important. But I discovered that all the collectors in New York and Buenos Aires and Paris already know about them. I just have to describe the condition. And the bids come in."

"How much have you made so far?" I asked.

"Twelve thousand, three-hundred and twenty-six dollars."

I whistled. "That's some nice pin money, Mom. You going on a cruise?"

"It isn't for me."

"Mom ..."

"It's for the girls. It's for a down payment on a house in Toronto."

"What in the world are you talking about?"

"What else are you doing here then? Coming home after all these years. You're thinking of moving back, I know it. But you don't have any money, I know that too. All that time that your father spent in record stores, going through catalogues, browsing in flea markets and garage sales and Salvation Army stores. I resented it then but I'm glad now. It'll help put a roof over his granddaughter's heads."

I felt my heart start to beat fast again and it became hard to catch my breath. "Mom, this is crazy. I'm not planning to move back. I've never thought about buying a house." But I was thinking: could she be right? Maybe, somewhere in my crazed brain, I was thinking of coming back.

"Now go find something to do," my mother said. "I've got to put more records up for auction and I've got a dozen completed sales to package up and take to the post office. LittleOnline-Mama is back at work."

20
Sorghum Boy

AT SEVENTEEN, I DIDN'T KNOW any bluegrass music. I knew only a few old-time songs by the Carter Family from a record that my father had got in a box at a garage sale. My father never listened to the album, but I liked to put it on when nobody was home and hear the simple, elemental singing, accompanied by guitar and autoharp. I never played it for anyone. Everyone else I knew listened to the CHUM radio top-twenty countdown every week and bought 45s of "Joy to the World" and Alice Cooper's "School's Out." I didn't think they were going to appreciate Maybelle Carter's fingerpicking "Wildwood Flower" or A.P.'s harmonies on "Keep on the Sunny Side."

My father complained that there were no good finds in the local used record shops in Toronto, but he would visit them once a month or so anyway, and sometimes I would go with him. That was how I got my first mandolin, which was sitting on a shelf next to a clock that didn't work. When I asked the man behind the counter if I could see it, my father said that a guitar was a lot more versatile and offered to buy me one instead, but I told the man that I would take it and paid the twenty dollars out of my own wallet.

The mandolin was made in Taiwan and sounded like a tin cigar box. It had a gourd-shaped back and short neck, an instrument to be played by a strolling musician in an Italian restaurant with checked tablecloths and candles stuck in wine bottles. I didn't know a thing about mandolins, I just liked it because it was small and different and it wasn't a guitar. I used it to pick out single-note melodies and two-finger chords to accompany the songs on that Carter Family album, which was the only such record I had until I went clothes shopping with my mother at the Yorkdale Shopping Mall and found a copy of the Nitty Gritty Dirt Band's *Will the Circle Be Unbroken* in the record store. That was an album that introduced a lot of people to old-time and bluegrass music. The band had brought in a bunch of traditional musicians to play with them — Roy Acuff, Earl Scruggs, Doc Watson, Vassar Clements — and it sounded like a loose and friendly acoustic jam. I loved it from the first listen. It let me imagine that making music with other people might be the kind of pleasure that I was looking for.

Those records were my only instruction in playing the mandolin until after my father died and I went to Tennessee. I'd come farther than any other student, most of whom were from within two hundred miles. I took courses in history and philosophy and read the assigned books, but I was too restless to sit in classes and I didn't go to half of them. Some of my dormmates and I started hanging out on weekends at a bar off campus, where I became familiar with that Tennessee institution called Jack Daniels. The bar had a house band called the Sorghum County Boys, the first bluegrass band that I ever saw live. Actually, none of them had been a boy for a half-century or so. My friends took the music for granted; they were more interested in the booze and the girls, but I watched and listened with barely restrained excitement to that band, especially the mandolin player. He was white-haired and paunchy — his mandolin sort of lay slanted on his stomach — but he could make it smoke on the fast fiddle tunes. And on the ballads and waltzes he made it shiver and weep with his slides and pull-offs and tremolo. I'd left my round-backed mandolin in Toronto, so I went to a swap shop in Knoxville and bought myself an old plywood-top Stradolin. Finally I got up the nerve to introduce myself during one of the band's breaks and discovered that bluegrass musicians were mostly easygoing, friendly, approachable people. And so I met Charlie Joyce.

He was from a little place called Siloam Springs, Arkansas, in the Ozark Mountains, but he'd lived all over the South. Mostly he'd worked in factories and metal shops, but in his later years he'd taken to woodwork and furniture building. That was where he got the skills to build mandolins, in a little shed behind his house, making two or three a year and getting five hundred dollars for each. When I met him he was in a small factory that made pressed-back rocking chairs. He'd never been a full-time musician, but he'd played all his life and had shared the stage at festivals with some big names — Red Allen, the Stoney Mountain Boys, the Cox Family. He'd jammed more than a few times with Bill Monroe, over at Monroe's annual Bean Blossom Festival.

It was Charlie who showed me how to play mandolin. Later I realized that he was a limited player, relying heavily on a couple of dozen licks, never varying his tone or his relentless, machine-gun firing of eighth notes, but he was more than good enough to be my teacher. I'd go over to his house outside of town where he and his wife, Holly, lived, one of those narrow trailer homes that I'd seen only in movies about white trash.

They had fixed it up comfortably, putting in a proper garden and fence and a vegetable patch in the back. We'd sit on lawn chairs with lemonade at our feet (Charlie having taken the pledge) and play together while Holly was in the kitchen making dinner for whoever might drop in, neighbours or grown-up kids with their own little ones. Right away Charlie made me get a new mandolin and I bought a used Washburn from a music shop in Nashville. It wasn't too loud, and its tone was only decent, but it had a bluegrass sound. He showed me how to move the chord shapes up the fretboard and help drive the music with a surging rhythm chop. He taught me breaks for the standard fiddle tunes — "Big Sandy" and "Red-Haired Boy" and "Temperance Reel" — and made me come up with my own variations. I learned fast, but then I practised endlessly, to the detriment of my university studies, and after six months Charlie let me sit in with the Sorghum County Boys for a few of the slower tunes.

For me, bluegrass was like finding religion. Of course I wouldn't have said that to Charlie, who'd returned to the church and asked me so many questions about being a Jew that I wished I'd paid more attention in Hebrew school. After two years of playing I was good enough to join a band of young pickers. Meanwhile I had delved into the history and tradition of old-time and country and bluegrass music. I listened to records, I drove two hundred miles and more to hear other bands play at bars or in concerts. I camped overnight at festivals, listening to music during the day and jamming all night, first keeping to the outside of the circle, quietly playing along with the fiddles and banjos, and then moving into the circle itself. And at the end of those two and a half years, I'd had enough of university. Everybody tried to persuade me not to quit when I was so close to graduating, including Charlie Joyce, who thought education a wondrous thing he hadn't had much opportunity of, and who knew plenty of musicians who had tried and failed to make a decent living. Holly tried even harder to persuade me to stay in school; later I learned that she was having telephone conversations with my mother and had agreed to act as a maternal substitute. But though I came back to Toronto to take the law-school exam, I wouldn't give in.

I remember Charlie sighing and saying to me at last, "You can't be playing that Washburn anymore. Not if you want to get somewhere."

I knew that well enough, but I didn't have the money for a good mandolin. The best players all had either vintage Gibsons or instruments hand built by luthiers, and I couldn't afford either. That was when Charlie said he would build me one as "a graduation present even if you aren't going to graduate." By now he had a reputation and was getting more money for his mandolins, money I knew he counted on since the factory had cut back his hours. I didn't want to take it, but he said that he felt responsible for encouraging me and anyway, he'd just build an extra one this year to make up for it.

I didn't much help build it — Charlie didn't like anyone interfering in his shop — but I watched my mandolin being made, dropping in as often as I could over the next weeks. I saw him cut and bend the sides from old maple boards he had stored away. I saw him carve the gradual arch into the spruce top, using calipers to gauge the thinness of the wood. The neck was fitted with a dovetail joint for strength. Then came the ebony fretboard, the mother-of-pearl inlay in the headstock. At my request he didn't use a traditional reddish sunburst for the finish, but a deeper stain, lightening just a little towards the centre of the top and back. The finishing itself took hours and here he let me help, rubbing the wood in small circles, working the varnish in. Then came the day when he finally strung it up. "It needs time and lots of playing to open up, especially in the bass end," Charlie said, before handing it to me in the shed. "But go on, give us an idea of what it'll sound like."

I could hardly believe it was in my hands. I fished a pick out of my jeans' pocket and started to play the "Lonesome Moonlight Waltz." It sounded wonderful from the first note. Pure highs and deep vibrating lows. A great bark of a rhythm chop that could drive any bluegrass band. I hardly knew what to say to Charlie, so I put the mandolin down and hugged him, which he let me do for all of three seconds.

He was around for only another seven months, the third in the trilogy of deaths that I knew as a young man. Like most of his buddies, he'd been a heavy smoker since the age of fourteen. His last month in hospital was a cruel trial for him and Holly and their children. I would have liked to be a pallbearer, but there were too many people who knew Charlie longer and better and who wanted to walk him to his final resting place in the Baptist cemetery outside his hometown in Arkansas.

The mandolin wasn't all that Charlie gave me. He had told the other members of the Sorghum County Boys that they might ask me to step in for him. Gordy Pike, the bass player, approached me two weeks after the funeral. He would have preferred to wait longer, out of respect for Charlie, but the summer season was coming up and they had bookings for festivals in Tennessee, Kentucky, Illinois, and Ohio. They were all going to take partial leaves from their jobs like they did every year and they needed to know whether I would come with them. I didn't feel ready but I said yes. I became a Sorghum Boy. We played two or three sets a day on outdoor stages plus the Sunday morning gospel hour, sometimes in brutal heat that made you sweat so much it was all you could do to keep a pick between your fingers. The fans (I had been one just weeks before) expected you to do some parking-lot picking with them between times. If I wasn't a real musician at the start of that summer, I was by the end, I learned to sing lead and harmony, I took more melodic breaks, I played a more interesting rhythm backup. Whenever I could, I'd pull aside a more seasoned mandolin player to show me a lick or two. I learned to get along inside the family that was a musical group, learned when to laugh and when to be firm and when to just shut up. And I discovered that place you go to when your mind and your heart and your hands have merged with the sound around you into some pure, driving, life force. The only place I've ever really felt at home.

21
Deep

LARRY NUSSBAUM, WEARING HIS SUIT trousers but with his jacket replaced by an apron emblazoned with the words *This Wasn't In the Job Description*, worked frantically at the stove. He looked like an inexperienced short-order cook during the morning rush. As the door was open, I had walked in, carrying a bakery box and a paper bag from the wine store, past the discarded high-tops, baseball gloves, skateboard, and knapsacks. The hall closet was so stuffed with tennis racquets and Rollerblades that the accordion door had jammed, as I discovered on trying to hang up my beat-up leather jacket I'd bought in the Prague flea market.

Before I had a chance to say hello to Larry, two boys appeared out of nowhere, tumbling across my feet as they wrestled for a football. The younger one was trying to pry it out of the older one's hands, calling, "You didn't touch it with both hands!" The older one had a smart-alecky grin on his face; he knew how much stronger he was. But then the younger one ran his nails over the older one's hands — clearly he'd learned some compensating skills. As the older one yelped and let go of the ball, the younger one snatched it and took off up the stairs. The older one followed, screaming vengeance.

"Remind me to punish one of them, or maybe both," Larry said, waving a wooden spoon in greeting. In the kitchen three pots were going on the stove, two chickens were roasting in the oven, and the makings of a salad were spread over the counter and chopping board. Through the archway to the dining room, I could see plates stacked but not yet laid out.

"Everything under control?"

"I'm a fly-by-the-seat-of-my pants sort of chef. I don't think the male mind is designed to do four things at once. Oh shit, I've got to drain the potatoes before they disintegrate. Hot water coming through!"

He picked up the pot with an oven mitt on one hand and a T-shirt wrapped around the other. While pouring into a strainer, he splashed his arm.

"Fuck! That hurts."

"Fuck that hurts," repeated a much higher voice. We both turned to see the youngest Nussbaum standing in the kitchen doorway. For some reason he was in his pyjamas, which were inside out. He also wore a generous application of lipstick and rouge on his face.

"Natey, this is my old friend Huddie."

"Hi, Huddie."

"Hi, Nate. It's very nice of you to invite me for dinner."

"Did we invite you for dinner?"

"Yes, we did," Larry said.

"Why didn't we invite Will Higgs?"

"Will Higgs is a terror. The last time Will Higgs came over he put the goldfish in the toilet bowl."

Nate thought for a moment, shrugged, and turned around again.

"Please wash off the makeup before dinner," Larry said. And then to me, "He gets into his mother's stuff. I don't know if he likes the makeup because it belonged to his mom or because he's going to grow up to become a drag queen."

"Cute kid either way," I said. "Can I do something to help? I'm pretty good at messing up a kitchen myself, if you don't mind my bragging."

"You can make the salad. Just don't do some fancy European thing to it."

"Trust me, you don't want to know what a salad in Prague is like. The Czechs are a carnivorous people." I started to chop the cucumber. "The boys look like they're doing all right," I said, awkwardly trying to slide into the subject.

"Pretty well now. The first year was rough. We were all lost. I couldn't hide my own grief from them. We'd set each other off. Daniel stopped doing his work. He almost lost his year. Mark got into fights with other kids. Natey just cried. He clung to me wherever we went, like he was afraid I would disappear too. Laundry piled up. The fridge was empty half the time. My mother wanted to move in and help, but I wouldn't let her. Every so often people rescued us. Your mother a few times."

"My mom?"

"I don't know how she heard, I hadn't seen her in years. But she showed up one day with a carload of groceries. Cleaned the bathroom, threw in the laundry, made dinner. Like a fairy godmother. I should have thought to ask her for dinner tonight."

"I took the liberty of asking for you. She's out with my uncle and aunt. I'm sorry I wasn't here to help, Larry."

"No reason you should have been. Everyone shouldn't have constructed their lives to help the Nussbaums."

"Can you afford to get someone in?"

"I tried at first, but that was a worse disaster. The kids hated having a stranger around. We've developed a routine that works, more or less. Laundry days. Take-out dinners. The kids have learned to help. I'm pretty proud of them. And it'll get easier, at least that's what I tell myself. Sometimes I think I don't deserve them, the mistakes I make, the way I lose my temper, break pencils in half —"

"You break pencils?"

"Pencils, pens. Once I was so frustrated by Daniel refusing to get in the bath that I ripped up an entire box of Kleenex. Like confetti everywhere. My kids stared at me as if I was a lunatic."

The salad ready, I tossed in the bottled dressing and put the bowl on the dining table. "You haven't told me anything about your life," Larry said, taking the chickens out of the oven. They looked more than a little dry. The smell from the open oven must have wafted upstairs, for the three boys came racing down, all claiming to be the most ravenous. Larry realized that he had forgotten to mash the potatoes so I did them while he and the kids finished setting the table and pouring drinks. Larry opened the bottle of wine. Natey solemnly handed us each a yarmulke and then together Larry and the boys lit the Shabbat candles and made the *bruchas* over the wine and the bread. Natey fidgeted and Daniel smirked, but they got through them.

Throughout dinner, Larry was telling one to sit down, another not to grab, a third to move his glass from the edge of the table. The two older boys ate like starving wolves, but Natey had to be reminded every few minutes that there was food in front of him.

Larry knew their friends, their teachers, what books they were reading, the standings of the teams they played on, and it gave me a keen pleasure to watch them all. I was permitted to bring out the dessert I had brought, a double chocolate cake that received tremendous cheers. "I forgot it's dairy," I said. "Do you keep kosher?"

"What are we, fanatics?" Larry said. "Make sure I get the biggest piece."

It took considerable effort, but the four of us managed to finish the cake down to the last overly sweet bite. Then the boys cleared the table with frightening speed — I thought the dishes would shatter in the sink — and took their hockey sticks and tennis ball out to the front drive. "Daniel, you keep an eye on Natey," Larry yelled. "No running after the ball onto the road."

"I know, I know."

Larry and I began to tackle the mess in the kitchen, he washing and I drying. Before he had a chance to ask me about myself again, I said, "Are you going to go to Valentine's memorial?"

"Marjorie Bluestein, formerly Luckenbill, hardly gives one a choice. Believe it or not she roped me onto the planning committee. Me, who refused all school activities. I can't believe you've come back," he said with a half laugh. "Huddie Rosen. You were different from a lot of the other kids at Arthur Meighen. Not pampered."

"You know who I think about sometimes?" I said. "Annie Lynch."

"Yeah, you had a thing for her. That was obvious. She thought I was a clown. Or maybe an asshole. Or both. So did you sleep with her or what?"

"That I'll never tell. I wonder how she's doing."

"Why don't you ask her yourself?"

"What do you mean. She's in Toronto?"

"She's the principal of Arthur Meighen."

"Get out!"

"I'm dead serious. Three years now. Came from another school in the district, and a French teacher before that, I think."

"But she hated it here. Hated the neighbourhood, the school. She was the one person I thought would get out."

"Well, she came back. Like you."

"I'm not back. I'm just visiting. Why do people keep saying that?"

With the dishes done and the kids still hollering outside, we took our glasses and the bottle of wine into the living room. Photographs of his wife, Andrea, stood on the mantle, on end tables, were hung on the walls. Wedding pictures, babies in strollers, sandcastles by the ocean. But we were done with personal things for now and talked instead about the Toronto Maple Leafs of our high-school days, the team of Sittler and Keon and Salming, the playoff series against the Bruins and the Flyers. I noticed Felix Roth's novel, *Rattsmann*, lying open on top of the stereo. I asked about it, and Larry said he really shouldn't leave it lying around, considering how full of sex it was, even if it was mostly sex between a human and a giant rodent.

It was getting dark beyond the windows and Larry called in the kids. He cajoled the two younger ones into getting into their pyjamas. Just as they were to get into bed they remembered that I had not been introduced to the guinea pigs. I was escorted down to the basement to meet Ruffles, Hank, and Beep, and to offer each of them a carrot as a goodwill gesture. Then it was back upstairs.

Nate said, "What's your name again?"

"Huddie."

"Can Huddie read to me?"

Larry said, "All right. But just one book because it's late."

"Two."

"Okay, two."

Nate kneeled down before his bookshelf and made a careful choice: *Miss Nelson is Missing!* and *Come Back, Amelia Bedelia*. "They're both funny," he said solemnly, handing them to me as he got into bed. He sat up waiting, face washed, hair combed, pyjama top buttoned up.

"Which one do you want first?" I asked.

He looked at me. "Are you a dad?"

"Uh-huh."

"What are your kids' names?"

"Maggie and Birdy. Well, that's what I call them. Their real names are Margita and Bela. Birdy's your age. Maggie is the older one."

"Do they like guinea pigs?"

"I don't think they've ever seen one, but I'm sure they would."

"You can bring them over."

"I would like to. But they live far away."

"Why?"

"Because that's where they were born."

"They didn't come with you?"

"No, not this time."

"What do they do?"

"I'm sorry?"

"What do they do?"

"You mean, what do they like to do? Let me think. Well, one thing we all like is to go to the zoo. We ride this very old wooden tram to get there — that's a lot of fun too. Our favourite animals are the elephants."

"I like elephants too."

"Do you? Well, the girls have one particular favourite. She's the smallest and her name is Klára. She has very pretty eyes. We buy a bag of peanuts and the girls feed her. She takes the peanuts very delicately with the end of her trunk. It tickles your hand."

"I would like to feed her."

"She would like that, I'm sure."

"How come you call them Maggie and Birdy?"

"I don't know. I just gave them nicknames when they were little and I used to sing to them in their beds at night. Now they don't want me to call them anything else. Do you want to hear their songs?"

"Yes."

"Some of Maggie's goes like this." I came closer and sang quietly.

> *Last time I saw little Maggie*
> *She was setting on the banks of the sea,*
> *With a forty-four around her*
> *And a banjo on her knee.*
>
> *Lay down your last gold dollar*
> *Lay down your gold watch and chain.*
> *Little Maggie's gonna dance for daddy*
> *Listen to this old banjo ring.*

Nate said, "Does she play the banjo?"

"No, not really. She's taking piano lessons, though."

"And what about Birdy's song?"

"Okay, here goes.

*I'm a free little bird as I can be, I can be,
I'm a free little bird as I can be.
I built my nest in a willow tree,
Where the bad boys, they cannot bother me.*

"Are there bad boys on your street?" he asked, looking keenly interested.

"No, they're just in the song. It's very old."

"Actually," he said, "Beep is a replacement guinea pig. We had another but he got away from us when we were playing on the front lawn. A car squished him."

"How awful."

"That's why we named this one Beep. So he can, you know, 'beep-beep' if a car is coming. You can read now," he said, putting his hands behind his head.

22

The Band Is Not Resembling Itself

LARRY LEFT THE TEENAGE GIRL from next door in charge while he drove me back to Finchley Crescent, waiting in the battered Mercedes until I got in, like I was a date he had to see safely home. The light in the kitchen was on and as my mother had neglected to pull the curtain I could see her sitting at the kitchen table. She had a cup of tea by her hand but as I approached the house in the dark she didn't touch it. She stared across the kitchen somewhere towards the toaster oven, her face almost expressionless except for a slight downward turn of her mouth. Living in Prague, I had sometimes wondered whether my mother kept secrets from me, whether she had a life that I didn't know about. A gentleman friend perhaps, a retired widower, well-mannered, who would take her to restaurants and plays. Looking at her now — she did not move, she might have been made of stone — I knew that she had no secret life. What I saw through that window *was* her life. That morning I had seen her take a pill at the kitchen sink, the prescription name blacked out with marker. What was it for? I'd given her no chance to speak of such things.

At the side door I made a deliberate noise of rattling and jangling. By the time I came into the kitchen she had the teacup in her hand and was smiling brightly. I noticed a stack of sealed and labelled mailing envelopes stacked neatly on the floor: my father's records about to disappear into other people's collections. "Did you have a good time?" she asked.

"I did. His kids are pretty great. How about you?"

"You know your Uncle Norman and Aunt Min. They sent back their meals twice. But I spent an hour on eBay when I got home. Did very well on the auctions that ended today."

"What did you sell?"

"Let me think. Records by Charley Patton, Bukka White, Furry Lewis, Texas Alexander and someone else. Oh yes, Victoria Spivey."

"Patton and White were favourites of Dad's."

"Were they? I never listened to them. I tried in the beginning, you know. I just didn't see the attraction. All that moaning and complaining. Or else they winked at you, with their little word games. Always to do with fucking, of course."

I stared at my mother. "What did you just say?"

"Jelly roll. Walk my dog. Let me play with your poodle. I'm not stupid, I get what they're saying. Maybe your father liked that about them too, I really wouldn't know. Well, I was just waiting to see you come home. Now I'm going to bed to read my book."

"We can stay up and chat if you want."

"Not tonight."

She went upstairs and I followed a minute later, closing the door of my room. Taking the mandolin from its case, I sat on the bed and started to play, a little slower than usual, Monroe's

"Evening Prayer Blues." I tried to understand why my mother, why Larry for that matter, thought I was coming back, whether it was a figment of their own imaginations or whether I had projected something. An image came to me of all of us — Marta, Maggie, Birdy, me — living in one of the houses around here. Or maybe downtown where I'd first grown up. With a room or separate apartment suite for my mother. The kids going to a good school, having so many advantages they couldn't have in Prague, spending weekends or summers up in Muskoka or Georgian Bay, breathing in fresh air and the scent of pine needles. Maybe that was the change we needed, the change to save us as a family. I didn't want to consider whether it was possible for Marta and me to be together anymore, I just wanted to think of my kids with their mother and father, sitting around the dinner table. And me responsible for making everybody happy.

It was too simple, and it was impossible. But what if it wasn't? I suddenly felt tired of Europe, tired of beautiful Prague, tarted up for the tourists, and its less beautiful surroundings. I thought of all the train trips with Marta and the girls to get out of the city, past abandoned and collapsing buildings, houses with the plaster flaking, smashed windows, quarries and mines, oil tanks, rivers burdened with rusting barges and crumbling bridges. I wanted something cleaner, easier, more open. Somewhere I could breathe. I didn't know how I would make a living; scrambling to survive as a musician seemed all right in Prague but not in Toronto. And maybe I was tired of being a musician too, half the time playing to audiences too drunk to care, hoping to be paid at the end of the night, sick of the smell of spilled beer and stale cigarettes. Feeling old, feeling tired. I didn't know how Marta could possibly adapt to moving. But the idea of giving more to Maggie and Birdy, of ending my mother's loneliness, of learning to love Marta again and be loved by her, was all too seductive to focus on the difficulties.

The telephone rang. It stopped during the second ring, which meant that my mother had picked it up. My heart raced; I didn't want it to be Marta, I wasn't ready to share this crazy idea with her. I heard my mother's hurried footsteps along the hall and then her knock.

"Is it Marta?" I said.

"No," she said through the door. "It's some other woman with an accent. A weird German accent."

"Maybe Dutch," I said, picking up the extension phone. "Annet?"

"Do you miss me, Huddie?"

"Very funny." I looked at my mother, to say she shouldn't worry, and she closed the door again. "It's expensive to call."

"We just got back from the Rodeo. I thought you would want a report."

"Of course." I'd forgotten what day it was. The band played at the Rodeo Fun Bar on Panská Street two nights a week. Last night had been the first gig without me. "How did it go?"

"Terrible. Grisha and Lukáš both want to lead. They fought over the mic and Grisha made the most awful jokes. Saburo was upset — I think he had a fight with Edo. His timing was off."

"Saburo's bass is never off."

"Well, it was tonight. And that mandolin player you found is only so-so. He doesn't drive the music like you. I have to fill in so much on my banjo, but then the others think I am hogging the lamplight."

"Spotlight," I said. "And your voice sounds very, very stoned."

"It makes me feel better."

"Listen, Annet, try and make the best of it. After all, it's just the first time. Everyone will get along. And the mandolin will get better. He was probably holding back."

"You should be glad to hear that you are not able to be dispensed with."

"Just hang in there, Annet."

"Did you hear from Margita and Bela?"

"From Marta. At least we're talking."

"Oh, Huddie. I'm so sorry to bother you with all this band nonsense. You have other things to worry about. Don't lose hope. It will work out. Marta is just confused right now. You both are. I know you both want what's best for the girls."

Annet sounded almost as worried as I was. My closest friend in Prague, she yearned for kids of her own. Maggie and Birdy called her Auntie and loved her to death. "Listen, this call is going to cost you a fortune," I said. "You'll have to sell your banjo. Let me know how things go at the next gig, okay?"

"I will. And I want to hear good news from you."

"Sure."

I put down the phone and slumped onto the bed. Somehow, talking to Annet and hearing her attempt to cheer me up had brought me back to reality. The idea of moving here had been totally unrealistic. It would be best to get it out of my head.

23
The D.B.A.M.C.

IN THE FIRST DAYS OF school I sometimes met Marshall Ornitz beside the playing field at a tree stump he liked to call the Round Table. He would lay out his calculus and chemistry and physics books and work through problems while punching numbers into his calculator. He had the first calculator I had ever seen, almost the size of a hardcover book. Meanwhile on the field, an intramural football game would be in progress. Mr. Tanhauser had already learned not to ask Marshall to hold the down markers; despite his ability with numbers, he couldn't seem to understand the rules of football.

But once Valentine returned, I spent most of my after-school hours with him. Marjorie participated in a lot of extracurricular activities, so she was occupied, and Valentine liked my company. But on this day, near the end of Valentine's first week back, he had to catch up in French, so I joined Marshall at the stump. A girls' field-hockey game was going on, the girls in one-piece bloomers and shirts with puffy sleeves, swinging their club-like sticks at the wooden ball. Marjorie Luckenbill was on one of the teams and I watched her running up the field, striding on her long pale legs, her black hair streaming behind her.

"What sort of a name is Luckenbill anyway?" I asked.

Marshall didn't look up from the protractor and compass he was using. "I think it's Swiss Jewish or something. Her grandfather was a diamond merchant. She was in my biology class last year. I beat her by two marks. I hate the way she sneezes. She makes this little *pppttt* sound, like she's afraid to let it out. That means she doesn't have orgasms."

"Oh, come on."

"I'm serious. I can't believe Valentine is walking around school in that neck brace like he got it rescuing kids from a flaming orphanage or something. Hail the conquering lunkhead. And did you see that his daddy bought him a new car? Maybe next time he'll jump into an empty pool and get a private jet."

I figured that Marshall's remarks were directed at me; he resented my becoming Valentine's friend. I picked up my knapsack and hefted it on my shoulder.

"Where ya going?"

"Home."

"If you want to hang out with Valentine," Marshall called after me, "you better bone up on some comic books."

It was a stupid comment; Marshall himself collected comics. But I ignored it and kept walking along the side of the field. Marjorie, playing the right side, took a pass from the centre. She went straight for the goal, head up, keeping the ball ahead of her. The girl in goal backed up with a look of fright while Miss Mickelberry, the girls' gym teacher, screamed, "Challenge her! Challenge her!" Marjorie cracked the ball past the post. Her teammates cheered but Marjorie ran up to the girl in goal and, putting her arm around her shoulder, pointed to where she ought to have been standing.

Watching, I'd stopped a moment, but now I kept walking. Into my line of vision the wooden ball appeared, rolling to a stop on the dirt path. I picked it up and turned as a girl ran up and lifted it with exaggerated delicacy from my hand. She had dark eyes, hair cut in bangs, a long face, a slightly protruding lower lip.

"I see you've been admiring the D-B-A-M-C," she said.

"Sorry?"

"The Dark Beauty of Arthur Meighen Collegiate."

She laughed and ran back onto the field. That was my introduction to Annie Lynch.

24
The Principal of the Thing

FROM EVERYTHING THAT I'D READ about North American schools, I expected to be confronted at the front door of Arthur Meighen by a couple of guards with crossed rifles. Or at least have a metal detector run over me while I stood with my arms and legs outstretched. But there was nobody around and I just pulled one of the doors open and walked in. No security inside either, just a teacher walking at a good clip down the hall and disappearing around the corner. It was after the morning bell so the kids would be in their classes by now. I took in the unmistakable school smell (chalk, gym suits, luncheon meat, ammonia), the rows of battered lockers along the walls, the hanging banner announcing an upcoming dance. I half expected a young Larry Nussbaum to sneak up behind me and put me in a headlock, or to see Valentine leaning into Marjorie while she stopped his hands from sliding too far.

"Are you looking for something?"

A small, pleasant-looking man gazed at me over a pair of bifocals.

"Yes, for the principal. Ms. Lynch."

"Anne? She should be in her office."

"You're a teacher?"

"Board guidance counsellor. Gender issues. Are you a parent?"

"Not at this school. I've just come to see Annie."

"The office is just at that blue sign. Very supportive, Anne."

"Yes, thank you."

The man nodded amiably and walked on. I had a sudden flash of memory: Ricky Minsk. The boy who got the lead in the school play every year, had a million friends, charmed all the teachers, girl buddies hanging around his locker. And then the day in early spring when somebody pinned to the outside notice-board a girl's gym outfit with Ricky's name embroidered in pink across the chest. Everyone laughing and pointing. Somebody saying, "Ricky's such a faggot," the first time I'd ever heard the word out loud or even thought about what it meant. And then Ricky himself showing up for school. Looking at the board, breaking into tears as he began to run home again. And we all left standing there, having the decency at least to feel shame.

The Arthur Meighen offices hadn't changed, except for the computers on the secretaries' desks behind the counter, but the atmosphere was different. In those days students came into the office only if they were in trouble or had to deliver a note; it was enemy territory. Now I saw students milling about — one girl pulling out a box of bandages from a drawer, a boy answering the phone, two more girls sitting on the bench eating granola bars and giggling. As if they belonged here, as if the school belonged to them.

A secretary looked my way. "May I help you?"

"I was hoping to see Annie — Anne Lynch."

"Just a minute. I'll see when she's going to be free."

I could see Annie's name on the door. The secretary knocked and entered. A moment later she emerged with Annie and a couple of parents of Asian background. "I knew that Lucille of yours was an original," Annie was saying, and they all laughed. She was still small and slim, with a boyishly short haircut, but she had middle-aged skin like the rest of us, and the way one side of her mouth pulled fetchingly down had become more exaggerated. She had lost that bright pixy look; she'd grown up.

And she was wearing a pantsuit.

Annie brushed past me with scarcely a look, ushering out the parents. Turning back again, she gave me a professional smile and said, "Please, come into my office." I followed, deflated by her not recognizing me. I wondered what to say. Her office was a cluttered mess of papers and files and printed reports that covered the desk, the shelves, the floor. "Hang on a second," she said, leaning over to scrawl something into her agenda while kicking the door closed with her heel. She put down the pen.

"Annie, you don't —"

Which was when she threw herself at me, whomping me against the desk and wrapping me in her arms.

"I thought you'd never come back."

Her voice was muffled against my chest. We both pulled slowly away. "I — I can hardly speak," she said.

"I thought you didn't know who I was."

"As if that was possible. I've imagined you walking in here more times than I want to admit. Look, you've got grey in your curls. It's sweet."

I reached out to hold her hands and the two of us grinned at each other like a couple of kids. "I find it very hard to believe that you're the principal, Annie. You've taken over the place."

"Yup. The principal of the thing, as I like to say. It was the only way to get my revenge."

"But honestly. You hated Arthur Meighen more than anyone else."

"Maybe it wasn't so much the school as myself. It's complicated. Besides, the system has changed for the better in the last twenty-five years. Although I still have to watch my fucking language. But I can't believe you're really here. Oh Jesus, you've come for Valentine's memorial on Saturday."

"That's what everybody says. It's more a coincidence than anything else."

"Sure, I believe that."

"Marjorie did ask me to play at the ceremony. I've turned out a musician, believe it or not."

"You think I don't know it? What's the Internet for? If I were you, I'd agree to whatever Marjorie wants and then stay out of her way."

"That sounds like what Marjorie would have grown into. She called me this morning to talk about what I'm going to play. I'm supposed to go over to her house. I guess she doesn't trust me."

"Really, I'm fond of her. More so than when we were kids. She's been a good parent for the school, even if she can be a pain in the ass. If you want to know the truth, when she brought up the memorial idea I was against it. It just seemed a tad too morbid and surreal for me. But Marjorie charmed the school trustee and the board. I'm not completely sure what's driving her. Maybe it's just plain guilt. Anyway, I'm hoping it will turn out to be a good thing, since I don't have any choice."

"So can I see the statue that the shop class is building?"

She gave me her ironic smile, just like she used to. "Uh-uh. Top secret."

"It's that bad, is it?"

"Don't even ask. And can you believe it, for Valentine of all people."

"He was hard not to like."

"Impossible not to like."

"And he did love Marjorie. Maybe it was unhealthy, overly dependent, but it was impressive. I'm not sure I've ever felt anything like it."

"Easier on the women in your life," Annie said, touching my wrist. "And speaking of women, Mr. Rosen, are you married or what? I see no ring on your finger, but that might be a musician thing."

"That's a long story. I think it'll take a bottle of wine. And I notice there isn't one on yours either."

"A less interesting story. Where are you staying?"

"With my mother."

"No!"

"Same house. She's out for her bridge game tonight."

"Mom's away? Perfect. I'll come by at seven."

"That would be great."

"Oh, I almost forgot."

I reached into my pocket and drew out a well-folded sheet of foolscap. I unfolded it to show typing — not from a printer but a typewriter, with corrections on whiteout. It might as well have been an ancient document. I said, "I thought this might be useful for the memorial."

"What is it?"

"Valentine's essay on Canadian identity. The one that Mr. Tillitson made us write."

"I remember it. You actually have it?"

"Val gave it to me after class. If he hadn't died I probably would have tossed it. But I kept it instead."

"Let me see."

She came beside me as I held it out. Mr. Tillitson, our history teacher, had sprung the assignment to write a single paragraph on what being Canadian meant to us, making it due the next day. Of all the teachers, he was the most exasperated by our indifference, ignorance, and laziness. Valentine had planned that night to see Marjorie compete in a city-wide figure-skating competition. I offered to write it for him but he'd refused, even getting mad at me. "You think I'm stupid," he'd said. "You think you're Doctor Huddie Frankenstein and I'm your monster. There are lots of ways to be smart, that's what Marjorie says. I'll write my essay myself, don't you worry." But in class the next day he wasn't mad anymore. He'd written his paragraph while eating breakfast. Mr. Tillitson had liked it so much that he'd read it aloud to the class and even made a copy and posted it on the door, which was how Annie saw it. Now Annie and I silently read it to ourselves, she for the first time in twenty-five years.

What is Canadian identity? That is too big a question. That is a question impossible for me to answer. Because I am not a prairie farmer, not a maritime fisherman, not a Mountie standing in front of Parliament in Ottawa. I don't know what it feels like to be an Indian woman trying to bring up my children on a reservation. I haven't even seen most of the country. It is such a big country. Perhaps it is too big to really know, just like your question is too big to

> *answer. But I know that I am Canadian the same way that I know I breathe. Most of the time I am not aware that I am breathing, but without air I would die. Without this country I would not be who I am. I never think about the British North America Act or our legal system or the right to vote. I don't think about the Canadian soldiers buried at Diepe. I do not think about the Chinese people who died building our railroad or how Metis people feel about the hanging of Louis Riel or the Jews about the way Canada wouldn't let in refugees before the war. But I know I am a Canadian because of all of these things.*

"He spelled Dieppe wrong," I said. "He never was much of a speller."

"It sounds just like Valentine. Oh, we've got to use this. It's just great that you brought it, Huddie."

A knock sounded on the door. The secretary opened it.

"You wanted those grade stats, Anne."

"Thanks. Leanna, this is Huddie Rosen, one of Arthur Meighen's most prestigious alumni. He's a musician and has just agreed to speak to our senior music students."

"That's wonderful."

"Yes, it is." Annie smiled at me.

"It's the least I can do for the old alma mater," I said.

25

I've Done Just Everything Wrong in My Life

THE FORMER DARK BEAUTY OF Arthur Meighen Collegiate lived in an enclave of near mansions on the other side of Bayview Avenue from the school. Her house had the look of a rambling English country home, with a genuine terracotta roof (how much had that cost?) and ivy creeping up the chimneys. The *three* chimneys. The front garden was English too, crowded with roses in tangled array and wildflowers and a small pond on which three lily pads bloomed their white or pink flowers.

The front door, like the brick, had been made to look weathered, but the effect was more successful from a distance, like a stage set. Before I could even knock, Marjorie greeted me with an efficient kiss on the cheek and asked me to follow her inside. She had pulled her hair back in a bun and had a pair of reading glasses on her nose, like someone afraid of her own beauty.

"We'll sit in the library," she mused. "It's a pleasant place to work."

"You have a lovely house."

"Grant's been generous about letting me decorate. He likes being surrounded by beautiful things."

I thought for a moment that she was being ironic about herself, that she was also one of Grant's beautiful things, but she didn't show it in her face, and I remembered that Marjorie had never understood Annie's sardonic tone. The library was no casual inspiration; a tray awaited us with a teapot and cups, finger sandwiches and pastries. The room itself was the perfect English library: warm wood panelling, shelves of uniform leather spines, piles of oversized art books on tables, a large antique globe, hand-tinted etchings of hunting scenes, Persian carpets.

"Help yourself," Marjorie said as we sat in the leather chairs. Help myself I did; a musician knows how to eat at another person's table. "This egg salad is delicious," I mumbled.

"It's the anchovy. Shall we get down to work?" She picked up a file from beside the tray. "Let me give you a rundown of the ceremony. Chairs will be set up on the lawn just in front of the statue by the pit. We'll have to hope for good weather. I had wanted the entire school to come out for the ceremony, but Annie balked at that. So it'll just be invited adult guests and a few representative students. The statue itself will be veiled, of course. Flowers will be tasteful, understated, and definitely not funereal. Annie will represent the school with some opening remarks. I asked to vet her speech but she just looked at me. I think there are certain things that should and shouldn't be said in particular circumstances. I'd like to encourage her to use the memorial to get the kids to think about the sacrifices of past generations. Like Remembrance Day."

I tried to fix a solemn expression on my face but it wavered. "Remembrance Day?" I said. "Do you really mean it, Marjorie? I mean, Val's death was awful but it couldn't exactly be compared to some young Canadian soldier taking a bullet at Vimy Ridge.

I mean, forgive me, but if he hadn't been such a lovestruck moron he would still be alive today and nudging into middle age like the rest of us."

"Forty isn't middle-aged," she said. "Fifty is the new middle-aged. Anyway, I don't agree. And you've interrupted my flow. So then it's my turn. My speech is going to be called 'The Real Valentine Schwartz.' I want people to know what an incredible person he was."

She touched a handkerchief to a tear in the corner of her eye and then blew her nose. It didn't look studied; if anything, she seemed embarrassed by her feelings. "I know, you think I'm an idiot, like everyone else."

"Of course I don't," I said, though I wasn't sure.

"Anyway, finally we come to the unveiling. A boy and a girl from the youngest grade — I've chosen the Chung twins, they're quite adorable and impossible to tell apart — will take hold of the silk ropes attached to the cover on the statue. Then I'll give you the signal to stand up with your mandolin. And you begin to play. We'll put you in the front row. Do you know that Bette Midler song, 'Wind Beneath my Wings'?"

"I've already chosen something," I said quickly. "A traditional song called 'Bury Me Beneath the Willow.'"

"You don't think that isn't a little dreary?"

"I don't plan to sing the words. The melody is beautiful and haunting."

"Okay, if you say so. So you'll start playing and I'll signal the twins to pull the ropes. I've made sure the cover can't get stuck; I don't want this to become some *I Love Lucy* episode. We'll all gaze on the statue and think of Valentine while you play. And then it'll be over. People can linger a while and drift away."

Her voice faded. I waited an appropriate length of time before picking up the last chocolate eclair. "Do you know where Valentine is buried?" I asked.

"I've tried to find out. Remember how Val died in the night? His body was gone by morning. The school office said his parents took the body to New Jersey or maybe New York, I can't remember which. I've searched through lists of cemeteries on the Internet but there are a lot of people buried. I don't even know which town or city. If I knew, I'd go and put flowers on his grave. I don't know why that isn't a Jewish tradition, it's so lovely. I'd do it anyway, though. But now at least I can put flowers by the statue. Valentine was so ... oh damn —"

She started to cry but this time she couldn't hold it back. She made little hiccup-like noises and tears streamed from her dark eyes and she took out the handkerchief and blew her nose. I thought she was finished but now her body started to tremble and the noise from her open mouth got louder until it became a wail. With someone else I would have known what to do, but with Marjorie I wasn't sure. I tentatively put my arms around her, and although she didn't fall into me, she didn't resist either. And then she grasped my hands and pressed them to her warm breast.

"Oh God, Huddie, I'm so unhappy."

"Marjorie. Jesus."

She kept crying, her sharp chin now digging into my shoulder. For a while she could hardly catch her breath and we remained there, me half-kneeling before her chair. Finally she calmed a little.

"I've done just everything wrong in my life. It's a terrible disaster."

"You're upset. It's understandable. You don't have to punish yourself. Or feel that you don't deserve a good life."

"It's not a good life! It's not a good life!"

She slapped her hand against my chest, startling me. "It only looks good from the outside. Grant is horrible. I don't love him. I don't even like him anymore. He seemed so glamorous when he transferred to Arthur Meighen. He was the sort of person everyone expected me to be with. How was I supposed to resist? But I was just some prize to him. He never loved me the way Valentine did. I deserve to be punished, and I guess I have been. If it wasn't for my son, I think I'd kill myself. My daughter hates me. Grant is having a disgusting affair again, I've lost track of how many he's had. And I don't want to do it anymore. Any of it. I don't want to!"

Her crying overwhelmed her again. What had I come back to? As Marjorie leaned against me again, I put my arms around her and felt the dampness of her shoulder blades. It seemed as if she would never stop.

26
The Age of Chivalry

VALENTINE WOULD NEVER HAVE THOUGHT of stealing that armour if it hadn't been for Mr. Tillitson. I could not understand what made him so angry, a barely repressed fury smouldering beneath the surface of his excessive formality. Compared to him, other teachers seemed almost human. Perhaps it was as simple as the disappointment of teaching history to a bunch of indifferent kids who drove better cars than his own wheezing Buick. One Monday morning he sprang a surprise quiz on us, the questions based on the weekend's assigned reading. Half the class failed. Valentine, fresh off his success on Canadian identity, got zero.

"Very well," Mr. Tillitson said, running his comb through his hair. Some of the other male teachers were aging hippies with hair down to their shoulders, but Mr. Tillitson, who was only in his thirties, kept his short and his comb in his back pocket, which the girls in class thought disgusting. "Since you all insist on acting like children instead of the adults that you are supposedly becoming, I've decided that you need an activity more appropriate for your developmental age levels. So we're all going on a field trip. To the Royal Ontario Museum, just like when you were little kids. Maybe seeing some actual objects older than your toaster might give you some inkling of the historical past. Before you look too pleased, however, you ought to know that this trip will be the basis of an extra assignment, above your regular work. Ah, now you don't look so happy, do you!"

Everybody knew the ROM from family visits and trips in the lower grades. We all thought that he was joking, but the following Monday morning a yellow school bus idled in front of the school. I got in, holding a seat near the back for Valentine, who was going to be my partner, but when he didn't show I reluctantly gave it up to Marshall Ornitz. The bus pulled into the street, spewing black diesel fumes. "What do you think you're going to choose?" Marshall asked me with unconcealed excitement. "Nothing corny, no birchbark canoe or suit of armour for me. That's for people with no imagination. I want something really old. Etruscan maybe. I see that Valentine didn't bother to show. I guess you need a partner, right?"

But I didn't get to answer because someone started honking behind the bus. We all turned to look out the back window to see Valentine's apple red Celica behind us, and Val himself waving out the window. He kept behind us the whole way down into the city, roaring past just as we pulled up in front of the museum.

He must have found somewhere close to park, because as we filed out of the bus he came running to join us. Mr. Tillitson made us stand on the sidewalk so we could hear him. "Ladies and gentlemen," he said above the noise of the other school groups of actual little kids, "today you are going to see fragments of the history of our race. Open your eyes. Wander about. Really *look*. Don't be in a hurry to read the little card. See if you can guess what it is. Who might have used it? Imagine the hands that made it, the person or people that used it, the voices once spoken around it. This is a chance for you to take a journey through time. You've got two hours."

We went up the long stairs, through the doors, and immediately forgot Mr. Tillitson's warnings to be respectful: everyone ran, their voices loud, across the rotunda floor. I suggested to Valentine that we wander separately for a while and see what we came up with. I decided on two possibilities: a Roman pull toy and an Indian elephant-headed god. But when I found Valentine he was staring at a suit of armour. It looked like every other suit of armour — visor, breastplate, broadsword, the works.

"This is it," Valentine said. "We've got to do it, Huddie."

"But Val, isn't it kind of obvious?"

"Look at it! It's so neat. Some knight wore this, Huddie. Some knight fighting for honour or maybe for his king or even some hot-looking maiden. It's from the age of chivalry. I tell you, I should have been born back then. I would have made a great knight."

"It's probably all bullshit from books and movies. Maybe it was owned by some rich guy who liked to strut around in his bedroom wearing a bunch of tin cans."

"You're wrong, Huddie. This is the real thing. Come on, what do you say?"

He turned and grinned at me, already sure I would give in.

27

The Permanent Assistant

MY MOTHER HAD AN APPOINTMENT downtown to get shots in her varicose veins, and so I caught a lift with her. I offered to keep her company at the doctor's office, but she said that she'd been going all these years without me and didn't see the point of my coming now.

I could see how much the downtown had changed since I'd left — all the new condominiums, the cafés with outdoor tables, the Gap, HMV, and other American stores — but I already had enough to take in, seeing my mother and my old friends, and the city would have to wait before I could pay much attention to it. My mother let me off at the corner of Avenue Road and Bloor, opposite the stone face of the museum. I felt a little sick at the sight of it but I crossed over, past the cart selling hot dogs and the one selling candy floss and popcorn, towards the long stairs up to the main entrance.

And stopped. Turned around. Took five steps back. To look at the hot-dog seller again. He had a short line before him and was working quickly, turning dogs over on the grill, opening buns, making change, dropping cans of pop into a bucket of ice. The wild Einstein hair had receded in two points up his scalp and the face was rounder, even bloated looking, but I was sure it was him. And then I heard the voice: "That's one Italian sausage, one bratwurst — excellent choice, by the way — one diet Coke, which will probably give you cancer, and a Sprite. Sprite's owned by Coke, did you know that? I'd rather carry 7-Up but the supplier won't let me ..." I heard the voice and I knew.

I came up on the other side of the cart. "Marshall?" I said. "Marshall Ornitz?"

He took a furtive glance at me and went back to turning the hot dogs, shifting them about with the tongs. "Marshall, do you remember me? It's Huddie Rosen, from Arthur Meighen Collegiate."

"I don't remember you."

"I was a friend of yours. Well, sort of. I used to meet you by the tree stump."

"I remember Lorne Nathanson. He works for Bawden, Cowper, and Livingstone. He has an office on the twenty-third floor of First Canadian Place, with a window. I remember Daniel Wolfe. He took over his dad's dry-cleaning chain. But I don't remember you. I don't remember most people from back then. They weren't good days. I don't think about them. If you want a hot dog, you have to get in line."

"No, that's okay, thanks."

I backed away and headed up the long steps to the main doors of the museum. If someone had told me back then that Marshall would end up selling hot dogs I might have laughed, but seeing him was sad and creepy. Not, somehow, impossible to believe. Perhaps the very traits that had made him so intense and annoying, that had encouraged other kids to mock him, had been signs of mental distress to come. I crossed the marble rotunda floor and went to the information desk. A young white woman with dreadlocks sat at a computer and telephone. "I'd like to see Madeline Day if she's in," I said. "She's in the medieval department. Or at least she used to be."

"Assistant head. What's your name?"

"Howard Rosen. I don't know if she'll remember me."

"Hold on and I'll ring her." She punched a code into the telephone. I watched as she repeated my name and raised an eyebrow at the reply. She hung up again.

"She seems to remember you quite well. Take the elevator up to the second floor. She'll meet you."

The elevator might have been going up, but I felt as if I were descending to my doom. When the door opened, Madeline Day was already standing there. Last I'd seen her she was in her early thirties, and now she was past fifty-five. She had grown heavier and more slovenly. Her grey hair was a mess, her white blouse had a faint stain above her heart, and a pen had leaked in her slacks pocket. She was not smiling.

"Follow me."

She turned brusquely and marched past the European collection. Perhaps this had not been such a good idea after all. Past silk bustles and inlaid tables and harpsichords we went while Renaissance music from hidden speakers faded into baroque and then romantic. We came to a recessed door, which she opened by punching in some numbers. A different world was on the other side, of fluorescent lights and work cubicles and people who looked like medical interns in lab coats. She took me all the way to the back, to an office with half a window looking towards Bloor Street. She dropped herself into the swivel chair behind the disaster that was her desk, but I kept standing because the only other chair was occupied by an iron mace.

"Why are you here?"

It was a good question. I thought I had known, but the reasons, or at least my confidence in them, had seeped away. "I suppose I just wanted to come and apologize. I know what I did back then but it was under duress. I was a kid, or nearly, and couldn't really understand the repercussions of what we'd done. But over the years I've been able to see what a real blow it must have been."

"Blow?" She laughed humourlessly. "You don't have the slightest idea what you're talking about. You and your buddy stole a sixteenth-century English suit of armour. Which happened to be one that I was going to include in the exhibit I was working on. The show still needed approval from the board of directors. The museum would have published my monograph. But after you stole the armour and embarrassed the museum, the directors didn't want to highlight the medieval collection. The exhibition was turned down. The monograph didn't get published. I didn't get promoted. I lost out on jobs at two other museums. My career stalled. And now, decades later, what am I? I'm *assistant* head of the department. They might as well change it to permanent assistant. George Mankowitz is head. George gets to go to the conferences in Geneva and Paris. George gets to write the catalogues."

"I'm very sorry."

She wriggled herself up out of the chair. "Do me one favour at least."

"Of course."

"Tell me where the armour is."

"I would if I had any idea. But I don't know where it is."

"Bullshit."

"No, it's the truth. Valentine was still wearing it in the ambulance. They took it off him at the hospital, but nobody knows what happened to it. We tried to find out back then."

"I believe that you have it."

"Of course I don't have it. What do you think I did, hide it under my jacket? Would I have let my parents, who weren't rich, make a donation to the museum if I had known where it was?"

"You did a perfectly adequate job of concealing it after you stole it the first time."

"That was Valentine. He put it in the attic of his house. He had a huge house. I guess the doctors just tossed it somewhere and some other doctor or an orderly or janitor took it home."

"So you think it's in somebody's living room, maybe with a shot glass in one hand and a Halloween mask of Richard Nixon inside the helmet? That exhibit was going to take me to the next step in my career. You stole my life, you and that lummox friend of yours. You know that I still dream about that armour? I dream that I'm wearing it. That I'm on a white charger, lance held with one arm, galloping towards my opponent. I really don't know why I'm telling you this."

"I'm sorry."

"Yeah, well that and two bucks will buy me a cheese Danish in the cafeteria, which is what I need right now."

"Let me buy you one."

"I can't be bought off with a piece of lousy pastry. You can find your own way out."

She sidled around the desk, pushed past me, and went down the hall without looking back.

28

Underwater

MY MOTHER AND I DROVE back from downtown with the windows open; unlike her brother Norman, she didn't like air conditioning. The shots in her legs hadn't hurt much this time, and the relief put her in a buoyant mood. Being a passenger while my mother drove was another infantilizing experience, and I dealt with it by fiddling with the radio until I found a country station. Most bluegrass fans claimed to dislike commercial country music, but I had a soft spot for the stories of honky-tonk seductions and broken dreams and remembering what your daddy used to say. "It's getting warm out," my mother said. "Why don't you go for a swim when we get back?"

"The last time I went to the Jewish Y, some old guy accused me of stealing his towel. I don't think so, thanks."

"I mean in the backyard."

"You don't have a pool in your backyard, Mother."

She turned her head and looked at me.

"Watch the traffic, please."

"You are kidding me, right, Howie?"

"Kidding you about what?"

"You didn't see the pool in the backyard?"

"I saw no pool. I haven't been in the backyard, but I know there's no pool. Nor trampoline either, for that matter."

She shook her head to show disbelief and possibly disappointment. "Well, trust me, there's a pool. Not a big one like your friend Valentine used to have, but a pool."

"You're pulling my leg," I said doubtfully. My mother wasn't the type.

"I told you on the phone, Howie. I told you when I was thinking about putting one in because the doctor said it would be good exercise. I told you when they dug out the hole. I told you when it was finished three years ago. Do you actually listen to me during our telephone conversations?"

"I listen," I said, but my face was burning.

"Maybe it's a kind of denial. You don't want the house to change from the time you lived here. You need your memories preserved in amber, to show how different you are now."

"You're watching too many talk shows, Mom. Why would I mind? It's your house."

"It's your house too. Anywhere I live is also your house, no matter how old you are."

She didn't say it warmly, though. "I don't believe you have a pool, but if you do, I promise to swim in it."

THE POOL TOOK UP MOST of the backyard, leaving room for just a narrow strip of patio stones and a couple of chairs against the back wall of the house. It was a new, prefabricated sort of pool; it looked like a giant cup sunk into the ground with the lip above the water level. My mother stood beside me, smiling with satisfaction. "Nice, isn't it?" she said.

"And you really use it?"

"I do arm and leg exercises. I learned it from a video."

"No wonder you're so slim."

"So are you going to go in?"

"It's warm enough out. But I don't have a bathing suit."

"You think I haven't seen your *tuches*?"

"That's a bit too Oedipal for me, Mom. I'll wear my boxers."

"And I'll go and lie down and then get ready for my bridge game. I've got to be in good shape for it. Elsie Hoffman, do you remember her?"

"Sure. Her son was a year behind me."

"Absolutely ruthless. I've never seen anyone so competitive. If she's my partner, I'm terrified that I'll make a bidding mistake. And if she's my opponent, I can't stand to watch her gloat when she wins."

"Kick her butt, Ma."

"I'll do my best."

"By the way, whatever happened to her son? What's his personal tragedy?"

"He married a nice girl. Three kids. A house in Richmond Hill. Believe it or not, sometimes things work out. I'll bring you a towel."

She went inside and I stripped down to my shorts. The pool had no deep end so I held my breath and slipped in. It was shockingly cold; my mom was no softy. I opened my eyes and saw undulating white and blue lines and the lowering sun yellowing the surface. I tried to let everything go, at least for a moment, and to be this simple underwater creature, anemone or starfish. And then I saw something plunge into the water — a hand signalling to me.

I came up, the water streaming over my face. When my vision

cleared I saw my mother with the cordless telephone in her hand. "It's Marta."

I waded across to her and she put the receiver into my damp hand. I thought she might linger to overhear the conversation, but she immediately turned around and went back into the house.

"Marta?"

"Huddie, I just have to talk to you."

"What is it? Is everything all right?"

"Please don't be mad, Huddie."

"Why would I be mad?"

"Margita begged me to let her sleep over at Irina's house and I said okay."

"But you know her father. He's a drunk."

"I know, I shouldn't have. But she begged me. And he isn't really a drunk, he's just —"

"Marta, I've seen the man. He's an alcoholic. I know how Margita can drive you crazy when she wants something. But I just don't think we can let her stay overnight there."

"I shouldn't have said yes. I don't know why I gave in. I was feeling so mean."

"It's not your fault. Why don't you have Irina sleep over at our — I mean your — place. Make up some excuse."

"But they don't want Bela around. The apartment is so small. They say she won't leave them alone and it's true."

"Maybe Bela can go somewhere for the night. I bet Annet would love to have her. They can eat ice cream and watch movies."

"Yes, maybe. I'm sorry, I can make these decisions on my own, I'm just tired and — it's just hard, you know?"

"You make them most of the time, Marta. Let's be honest. I'm not worried about that."

She began to cry. "It's just one thing after another. I had such a scare this morning. Bela was sitting on the window in the living room."

"Jesus, you just found her that way?"

"I screamed and ran and pulled her in. It's five flights down! She was sitting and holding a book and pretending to read. Some of the other girls in her class can read already. She thinks she's stupid. I had to act so angry with her, so she will never do that again. But she was so upset after and I had to make her feel better. It was so exhausting."

"I shouldn't have come here. Even if I'm not staying with you I could be helping."

"No, no, I don't mean that, it's just a bad day, I need to talk sometimes. I need you to tell me that I'm not a bad mother."

"You know I think you're a wonderful mother."

"It's ridiculous. I know you'll say that but I need to hear it anyway."

I took a deep breath. "Marta, I've been thinking. What if you and the girls came to Canada. We could live here. In a house with more room and a yard. The kids could have so many chances in life. Everything could be better."

"What are you saying? Move to Canada? You never even let me visit."

"I know, it was a mistake."

"I don't know Toronto. I can't even make a picture of it in my mind. What job would I do? Would you be a musician?"

"I don't know. But everything would work out, I'm sure."

"Just thinking about it scares me. I'm Czech, Huddie. This is what I know."

"The kids could have their own rooms. A swing set in the backyard. More room and more money and —"

"Oh, I don't know. I can't talk about it more now. We're still separated. We've decided nothing, you understand?"

"But you said you —"

"I have to go. I will think about it, Huddie."

I heard the phone gently click. I put the phone down on the lip of the pool. Trembling, I pulled myself out of the water. The ringing phone had made my mother forget to bring a towel and I stood with my arms around myself, shaking in the cold.

29
Hardy Har Har

MY MOTHER HAD LEFT FOR her bridge game by the time I was out of the shower, but I found that she had done my laundry, leaving it neatly folded on the bed. I was getting dressed when the doorbell rang.

It was Annie, holding a bottle of champagne in one hand and a bag of Chinese takeout in the other. The phone call from Marta had put everything else out of my mind. It must have shown on my face because Annie dropped her smile as soon as she saw me.

"What is it?" she said, walking in as if she had been visiting the house every day for the last twenty-five years. But of course we didn't really know each other at all. I wanted to speak, to tell her the crazy way I was trying to save my marriage and my family, but I could find no words. I swallowed hard and said, "It's nothing. I like a guest who brings both the chow and the drink."

"You always did keep things to yourself," she said, walking into my mother's kitchen. I could see the emotions brought by recollection cross her face. "This feels so, so strange," she said. "Like stepping right into the past. I have goosebumps. At the same time, it just hits home how much time has passed, how damn fleeting it all is. What is that smell? Could it really be honey cake?"

"The real thing. I'm starving, not to mention thirsty. Where do you want to eat? Casual here or formal in the dining room?"

"The kitchen," she said. "It'll get us to the food faster."

I brought out dishes and glasses while Annie popped the cork on the Spanish knock-off. Then we dug in. I was ravenous. "It's weird," Annie said. "I feel like Valentine's going to walk through the door and hog all the food."

"I know. This won-ton soup is everything I remember it to be. But really, Annie, tell me what's going on with you."

She sighed. "This is going to take some strength. Give me more of those chicken balls in red dye. It's a thrilling tale really. I went to university, spent my summers working abroad for different aid agencies, and then did teacher's college because I thought it would give me more freedom. I taught in Japan for a couple of years and then met this other teacher, Canadian. We lived together, he turned out to be a junkie, we came back to his hometown of Vancouver. He got worse, promised to go to rehab, I stayed, he didn't, I left, he OD'd."

"That's really terrible."

"It was worse than it sounds. I went away again for five years to France, taught at a private school in Bordeaux, came back again, met a woman nine years older than me. We moved in together and it was great for a while, but the depression she suffered from returned. I stayed, she got better, I stayed, she got worse, then she made me leave her. Three months later she, well, she killed herself."

"Jesus."

"Do you see perhaps a pattern here? That was six years ago. I haven't allowed myself to have a serious relationship since. A few casual, all men, I think she was my one woman and maybe the love of my life. But heck, look at my career, I'm queen of Arthur Meighen Collegiate. It doesn't get better, I'd say. Come on, pour some more of that cheap bubbly. By the look on your face, you need it too. And see if you can manage to tell me something about yourself. Nothing too personal, it might shock me. Tell me about your band."

So I told her about the Don River Boys. About our Russian fiddle player, Grisha, who was first violinist for the Stalingrad Symphony Orchestra before communism imploded and half the musicians in Russia lost their jobs. Morose, cynical, misanthropic, semi-alcoholic, but a great fiddler, a Russian Vassar Clements. About Annet, our banjo player. Dutch, a shade under six feet tall, blond, with a big voice and a bigger heart that was always getting stepped on by the short men she favoured. About Lukáš, our guitar player, who was the only native Czech. Young and good-looking, if he had spent as much time practising as he did standing in front of a mirror getting his hair to fall right, he'd be an even better picker. Last was Saburo on bass. From Tokyo, where bluegrass was remarkably popular. Saburo didn't like it when anybody in the band argued and would take the blame for everything. He was also gay, which explained why he had left Japan.

With the champagne affecting us a little, we got into some reminiscing. How Annie wore a pair of jewel-encrusted sunglasses belonging to her aunt to school one day, claiming that she had an inflammation in one eye. How another time she announced that she didn't like her laugh and would now say "Hardy har har" like Jackie Gleason on *The Honeymooners*, which she did, driving me crazy for a week.

"And there was our last night before you went off to college," she said. "That's worth toasting."

"Mmm," I said, my mouth full. "I don't remember."

"You shit." She batted me with the end of her chopsticks.

"I was pretty much a wreck," I said.

"I know. Over your dad."

"You were very beautiful to me. Very tender. I didn't know what I was doing, I was very scared, I was sick at heart, and you took me into your bed."

"Actually, it was the fold-out sofa in the basement of my parents' house. I didn't know if I should have been doing it. You looked like you were going to cry."

"Shit, I did cry after."

"And you never answered my letters."

"I'm sorry."

"That's all right." She sniffled a little. "Now, tell me about those daughters of yours. As if I wouldn't know about them."

30
The Woman who Sold Shawls

I PLAYED WITH THE SORGHUM County Boys for three years, and in the winter, when we didn't have enough gigs to pay the rent, I put up drywall, helped to winter livestock, and worked at becoming a better player. But the boys were in their late sixties and losing their taste for the road, so I joined another band and played in that one for a while until the manager disappeared with our festival earnings and the fiddle player had to sell his van, which was our means of transportation. After that I went to Nashville, although reluctantly, since it's a commercial country rather than a bluegrass town. I managed to survive, if barely, as a session player, performing on demos for songwriters hoping to sell a tune to Waylon Jennings or the Judds. But Nashville struck me as the worst of Tennessee, a suspicious-minded small town without the beauty of the country landscape or the generosity of rural people. So I formed a band of young players and moved myself to a rented cabin in a town called Lonesome Furnace that used to have a forge. We named ourselves after the town and earned a reputation for lots of energy and spark, got a regular spot at the Station Inn, and even played the old Ryman Hall as the opening act for more famous bands. By now Charlie

Joyce's little mandolin had really opened up. It had a terrific bark, highs that could be sweet or cutting, volume, and power.

As a late starter, I was still learning everything I could about bluegrass, expanding my repertoire, listening to every hot player who came through. My love for the music and the culture it came from only deepened, but what I did not develop was a sense of personal belonging to the South as an actual place. I had my friends and bandmates, I was welcome at the local jam on Saturday afternoons inside Hargreave's Dry Goods, I had a few girlfriends who were drawn to me as an exotic northerner and mysterious Jew. But I remained on the outside, a result somehow of my own nature as much as the southerners' uneasiness around those who might judge them. I met people who were as open-minded and generous as any I'd ever known and others who were narrow, suspicious, or simply bigoted. Half the players I met would fight you for suggesting that the banjo was descended from an instrument played by African-born slaves. I didn't go to church or vote Republican. I could never get used to that blazing summer heat. Maybe all of that was why I pushed the other band members to accept an invitation to perform at a summer bluegrass festival just outside of Prague.

I hadn't even known that bluegrass was popular among Czechs. It was only later that I learned of the first local bluegrass band, the Greenhorns. In 1964, the communist government had allowed Pete Seeger to play a concert in Prague, bringing an instrument never seen before: the banjo. The Greenhorn's own banjo player had to build his based on a photograph of Seeger. Czechs took to the music so well that they put on the first European bluegrass festival, convincing the authorities that they wanted to celebrate the music of the oppressed working people of rural America. Still, it was only partially accepted, and American instruction manuals and reel-to-reel recordings were passed around like subversive literature. After the revolution in 1989, more bands started up — traditional groups who sounded just like the Blue Grass Boys or the Stanley Brothers or Flatt and Scruggs, progressive bands influenced by David Grisman and the New Grass Revival. They sang in Czech but also in English, the words sounding clipped and with occasionally peculiar emphasis.

None of the other band members had ever been anywhere east of Charlotte, the commies had been kicked out only a short while before, and the money was barely enough to get us over there. I wouldn't let up until they agreed, but boy were they glad. Back home we were just another bluegrass band scrounging for gigs, but at the festival we were stars. The real thing. Thousands of people crowded the hillside before the stage to hear our sets. They cheered for more and wouldn't let us off. Between shows I jammed with young players who couldn't speak English, except to say "Cripple Creek" or "Flop-Eared Mule." They came up to touch the scroll of my mandolin like it was the Holy Grail. We all soaked up the adoration, but after ten days the boys were ready to go home. Only I stayed. Because I'd met Marta.

Her straight hair was cut in a slanted bang that showed off her wide face and pale skin, her faint freckles and small nose and green eyes. She had a small mole near the corner of her mouth; later I would discover that it was part of a constellation on her body, another on her left breast, a third near her navel, one on her thigh, and one on the ankle of her other leg. She wasn't very tall, was narrow-waisted and fuller in the hips, and wore corduroy jeans. It turned out that she almost always wore corduroys; she didn't wear dresses like other Czech women.

When I first saw her, she was standing by the plywood booth that she had set up in the market section of the festival to sell shawls that her mother knit, tidying up after someone had browsed through them. *Bohemian Shawls Authentic* said the homemade sign, although I later discovered that the hippy colours had nothing authentic about them.

Another band was playing on stage and I had wandered to the market area. She smiled at me, perhaps hoping to attract a customer, but I took it as an opportunity to come over and talk. I didn't think that I had much chance with her, but then I didn't have anything to lose either. I went up carrying my mandolin case, hoping that would impress her (it didn't). I looked at the pile of shawls and felt one between my fingers. The wool was very coarse.

"Two thousand koruny," she said. "Very good deal. Handmade in Šumava Mountains."

Actually, they were made by her mother in a new building in the industrial outskirts of Ostrava. She knit them while watching Czech soap operas.

"You speak English," I said. She answered with only a charming shrug. "I don't have two thousand koruny."

"Ah. So musicians in America also have no money."

"My band is on in half an hour if you want to come and listen."

"As you can see, I have a great deal of work to do."

"My name is Huddie. Huddie Rosen."

"Huddie is a name?"

"A nickname."

"Look, Huddie which is a nickname. I think there are many of nice Czech girls who like to have an American boyfriend for three days. But I don't wish for it."

I was a little taken aback by her directness. "People here are certainly different."

"Why people? Maybe it is just me. Are you Jewish?"

I stared at her. "Well, yes, as a matter of fact."

"I'm interested in Jewish. There are not many here anymore of course. I don't even know one if you can believe it."

It seemed ironic that my Jewishness was what might attract her, but I was willing to exploit anything. "I've got to head back and get ready. So you won't come and listen?"

"I don't know. Are you good?"

Now it was my turn to shrug; I hoped it looked charming too. I went back to the stage, a wooden platform with a bad sound system at the bottom of a grassy slope crowded with people. Halfway through the set, I saw her standing off to the side. When the set was over some fans asked if I would come and pick with them, and then I had to give a workshop, and after that sit in with a Czech band for half a set. It was dark when I next walked past the closed booths of the market section. I stood listening to the crickets and feeling disappointment when a hand touched my shoulder.

Marta drove us in the little Škoda to her apartment in Prague. We had to go up a back fire-escape and through a window to get in. It was the smallest apartment I had ever seen. It had a pullout sofa bed and a rack for hanging clothes that came down from the ceiling by a pulley. The sofa creaked so much that I thought it might fold up again. Because Marta made love with such abandon I assumed that she had done this sort of thing often, but I was wrong. I should have known by the way she looked at me. How she never closed her eyes.

31
Maybe We'll Start With Some Questions

"ALL RIGHT, CLASS, LISTEN UP. We have a special guest in class today. Mr. Rosen."

"Please, call me Huddie," I said to the teacher, whose name I'd already forgotten. Shaven head, earring, lean runner's body.

"Huddie is a graduate of Arthur Meighen Collegiate."

"Well, technically not a graduate. I left at the end of grade twelve when there was still a grade thirteen in Ontario."

"A former student, then. And he is now a real, live working musician. Jonathan, kindly cease jabbing Lucille with your bow. So does anyone know what the instrument is that Huddie is holding? Don't even try, I'll tell you. It's a mandolin. Mr. Rosen — I mean, Huddie — plays in a country and western band."

I let that pass. The teacher leaned slightly towards me and said under his breath, "I've got a '72 Les Paul. Man, does it put out." He raised his voice again for the class. "Huddie's going to demonstrate for us his instrument and tell us something about the life of a musician. I'm sure it isn't romantic like we sometimes imagine. The road trips, the bad food, poor attendance, bandmates who don't show up on time, growing older while the young punks get all the attention. Those of you who are interested in a career in music will no doubt find Huddie's insights fascinating. So Huddie, how would you like to do this? Do you have a program?"

"Not exactly. Maybe we'll start with some questions."

"Fine. And a show of hands already. Yes, Albert?"

It was a heavy boy at the back, clutching a bass. I could tell by the grin on his face the kind of question it was going to be.

"Do you, ah, get a lot of chicks?"

Laughter and groans from the class. "Can I answer that?" I said.

"No. Next question."

There were no more hands and I wondered how I was possibly going to fill the time when a voice said, "I have one."

"Go ahead, Grace," said the teacher. I looked among the viola players and saw Marjorie's daughter. Hair dyed jet black, eyes ringed by black mascara, the nose ring that I had glimpsed from afar. Her expression unreadable.

"Were you a friend of the guy who jumped off the roof?"

"That's not a music question," said the teacher.

"Yes, I was his friend." I looked directly at her. She must have known that already; I could see it in her sly, suppressed smile. She was trying to get at me.

"Did he really do it because he was in love with some girl who told him to take a hike?"

"Now, Grace," the teacher said, "suicide is a complicated thing. There isn't usually just one reason. Depression. Stress. Mental illness. Chemical imbalance."

"Your teacher is right," I said. "But, yes, he did it for a girl. He might have just fallen. But whatever he did, it was for her."

"For her or to punish her?" Grace asked.

"He should have sought help," the teacher jumped in. "Help is available, kids. You should always know that. We have expert guidance counsellors in the system to call on. Now, does anyone have a music-related question?"

"Okay, I do."

The first violinist, judging by his place. "Yes, Matthew," the teacher said.

"The strings of a mandolin are the same as a violin, right?"

"That's right, except of course they're in pairs."

"Why don't you play the violin, then? Aren't you good enough?"

More groans. "That's all right," I said. "Every bluegrass band has a fiddle player. And actually, I can play the fiddle, just not that well. Here, loan me yours. Is it your own? Don't worry, I won't drop it. You know, in the American South, long before bluegrass, the fiddle was often the only instrument around. Some people used to believe it was the instrument of the devil. It could seduce the listener with is entrancing rhythms, or even bring out sexual desire." Titters from the class. "There's a fiddle tune called 'Devil's Dream.' I'll try to play it for you."

As a fiddle player, I didn't have much tone, and without frets my intonation wasn't spot on, but I could saw away at a pretty good pace, and every go round I sped up a notch, finishing with a rather messy flourish that I slurred to cover up my imprecise fingering. The class hooted as I handed back the violin.

I picked up the mandolin again, counted in with a quick shuffle and galloped through Monroe's "Rawhide." When I finished this time the hooting was accompanied by foot stomping. I wanted to give them a larger sense of the instrument, so I played something more raucous and bluesy — the old jug-band tune,

"Vicksburg Stomp" and then the simple and lovely "Westphalia Waltz" to display the effects of tremolo. I told them something of the origins of the music and about the early players, not only the Blue Grass Boys but also the Stanley Brothers, Jimmy Martin, Reno and Smiley. About how women travelling around the South playing music were considered morally suspect and had to be married or pretend to be the sister of one of the other band members. I told them that the great thing about bluegrass was that a lot of the fans were players too, jamming with friends and even strangers in back parlours, on summer porches, in taverns, or around campfires at the summer festivals. You didn't even have to be particularly good, as long as you were feeling the joy of making music. And then because I'd had enough of my own talking I had the idea of teaching them "Will the Circle be Unbroken" on their own instruments. I started to write out the notes on the blackboard, but changed my mind and taught them by ear instead, the way the old-timers learned a tune. I taught them the words of the chorus too, and divided them into low and high harmony sections. Ten minutes later we were all making an enthusiastic din. I would sing a verse, then we would sing the chorus together — *There's a better home a-waiting, in the sky, Lord, in the sky* — and then I would point to somebody to take a solo, and it didn't matter if they got half the melody wrong.

I looked over at Grace to see that she was plucking her viola rather than bowing. It didn't look like she was singing at first, but then I could see that she was, under her breath, more to herself than to the rest of us.

32
Red Cavalry

THE DAY HAD TURNED WARM and I sweated as I walked up Bayview Avenue. A mandolin case is small, but on a hot day, with your hand sweating, it still gets to be a pain. There was a sidewalk along Bayview, running beside the long green lawns, and I was the only pedestrian, with the traffic pulling past and spewing fumes into my face.

I was heading for the Bayview Village Shopping Centre. My last visit to a mall had been two years ago in Fort Lauderdale, where I'd taken the girls to meet my mother and Uncle Norman and Aunt Min for a holiday. Maggie and Birdy had been wide-eyed and giddy with the excitement of American goods. My mother kept taking out her wallet to buy them anything they pointed at; I practically had to restrain her. She kept giving me a look: *You see how they'd be happier over here?* And the sorry truth was, it made my heart glad to see them, back at the hotel, looking angelic in their sweet new clothes and playing co-operatively, at least for a while, with all their new toys.

My mother had told me there was a liquor store in the mall and I was going to buy a couple of bottles of wine for me and Annie. She was coming over tonight, after Norman and Min picked up my mother for some touring musical at the Royal Alexandra Theatre. It was a little humiliating to have to ask my mother if I might have Annie over, but it was her house after all, and I decided that I'd been a lousy enough son as it was. She said it was fine as long as we didn't leave a mess in the kitchen.

In my day, the mall had been a modest strip plaza, with an ice cream parlour where I'd eaten my first banana split, wishing that I had been sharing it with Annie. Larry and I had gone together a few times to race miniature cars on a figure-eight track at the model car shop. I doubted whether kids raced cars anymore, or learned Morse code, or built balsa-wood airplanes that could fly. Now it was just computers and video games. When I finally crossed under the 401 overpass and reached the mall, I saw that it was surrounded by an enormous concrete moat of a parking lot. It had been expanded, roofed over, and glitzed up inside too, with polished granite floors, sparkling lights, and palm trees in planters, wooden benches and café tables, all very pretty and soothing.

On the way to the LCBO, I passed a toy shop and looked in the window. There was a Barbie display — a Barbie horse that walked, a Barbie camper van, a Barbie rock-'n'-roll stage with music and flashing lights. There was a beautiful stuffed bear with dark velvety fur, and an equally cuddly tiger, both large enough to need two arms to hold, and I knew instantly which one Maggie would fall in love with and which one Birdy would. I went into the store, pointed to them, and handed over my credit card. As I signed the receipt I stopped myself from looking at the cost.

A moment later I was out again, carrying with one hand the animals in an enormous carry bag and with the other my mandolin case. In the wine store I bought a couple of Chilean reds, cheaper than I had intended before the toy store, and I walked out again, another weighty parcel under my arm.

I was on my way out when I switched direction and headed into Chapters. I had never been in one of those giant bookstores with big reading chairs and a café, but I'd heard about them. Books in English were expensive in Prague and I wanted to bring a few home for the kids, if my credit card still worked. I was always trying to improve their English, whereas Marta always spoke to them in Czech and read them Czech books. I lumbered past the leather armchairs, the tables of books, the artful displays of candles and incense and bubble bath, as if somehow these were necessary components, along with literature, in the art of seduction. Then up the escalator to the second floor where I got momentarily distracted in the Country/Folk section of the CD shop. But I resisted buying anything and started looking about for the kids' books when someone familiar caught my eye.

I could see him only from the back — hunched over, unruly hair thinning at the top. He was engaged in some furtive activity, glancing to the sides and then shuffling books about. For a moment I thought he might be slipping one under his jacket but, no, he was merely rearranging the books on the shelf, moving one title so that the cover faced out. And then I realized the person moving the books looked familiar, the curly hair, the slight shoulders, even the blazer and jeans and Converse runners. It was Felix himself, Felix Roth from Arthur Meighen Collegiate.

I came up behind him, lugging my goods. "Hey, Felix."

He started and turned around. "Shit, you scared me. I know you, don't I? Huddie! Huddie Rosen."

Felix held out his hand and, realizing my own were occupied, gave me a pat on the shoulder. "Well, you caught me in an embarrassing position," he said. "I feel like I've got my pants down."

"Because you were making your books more prominent? I can't blame you."

"Whenever I go into a bookstore I play this stupid game, I can't help myself. I try and see how long I can last before checking under the Rs. I average about seven minutes. Usually it's a big thunking disappointment. There's always half a shelf of *Philip* Roth and usually none of me. You try being a Jewish writer living in New York with that last name and see where it gets you. So how long has it been since we've seen each other?"

"Twenty-five years."

"Of course, it has to be. Actually, I heard you were in town too. From Marjorie. I went to see her the other day, although she wasn't exactly helpful. I think I was always afraid of her, and that very same feeling came over me. Do you have time for a coffee?"

"Sure, if I can find a place to put this stuff down."

"Why don't we sit in the store café. In fact, we'll never have to leave this mall again. Is that your mandolin? Can I take it for you?"

We began walking. "I envy musicians," he said. "I always wanted to play an instrument but I never had the talent or the discipline."

"You certainly had it for writing. And you already knew back then what you wanted to do, which I thought was amazing."

"Or crazy. I heard somewhere that you play bluegrass. I don't know much about it but I do have the soundtrack of the latest Coen brothers movie, what's it called?"

"*O Brother, Where Art Thou?*"

"Right. I like that song that George Clooney sings, 'Man of Constant Sorrow.'"

"Dubbed by Dan Tyminski actually. We get a lot of requests for it. Better than 'Dueling Banjos.'"

"Is it an old song?"

"Yes, it's traditional."

"It's quite interesting. There's a passage in Isaiah known as the 'Man of Sorrows' that Christians later applied to Jesus. And here's this song about an ordinary man, as if maybe we're all Jesus in what life makes us go through. Sure makes it personal."

"I didn't know any of that. But they do take their faith personally in the South."

We reached the café's counter. "I'm sure it's tough trying to make a living in music, but when you're actually up there playing, it must be pure joy. At least that's how I imagine it."

"It is, at least some of the time. When everyone's in the groove and listening to one another and the musical ideas are sparking. At other times it's much more ordinary. What's writing like?"

"More or less the same, only I don't have anyone else to blame. You want a cappuccino?"

"Espresso, thanks."

Felix was quick with his wallet. We took our drinks to a little table. I said, "Everyone seems to be reading your book."

"Not everyone. But I have many followers in North York. My Canadian fan base. After every book comes out I have the same conversation with my publisher. He says to me, 'It didn't do as well as we'd hoped.' This book is a little different, though."

"Different how?"

"It ruined my life."

"You can't be serious."

"My wife left me because of it."

"She left you because of a book?"

"After I finished *Rattsmann* I gave her the manuscript to read, as I always do. She's been my first reader for fifteen years and giving the manuscript to her is an important moment for me. Sometimes she finds what I write painful but she has never before suggested I change anything for that reason. But this time she did. She said it was too personal, that I'd invaded our bedroom. And that I'd exposed all her vulnerabilities. That I'd violated our trust. I'd used myself even more ruthlessly but that didn't matter. I understood how she felt. I felt it myself. But I asked her to understand my need and that I couldn't change it. She didn't ask me to change it; she asked me to destroy it. She said that I had to make a choice about what was most important to me. What did one manuscript matter? After all, I'd been saying for years that the world could live quite easily without another book by Felix Roth. Maybe it had nothing to do with this book, maybe life with me was miserable, I don't know. I couldn't really answer her other than to publish the book. So she packed and left.

"I thought she'd come back. And when she didn't, I begged her to. I mean literally, on my knees in the Sheep Meadow in Central Park, where I came across her jogging. I hadn't seen her in two months. It turned out she'd already found another man. She was embarrassed to tell me. A television writer, if you can believe it. Much more successful, naturally. A man whose hobby is riding horses. What grown man rides horses? She said he didn't turn his soul inside out every time he wrote a script. I went from depression to black despair."

"What did you do?"

"I'm embarrassed to say. But I felt desperate and alone. I slept with the woman across the hall."

"Naturally."

"Her apartment was right across from ours. Upper West Side at Amsterdam Avenue. Before this happened I'd never even met the person behind that door. But I used to hear her sometimes during the day. Weeping. I'm serious. I must have stood in front of her door a dozen times, trying to decide whether or not to knock. But I never did, at least not until I was in that apartment alone, driving myself crazy. Writers aren't like musicians, Huddie. We've just got ourselves for most of the hours of the day. So I opened the door and heard the crying. I didn't hesitate, I just rapped. She opened the door in a half-second, like she'd been waiting for me. She was a mess — blotchy face, swollen eyes, limp hair. Actually, she wasn't a particularly attractive woman under any condition. She had a lot of reasons to cry, as she told me in the first half-hour. Her crappy job as a bank teller. Her young brother having hanged himself at the family farm in upstate New York. Her Bible-thumping parents telling her she was going to hell. She had no friends. She hated everyone."

"And this was the woman you decided on as your first lover after your wife?"

"Exactly. For a brief time we were a perfect match. A destructive energy being sucked into a black hole. We made the wall plaster crack from the shaking headboard. I would go to her apartment every night. I didn't even have to knock. It lasted two weeks and then suddenly I became terrified of her. And I did something very cowardly. I just packed a bag and left."

"Without telling her?"

"Not a word. I flew to Paris. Tried to begin a new book. Kept to myself. Looked at art. When I came back, she had moved out. Not a sign of her. That was two months ago. The work I brought back from Paris turned out to be shite, as the Irish say."

I got up. "It isn't a pretty story, Felix."

"You've got to go? Can I give you a lift?"

"If you wouldn't mind. I'm going back to my mother's on Finchley Crescent."

"In the subdivision across from the school, right? Sure, I'll take you."

We walked through the mall towards the exit. Felix said, "Don't take this the wrong way, but isn't your playing bluegrass music like being the one Jew in the Baptist choir?"

"I suppose, if the Jew is there because he loves the singing."

"Like Isaac Babel."

"I don't think I know him."

"He was a Russian Jew, a brilliant writer of short stories, terse and punchy. He rode with the Red Cavalry, the Russian Cossacks fighting the White Army during the Russian revolution. They were hard-drinking, violent, fraternal, exclusionary, sentimental, and cruel, and they disliked Jews and intellectuals both. But Babel, the Jew intellectual with glasses on his nose, loved them."

"I don't think I'd equate people who live in the southern US with Cossacks."

"Maybe not, but there is a strain of Jew who is drawn away from everything that is Jewish. Who loves what hates him."

"You're forgetting, or perhaps you don't know, that I don't live in Tennessee anymore. I live in Prague."

"Now that does complicate things. You adopt a Gentile culture and then return to the Old World, to a place where Jews once thrived but are now all but vanished. Interesting, if a touch messed up."

"Thank you."

We reached his rental car, a silver Taurus. Inside, a dog was gazing long-faced at us, its tail a slow metronome. Some kind of hound with bloodshot eyes, as if it were allergic to itself. When Felix opened the door, the dog bathed his face with its tongue.

"He belongs to the owner of the condo I'm renting," Felix said as he shoved back the dog. "Unconditional love. It works for me."

"What's his name?" I asked, getting into the car. Clearly he resented being relegated to the back seat and he laid his damp nose on my shoulder.

"The owner forgot to tell me. I call him Regret. I would have called him Sorrow, but John Irving used it first. All the good ideas have been taken. Listen, Huddie, I was actually going to call you. Talking about myself, I got off track. I'm really hoping for your help. I want to write a novel about Valentine."

"I hope you're kidding."

"That's why I'm in town. To attend the memorial. I haven't written anything worth keeping since *Rattsmann* and I thought maybe it was all over for me. Of course, writers have that fear often, but it felt real this time. And then I got this email from Marjorie and I thought about Valentine for the first time in years. I remembered that dive he took into the pool when he almost broke his neck. You were there too. And then the fall from the roof, a magnificent symmetry, almost too good. I started thinking about whether Val was more like Prince Myshkin in *The Idiot* or a Don Quixote type. You were a close friend, I wasn't. You know so much more about what happened. About what Valentine was like. If you would just talk to me it would be a huge help."

"I don't know if I want to go over it all."

"Don't kill me here, Huddie. You're an artist too. I need this story. I'm hungry to write, I *need* to write."

"Let me think about it."

"All right. Think about it and take pity on me."

He dropped me off in my mother's driveway. As soon as I was out of the car, Regret squeezed his way between the seats and took up his place on the passenger side. The dog watched me as Felix reversed back into the street. I almost believed it was going to wave.

33
But Seriously, Folks

"HUDDIE, THE KIDS WANT YOU to come visit again."

"That's sweet of them, Larry. I'd love to. Maybe in the next couple of days."

"Listen, I've got a client coming in a minute so I have to get off the phone, but I want to talk to you."

"About what?"

"About moving back to Toronto. Your mom told me you were thinking about it."

"Well, I don't know if I'm thinking about it. The truth is that it may not be possible."

"You've got to do it, Huddie! I want you here, boychik. And listen, I've got this idea for you. Why just one Jew in a bluegrass band? Why not an all-Jewish group? You'd be a real novelty sensation. The Goldena Medina Boys."

"I'm not sure that's quite what I'm looking for. I mean, I care about this music, Larry. It's not a joke to me."

"No, no, you can play the music straight. You just have to throw in some jokes in-between. In fact, I've got some material that I've been working on. You know, while sitting in the car waiting for the client to show up. Want to hear it?"

"How can I resist?"

"Okay, get this. The song finishes, the applause dies down, and you step up to the mic. You say, 'Thank you, ladies and gentlemen. I come from the only clan of Orthodox Jewish bluegrass musicians. At weddings, we played bluegrass music, but only the men could dance together. The bride and groom were lifted up on chairs to the tune of "I'm Going Back to Old Kentucky." Every Saturday night my mother would make kreplach and listen to Minnie Pearl on the Grand Ole Opry. And on Sunday mornings she would say, "Don't even think of going possum hunting without your galoshes, young man." My favourite relatives were Uncle Mosey, the fiddling accountant, Aunt Miriam, the Yiddish banjo sensation, and cousin Herb, who wrote the now classic "Brooklyn Heights Backstep."' That's all I've got so far. What do you think? You can do weddings and bar mitzvahs with this stuff, you'll have more work than you can handle."

"I admit it's funny. Thank you, Larry, but I don't want to be the bluegrass Jackie Mason."

"You're missing the opportunity of a lifetime here."

"I'll just have to take that chance."

34
Pathetic

MY MOTHER HAD LEFT A bowl of strawberries on the counter. I thought she must be out, but then I noticed the door to the basement open. There was something eerie about the light emerging from the top of the stairs, like the glow from an open coffin in a Bela Lugosi movie. Or maybe I'd go down to find a laboratory with electric currents running up metal rods, smoke rising from beakers, a grotesque human form strapped to the table, and my mother, wearing protective eye goggles and a mad grin, urging her creature to *Live, live!*

But she wasn't bringing something to life, she was killing something off once and for all. I came down the stairs to find her at the computer with a cup of tea and a portable radio tuned to a CBC program in which someone was reading listeners' letters on their most amusing gardening mishaps. Already there was another pile of packaged records on the table and after greeting my mother I looked at the addresses on their labels: Detroit, Spokane, Ottawa, Buenos Aires, and Ghent, Belgium. Next to them were more records waiting to go up for auction: Texas Alexander, Leroy Carr, Peetie Wheatstraw.

"Feels like Dad's ashes being scattered to the winds," I said.

She did not look away from the screen. "If you're trying to make me feel bad, you've come to the wrong widow. I've lived with these records for two and a half decades and I think that's more than enough. Let people have them who will appreciate them and let us have the money." She put her hands in her lap and turned to me. "Howie, do you really think that getting rid of these records is like forgetting your father? Do you think I could possibly forget him? But I'm tired of sentiment. And I've been a widow for long enough. I think I'd just like to be Fran Rosen."

"I don't mean to make things harder for you, Mom."

"Oh, you made things harder a long time ago. This is nothing. Anyway, at this point it's too late to stop me. By the way, there's someone here to see you. She's in the backyard."

"Who?"

"A teenager. Grace, I think she said her name is. Do you know her?"

"Marjorie Luckenbill's daughter."

"Yes, she looks like her. Not as pretty as her mother was back then. Probably a good thing. I lent her a bathing suit so she could go swimming."

"All right."

"Anyway," my mother called as I headed back up the stairs, "I think your father would have liked to be scattered to the winds."

I found Grace floating face down in the centre of the pool, her arms and legs stretched out. She rolled over to take a breath and drift on her back with her eyes closed. She wasn't tiny boned like my mother, and she still had some child roundness to her, so the suit pinched her pale flesh. I knew that I had irreversibly crossed a dividing line when seeing her did not make me think of my own teen years of unrequited lust but instead of Maggie and Birdy and what they might be like at that age.

I came up to the side of the pool and waited until her eyes opened. She righted herself and stood in the water, squinting up at me.

"Ah, hi," she said awkwardly. "You're a friend of my mom's."

"And you're Grace."

"You came to my music class."

"Of course. You asked the question about Valentine."

"Yeah, well. Dumb, I guess."

"Maybe not the most appropriate moment, but not dumb." I crouched down by the edge of the pool. "Am I mistaken, or is school not actually out yet?"

"Whatever."

"Seems like you're giving your mother a hard time."

"She's so pathetic."

"You think so?"

"Duh. My dad's screwing around on her and she just takes it? I call that pathetic. The weird thing is that I don't actually hate my dad."

I tried not to sigh audibly. Did kids have to know everything? It seemed remarkably easy for her to say these things to a stranger. I hardly felt qualified to offer advice, given the hash I'd made of my own affairs. I said, "Your mom tells me that you play guitar. We could do some picking one day."

"I brought it. It's in the living room."

"Really. Then why don't I get it, and my mandolin. You can dry off."

"Sure."

I went upstairs to fetch the Joyce and then back to the living room, where I found her guitar case by the sofa. I opened it and saw a brand new Martin D-28, the equivalent of a Mercedes sedan, high-end and dependable. It was a handful of guitar for a sixteen year old. Marjorie would have been smarter spending a quarter the amount for something decent and playable, so that Grace might hunger to deserve something better. But, no matter, I picked it up and took them both to the pool.

Grace had changed into jeans and a black T-shirt with cut-off sleeves. Her wet hair dripped onto her shoulders. My mother's bathing suit had been hung on the fence. I handed her the Martin and pulled up a couple of lawn chairs for us to sit in. "What songs do you know?" I asked.

"Not much. I'm not really into roots music. I mean, I've heard some Gillian Welch. I sort of liked the stuff you were playing in class."

"Okay. Let's try something slow. Maybe in waltz time. We can do 'Sitting Alone in the Moonlight.' One verse, a chorus, four chords. Have you got a capo?"

"I did but I lost it."

"Then we'll play in G. Which means the G is the 'one' chord. The four chord is four up from there — G, A, B, C. It's the C chord. So what's the five chord?"

"D?" she said uncertainly. She watched with concentration as I played it through once and then a second time while singing the words. Then she played it with me, getting the rhythm right but lagging behind on a couple of changes. When she had it down we started again. I sang the chorus and verse and then played a simple melodic break over her strumming. A mandolin and a guitar voice beautifully together, no matter how simply played, and I could tell she heard it too. The next time round she joined me on the words and I fell into singing harmony to her lead. She had a sweet voice with a pleasantly wavering pitch. I gave her a nod to finish but she didn't catch it and so we came to a ragged end.

She looked surprised, as if she had just stood on her hands for the first time. "Not half bad," I said. "Now let me show you a really simple flatpicking break, or solo, that you can do on the guitar. You'll have to really practise before you can play it fluently. Don't worry about speed. Get the rhythm and tone right. And watch your pick direction. Here, switch instruments."

She gave me the guitar and I thought a moment and then played the break. Simple was all I could do on the guitar, but I saw Grace's eyes widen.

"There's no way I can play that."

"Sure you can. We'll go slow until you've got it memorized. The trick is to break it up into bars and learn one at a time. Here's the first two bars."

I played slowly, paused, and played it again, then handed the guitar back. Grace started on the wrong string.

"One down," I said.

She got it right, managed a bar before messing up. "Shit."

"It just takes repetition. Everyone finds it frustrating at first, but after you work at it the notes will just flow without thinking. Trust me. I'll play it on the mandolin and you can use your ear."

She didn't get as far this time before hitting a wrong note and dropping her pick.

"Shit." She leaned over to look for the pick, which had fallen somewhere between the chair slats.

I moved to help. "Even pros drop their picks. If you don't ever drop a pick you're holding it too tight," I said, but I could see her looking more pissed off by the second as she hunted under the chair. She came up again, banging the back of her head on the metal edge of the chair arm.

"Fuck!"

"That must have hurt," I said. She stood up, holding — no, *strangling* — the guitar by the neck and took a step towards the pool.

"Grace, what are you —"

Splash. Into the water went the Martin.

"Jesus!"

I lunged towards the pool. She hadn't thrown it hard, and the guitar landed on its back, wobbling but staying afloat, only tipping back to the headstock and then flat again. I waded in, fully clothed, moving slowly so as to disturb the surface of the water as little as possible, and kept my eye on the guitar, which floated away from me as I approached it. "For God's sake, Grace. Are you trying to prove to me you're a rich, spoiled brat? Good work, you've succeeded."

I reached the guitar and lifted it straight up with both hands, a little stream of water dripping off the end. Quickly I turned around, waded out, and scooped up a towel from a pile on a metal table. I wiped off the bottom and sides and neck and saw that it would be all right. My shoes, socks, and jeans were plastered to my body.

When I thought to look for Grace, she was gone, the gate swinging open. "Oh, great," I said to nobody. Oh, bloody great.

35
Roses in the Snow

VALENTINE HAD A BEAUTIFUL OAK desk in his bedroom, but he brought in another, smaller desk for me so that we could do our homework together, eating the snacks that Mrs. Schwartz prepared for us. That was where we worked on our medieval armour project, reading books on chivalry and the history of combat. We wrote descriptions of how metal workers cast the sheets and beat them into shape, about changing armour fashions (like the pucker suit, which had ridges to imitate pleated clothing), and imagined who might have worn the armour and in what battles or jousting contests. Valentine drove us down to the museum in his Celica and we sat in front of the case staring at "our" armour. It was from the late fifteen hundreds, and made for some rich lord in the Greenwich workshop set up by Henry VIII. I had to admit it was good-looking armour, with intricate engravings and gilding on all the plates, a pointed breastplate, and a ridge like the spine of a reptile on the top of the visor. We didn't have a photograph so Valentine had decided to draw it, but with each visit he got only a little more done because of all the detail he was putting in.

Chivalry wasn't all that we talked about while Val was drawing. He had some crazy ideas about luck, which he insisted came to a person who was, as he put it, "pure of intention," a nice phrase that he was incapable of explaining. He believed that he was born lucky the way others were born with musical ability or a photographic memory, and he talked about this gift in solemn tones. It was the reason that he didn't worry overly about his mediocre school marks (improved from lousy since we began studying together), his lack of drive to get into university, or his not having any idea what profession he might pursue. This gift of luck would sail him from student life into adulthood with everything he wanted, which I took to mean Marjorie and the means to keep them both in style.

Even then I could see that this confidence was a mask for some pretty serious fears. It seemed to have something to do with his father. Mr. Schwartz, permanently tanned and dressed in the most beautiful suits I'd ever seen, liked to breeze into the room while we were working. He would glance at our notebooks, ask Valentine a couple of questions, shake his head at his "Einstein of a son," and go out again. Valentine would often be shaking with anger, but these terrible feelings about himself only made him hold more stubbornly to this weird conviction. Sometimes he had me believing in it too.

Most of the time we were left pretty much to ourselves. When Valentine was in a good mood, he would tell me about his plans to grow rich. Like flying people up to the top of Mount Everest by helicopter to take their photograph. Or producing a breed of dogs the size of mice. Or developing a tobacco that improved your health. Or — his latest — bringing back jousting as a sport. He would make a fortune manufacturing authentic reproductions of armour and running indoor stadiums all over the world where people could compete. My contribution was to suggest that participants sign a waiver so that they couldn't sue Valentine after getting hurt.

Valentine wasn't always in a good mood, not even when his father was out of town on one of his frequent business trips to Florida and Las Vegas. He was prone to mood swings that would attach themselves to whatever concern he might have at the moment, but since his concern was usually Marjorie, I thought that it was because of her he was so frequently unhappy. He worried that she didn't want to be with him all the time and that she didn't think of him constantly when they were apart. He worried that he wasn't smart enough for her. That they had gone all the way (as we put it) only three times and that Marjorie wasn't nearly as eager as he was to do it again. It even bothered him that they could not communicate through mental telepathy. He often tried to "send" her messages by projecting his thoughts while he lay in bed, something he read about in a paperback book, but the next day Marjorie claimed not to have picked them up.

Sometimes he would think up schemes for proving to her how he felt. There was March break, when Marjorie and her family went to Whistler on a ski holiday (a fateful holiday, it would turn out, when Grant Bluestein was also there). Valentine piled Marjorie's front door with a fortune in roses — six dozen of them. But her flight got delayed a day by a late storm, and by the time she came back the roses had been buried in snow and then removed by the company hired to clear the drive.

I remembered seeing a defeated Valentine at home the next night. He said to me, "I want so badly to prove to Marjorie how much I love her. Like if her house caught fire while I was walking by, then I could run in through the flames to save her. Or if someone tried to kidnap her and I got shot rescuing her, nothing that would be like a permanent injury and, like, wreck our lives, but that would show her. I just want her to know, Huddie. I *need* her to know."

He scared me, talking like that, but he excited me too, somehow. Of course there were also times when I just grew bored of hearing about Marjorie. Sometimes I would have liked to talk about my own future, if only I could have imagined what it might be.

36
Dead-Girl Songs

IN MY OLD ROOM, I picked up the mandolin and started to play "Down in the Willow Garden," a beautiful but unsettling melody with its repeated shift to the minor sixth. I began to sing the chilling words into the empty house.

> *Down in the willow garden*
> *Where me and my love did meet.*
> *There we sat a courting,*
> *My love fell off to sleep.*
> *I had a bottle of burgundy wine*
> *Which my true love did not know*
> *And there I poisoned that dear little girl,*
> *Down on the bank below.*

Not only does he poison her, he stabs her and throws her into the river for good measure. There were a lot of murder ballads — "Banks of the Ohio," "Pretty Polly," "Knoxville Girl," "Poor Ellen Smith," "Little Sadie" — in each one the man murdering the girl he loves, usually for no cause at all. Or, as in "Little Glass of Wine," where the man becomes irrationally jealous and poisons them both. There was a dark, pulsing rhythm to their lyrics, a murderous energy that came, or so I guessed, from severe sexual repression, from the intolerable pressure of social strictures and religious faith that turned the urgency of desire into blood lust. Yet their melodies were often the most hauntingly beautiful of all the old-time music.

Playing made me think of an evening in Prague, all of us sitting in the kitchen and me with the mandolin in my lap as it often was. Marta was dishing out a Czech delicacy, pancakes with whipped cream and jam. They were small, a little chewy, and good. Marta was saying to Maggie, "You can't talk to your teacher that way," and Birdy was giggling and pretending to slip off her chair. I began playing a melody without even thinking about it, softly, not even realizing it was "Banks of the Ohio" until Marta, placing a dish before me, whispered, "Not that, please. No dead-girl songs."

When Marta had become pregnant with Maggie, we had to find an apartment larger than a cupboard. It wasn't so easy, but then Marta's uncle died. He'd been a city street worker, one of the men in blue coveralls. With the help of some handouts to the landlord and a city official or two we got the place. It was a two-bedroom apartment in Vinohrady, a rather pretty neighbourhood that had been built in the 1920s and had been the site of street battles in '68. Ours was the one ugly building on Ripska Street, but it was just large enough and there was a lovely playground nearby.

Marta's father had been a professor of literature at the university in Prague, her mother an art historian. They'd been friends with the filmmakers of the Czech New Wave. Then the troops came and it all ended. Her father had died early, not out of despair but from lung cancer. Her mother grew depressed and couldn't teach anymore. She retired and began knitting the shawls that Marta sold, as if she'd stepped back two generations. Marta herself rejected an academic life under the new conditions and became something practical instead, a massage therapist. It was only in the last year that she had become involved with a group of young Czech filmmakers. On days when I was home she would go out and not come back until late. Or I would return from a gig and find her new friends, like the young man named Pavel, smoking at the kitchen table at 2 a.m.

The telephone rang, shaking me out of my sick feeling. I waited for my mother to get it but then she shouted to me from her room. I picked up the receiver.

"Excuse me. By any chance am I talking to Huddie Rosen?"

"Yes. Who's this?"

"Huddie, it's Art Lent."

"I'm sorry?"

"Arthur. Arthur Lent. You don't remember me?"

"I'm sorry, I'm not sure."

"From Arthur Meighen. I heard about the memorial for Valentine Schwartz. He was such a great guy, it was a terrible tragedy."

"Yes, it was."

"I'm just in town for a few days. Do you think we could get together? There's something about Valentine that I think you would be interested in knowing. Well, not about Valentine exactly. About the armour you guys stole."

"Do you know where it is?"

"It's better I explain in person. Meet me tomorrow at 10 a.m. I'll pick you up."

"It'll have to be the afternoon."

"Two o'clock, then. See you tomorrow, Huddie. Be there or be square!"

"Ha ha," I said humourlessly and hung up. That had been the tag line used by the high-school dance committee at the end of its announcements. Art Lent. I wondered if he was the skinny kid in English class who wanted to be a lawyer. I could remember a kid who walked around in a tie and jacket, carrying a briefcase instead of the usual backpack, and how everyone called him "counsellor." Maybe this Art Lent knew something about the armour, or maybe he was a scam artist trying to milk some money out of me. I hoped he did have it, and that I could get it back to Madeline Day at the museum. Like Marjorie, I could benefit from a little closure.

My mother came into the kitchen. "Who was that?" she said, going over to the sink. A colander of beans was sitting in it and she started to wash them under the tap.

"Just somebody from school. You're done making me a fortune for the day?"

"Yup. So do you have a hot date tonight?"

"Nope, nothing. I'm yours."

"Good. We'll have dinner and watch *Miss Marple*."

"Who?"

"She's an English detective. They made a TV series out of the book. I've got them on video from the library."

"Sounds good. Here, I'll cut the beans."

"It's about time you made yourself useful," she said, smiling. It was painful to see how much she felt just having me here.

37
The Valentine Schwartz Memorial Committee

IN OUR DAY, STUDENTS HAD been forbidden to enter the staff lounge at Arthur Meighen. Annie had imagined it as a smoke-filled den of iniquity, an eastern-style harem or opium cave, swathed in silks and softened by cushions embroidered in gold, where teachers removed their glasses and released their hair and, drawing on hookahs, ran their fingers over one another's pasty bodies.

The real lounge had been just an unused classroom with some beat-up sofas instead of desks, a coffee maker, and a chipped glass ashtray overflowing with butts. When I entered it this morning for the meeting of the Valentine Schwartz Memorial Committee, it hadn't changed much except for a smoking ban. Marjorie was perched at the end of a sofa with a stack of colour-coded files. Slumped beside her, Larry Nussbaum gave me a wink. Across from him was a woman who looked vaguely familiar and a couple of students. Annie was in a chair.

"Huddie keeps musician's time," Annie said, pretending to sound stern. "You know Marjorie and Larry. And I think you know Anita Gornkoff, who was also from our year."

"Of course," I said. "How are you, Anita?"

"Diabetes."

"I'm sorry."

"It's under control."

"And these are our student reps," Annie said, "Stuart Kwong and Krista Moghaddas."

Marjorie startled me by slapping her files on top of the coffee table. "I'd appreciate getting started." She hardly glanced at me and I wondered whether she felt some embarrassment over her confessions of the other night. "I've still got a million things to do to get ready."

"I'm in no hurry," the kid named Stuart said. "Right now I'm missing gym."

"Well, let's get on with it," Annie said. "I think as the first order of business —"

"Excuse me for interrupting, Annie, but as the chairperson of the committee it is my role to actually chair the meeting."

"Yes, you're right. Chair away, Marjorie."

"Thank you. I think our first order of business concerns this essay of Valentine's that Annie has brought to my attention. 'What is Canadian Identity?' We have Huddie to thank for preserving this important document all these years. I propose that the essay be read during the ceremony, and since at this late date it seems an unnecessary complication to bring in yet another speaker, I shall read it as part of my own remarks."

"May I bring up an issue?"

It was Krista, the other student. A smart-looking girl, of Iranian descent by my guess but likely born here, projecting as much confidence as she did. Diamond stud in her nose. Hemp necklace.

"Another issue?" Marjorie said with disdain.

"This ceremony is getting a little inflated, isn't it? Now you're going to read an essay by this dead kid? I mean, it can't exactly be the Charter of Rights. I still don't know why we're not just putting up a little plaque or starting a university scholarship, especially for somebody who died before any of the present students were even born. If we're going to put up a statue it ought to be of somebody like William Hubbard."

"William Hubbard?" said Larry.

"The first black Toronto city councillor. Or Abigail Hoffman, the track star."

"Or how about that kid with one leg who ran across the country," said Stuart. "What's his name again?"

"You don't know his name?" said Anita. "Annie, what are you teaching these kids?"

"I ask myself the same question."

"*Stop this!*"

We stared. Marjorie had actually shouted. In a voice of repressed fury she said, "It's too late for this nonsense. Valentine Schwartz's death was a tragedy that marked our lives."

"*Your* lives," Krista said, although quietly.

"Yes, my life. *My* life. The board of education approved the proposal for a statue months ago. And as far as I'm concerned, giving students a say in this has gone too far. We wouldn't have half the problems —"

"If I might say something," Annie stepped in. "It's only natural that emotions run high on occasion. And I, for one, am grateful to have students and parents who are so passionate. The simple fact is that we've gone too far with this memorial, including the statue, to put it into question. However, I have to agree with Krista that it would be a good idea for us to think about how we can make this ceremony more relevant to the present student body."

"That's simple," Krista said. "Give me a chance to speak at the ceremony."

"Over my dead body," said Marjorie.

"I think one dead body is enough," said Stuart.

"That's in bad taste," Larry said. He'd been playing with a game on his cellphone while everyone else spoke. "Funny, but in bad taste. Listen, Marjorie. Krista has a point. It really is their school now. And she is the president of the student council. Let her speak."

"I'm not going to make a scene or something," Krista said. "I've got my own reputation, you know."

"Fine," Marjorie said. "But that's it. No more student input."

"We ought to mention Huddie's musical role," Annie said. "Just so everyone knows."

"My blood sugar feels low," said Anita.

"Terry Figgs," said Stuart. "That was the name of the guy with one leg. Wasn't it?"

38
I'm Using My Bible for a Roadmap

PRAISE HIM WITH STRINGED INSTRUMENTS, say the Psalms. Words taken to heart in the South. The first gospel number I learned when I joined the Sorghum County Boys was the Louvin Brothers' "Are You Afraid to Die?" I played it with simple double-stop tremolos, a little softer than Charlie had, fading into the higher notes, and I sang the high-harmony part. I felt a little uneasy, but the first time we performed it on stage — there is always a gospel set at bluegrass festivals on Sunday morning — our voices in the early air sounded so ethereal that a shiver went through me.

That song was easy compared to the next one I had to learn, "Are You Washed in the Blood?" We played it at a fast tempo, with high, aching voices. After that came "Every Humble Knee Must Bow," "Talk about Suffering," "Gospel Plow," "To Be His Child," "I'm Using My Bible for a Roadmap." Inevitably I remembered my serious discomfort as a kid in school singing carols at Christmas time, fearful that our Old Testament God would punish me for being too cowardly to refuse. So I just mouthed the words, hoping to stay under both God's and Miss Callaghan's radar. And here I was, a grown man, an atheist by default, but still somehow a Jew, singing of death and resurrection, sin and salvation, of the lurking Satan and the never-lost promise of the loving Son.

And gradually I fell in love with those songs. With the barely restrained ecstasy behind the words. One morning in North Carolina, a Sunday of pouring rain but with the audience huddled under umbrellas and raincoats, we stood on the covered stage and sang "You're Drifting Away." No instruments, just voices in a five-part harmony. I realized that I didn't feel threatened anymore. I hadn't been converted either, except into loving the music, which was something I could believe in.

Besides, I'd realized that it was easier for me than for some of our other musicians who actually believed in what they were singing, or couldn't shake off what their mamas had taught them. Bill Monroe himself sang and played gospel with intense feeling, and there weren't many sinners bigger than ol' Bill, whose sad hunger for female attention was the worst-kept secret on the bluegrass circuit. Some of the boys I'd played with in Tennessee were worse in their way, using their money on drugs or Nashville hookers, leaving behind women and children, skipping support payments. Some of them dreaded those Sunday-morning gospel sessions as much as they would have being dragged to church. Me, I could just enjoy the music.

Strangely, what I never thought about back then was that my father used to listen to gospel blues. Blind Willie Johnson, Son House, Charley Patton and Bertha Lee, Sister Rosetta Tharpe — they made some of his favourite recordings. Faith and sin — another place where bluegrass and African-American music crossed. It was something else that connected me to my father, this unabashed love for a music that wasn't our own.

When I came to think of it, gospel blues provided another reason for Uncle Norman to feel hostile towards my father's passion. Expressions of Christian belief made him gag, a common Jewish reflex. Sometimes I wished that I had the imagination to conjure up my father's ghost, risen from the dead, hovering at the edge of a Sunday-morning crowd and listening to us sing "When the Roll Is Called Up Yonder."

39
The Family Discount

IT WASN'T LONG BEFORE UNCLE Norman arrived at my mother's door to take me to the shop. I tried to beg off, but Uncle Norman insisted — "I gave up a card game to get you, and Izzy Sharp was in it. I can read Izzy's face like an open book" — and before I knew it I was strapped into the passenger seat as we inched our way up Bathurst Street. Uncle Norman spent the drive talking about his weekly poker game and the way each of the regular members played — how Morris Finegold couldn't help widening his eyes when he was dealt a good card, how Freddy Gould bid incrementally no matter how good his hand, trying to gradually raise the pot. We reached the little row of businesses where C-Rite Eye Care had operated for forty years and Norman scraped into one of the diagonal parking spots. Everything was the same: the rusting bagel over the kosher bakery, the dusty boxes of enemas in the window of Seldan's Pharmacy, the dairy restaurant that emitted a smell of boiled chickpeas, the stairway up to the Posesorski Tailor Shop, where I'd been fitted for my bar mitzvah suit. Only the Triple-X Video Store with the painted-over windows was new.

Despite the changes that my aunt Min had mentioned, everything about the interior of C-Rite Eye Care looked the same to me, including the receptionist, Mrs. Nathanson, although she was heavier and wore a wig that sat too high on her head. "Is it really little Howie?" she said, pressing her damp palms to my cheeks. "I remember when you used to hide behind your mother's legs. And look at you, not a young man anymore. What does that make me, a hundred and fifty? So, what do you think? We've spiffed the place up."

"It looks great, Mrs. Nathanson."

"See?" she nudged my uncle with her elbow. "And how do you like the painting there by the mirror? I picked it up myself in Paris, France. In Montmartre, which is where Picasso lived. I bought it directly from the artist when it was still wet."

My uncle was frowning. He turned to peer at the closed office door. "Harvey's working?"

"He's got Mr. Zaretzky in there." To me she nodded. "Cataracts."

"We'll wait for the room."

I sat in one of the plastic-moulded egg chairs and glanced idly at the rack of eyeglass frames beside me. They were mostly aviator-style, gone out of fashion years ago, which explained the low prices on their tags. Norman picked up the phone and called Aunt Min to report that we had made it safely to the shop. "He talks too much to the customers," Norman said as he hung up. I wasn't sure whether he was speaking to me or Mrs. Nathanson. "He could talk all day like a yenta. There could be a lineup out here and it wouldn't matter to Harvey."

Only there wasn't a line. There was just us. However, at that moment the door opened and a woman came in with two boys.

She spoke in broken English to Mrs. Nathanson and then in Russian to the boys. The boys sat down, keeping their eyes lowered, and their mother sat next to them. All of them wore glasses. Harvey Greenbaum emerged from the examining room, leading a tiny, bald man with elfin ears. "Mrs. Nathanson, will you help Mr. Zaretzky choose a new pair of frames?"

"I want strong," Mr. Zaretzky said. "Must be very strong. I am always dropping them." He too had a Russian accent.

"Harvey, I need the room," my uncle said. "I'm going to check my nephew's eyes."

"You don't want me to do it?"

"No, I'll do it myself."

"I'm happy to do it," Harvey said, smiling. He was an obese man, but his enormous tweed trousers fit him well. Perhaps he went to Posesorski upstairs.

"Harvey, go next door and get yourself a bowl of borscht. Skip the sour cream. I'm doing my nephew."

"If you insist," Harvey said, pouting.

"Come in," Uncle Norman said brusquely to me. I followed him in and he motioned for me to sit back in the mechanical chair. He swivelled the optical apparatus in front of my eyes and began switching the lenses.

"You seem to have a large Russian clientele."

"Jews who immigrated in the last ten, fifteen years. They know nothing about being Jewish but they know how to bargain. They want a discount on top of a discount for what Stalin did to them. Then there's the Orthodox — don't even get me started. Tell me when the pictures match up."

"Now."

"And again —"

And so we went on, dropping the small talk. He had me read from the eye chart projected from a slide on the wall. He used a device to blow air into my pupils. As a kid, I'd come to have my eyes checked once a year, and my uncle had always pretended to be bitterly disappointed at my perfect vision. Now I saw a slight tremor in his hand. He pushed aside the apparatus and went to the metal desk, which must have dated from the fifties, to make his notes.

"You have trouble reading?"

"Sometimes. I have to move the paper a little farther from my eyes."

"Finally I got you."

"What is it?"

"I'll tell you exactly what it is. Middle age. Don't worry, I'll charge you the family discount."

"What's the family discount?"

"One hundred percent off."

"I can't complain," I said, getting up from the chair.

He rose from the desk and we stood a moment in the darkened room. I hadn't looked this closely at him until now and even in the dim light could see what an old man he'd become. "So, Howie," he said. "I want to talk to you about something."

"Sure, Uncle."

"Your mother tells me that you're thinking of moving back. This is a good business here. Not glamorous, maybe, but steady. Your cousins aren't interested in taking over. I made them owners of the building and they're satisfied to get the monthly cheques. But Min wants to spend more time in Boca. You can keep Harvey on and manage the place. Just that is a full-time job, trust you me."

"What exactly are you offering, Norman?"

"You can't live like you're twenty when you're forty with two kids. You could have a nice home, vacations. You can keep that *goyishe* music as a hobby. Of course I'd keep my hand in for a few months until you get the hang of things. I wouldn't want you to run the place into the ground. But you'd own it, not me."

"I'm speechless, Uncle Norman. You want to give me the business?"

"My kids would still own the building."

"I don't know what to say."

"Think about it. It's not a small decision. Maybe a regular job isn't for you. It never has been. On the other hand, maybe it's time for a change. Here you could have a life, Howie."

He pushed open the door, blinding me with the flood of light. "Howie needs reading glasses," he said loudly. "Gita, show him some frames. The ones we can't get rid of, even to the customers just off the boat."

40
Cowboy Hat

FOR HOURS AFTERWARDS I WAS in a kind of daze. That was after getting over the nausea that so overcame me I thought I would throw up in Uncle Norman's car. I couldn't make any sense of this image throbbing in my head — driving to work at C-Rite Eye Care, greeting customers, placing orders for new frames, bantering with Harvey and Mrs. Nathanson, grabbing a bite at the dairy restaurant, heading back home at the end of the day to be with Marta and the girls. Maggie and Birdy in their pretty rooms, doing their homework, running down the stairs to meet me. And on the weekends, taking them to the multiplex cinema, the mall, the park. Trying not to look at my mandolin in the corner of the room as I fell into bed. I didn't know if it was a dream or a nightmare.

When I got back to my mother's house, I found her putting away groceries in the kitchen. She had the little television on but with the sound off. I thought of telling her about Norman's offer — I had a feeling he'd kept this card up his sleeve — but I couldn't. I told myself that it would be better to talk about it with Marta first. So I just said, "Can I help?" and lifted a can of stewed tomatoes from one of the bags.

My mother removed it from my hand. "You don't know where anything goes. Do you want some dinner? I know it's a bit early but I thought I'd just have some cottage cheese and fruit. But I could make you something else."

"That would be perfect. I can't remember the last time I had cottage cheese. Do you think people who aren't Jewish eat cottage cheese?"

"Everyone on a diet eats cottage cheese. And no, I'm not crazy enough to be on a diet. Now if you want to do something useful, slice this banana."

"I'm surprised you trust me not to cut myself."

"It's a dull knife."

"What's on the television?"

"Some French police movie. I didn't see the beginning but it has something to do with stolen diamonds. Mostly they smoke and race around in little cars. And the women slap the men. I'm enjoying it."

We took our plates to the table. "Mom, do you remember a kid named Arthur Lent? Art Lent. Or his family?"

"There was a woman on the PTA. Maybe it was Lenz. Why?"

"Just somebody who knew Valentine. I have another question for you."

"Oh dear. You have a look."

"I do not."

"Trust me, you do."

"Fine, I guess I do. I was wondering whether you have ever had a relationship since Dad died. With a man, I mean."

"I didn't think you meant a squirrel. Now you're asking me, twenty-five years in."

"I'm a bit late for a lot of things. But I'm asking anyway."

"I'm not Internet dating, if that's what you think."

"I didn't expect you were. Mind you, you're pretty swift on that computer."

"I'm an old-fashioned girl. You really want to know? I've had a few."

"A few? What do you mean, a few? How many?"

"I'm supposed to keep count?"

"You're shocking me."

"It's not that many, for goodness sake. Three."

"Not bad. And none of them was serious?"

"One. I met him at the Speisman's cottage on Lake Simcoe. A very nice man from Houston. A Jew with a Texan accent and a cowboy hat. His company installs cable TV. He was a widower with five grown children. He came to Toronto a couple of times after to see me."

"When was this?"

"Maybe six years ago."

"Were you serious about him?"

"I liked him. He wanted me to come to Houston and meet his grown-up kids and the rest of his family. He has a beautiful house — I saw pictures."

"But you never went to Houston."

"No."

"Did you not want to get married again?"

"I wasn't saving myself in honour of Dad's memory, if that's what you mean. A person is entitled to a life. But I — I don't know. I just couldn't. It was too much change for me. Deirdre Speisman told me he married a girl from Montreal."

"Maybe he just wasn't right and your instincts told you that. There could be another coming along."

"Uh-uh. That's it. He was the last. I was depressed for three months after."

"You seem kind of down to me now."

"That's because my son deserted me for two and a half decades and deprived me of my grandchildren. I want you to come back for good, Howie."

"I know. Let's not talk about that tonight."

"Sure. Let's make an appointment for next Tuesday. You want some decaf?"

My mother made the coffee while I cleaned up. She sent me into the living room to get the album off the top shelf. It was where she kept the photographs of Maggie and Birdy and Marta and me that I'd sent her over the years and that she'd taken on her visits. I didn't wait for her but sat on the sofa and opened it. The photos sent by me were few and far between, every six months at best, the girls leaping in age — suddenly walking, or taller, or wearing school knapsacks with hair down to their shoulders. Maggie had her solemn look in some and was smiling in others, but always with her hands at her sides, posing. Birdy was usually laughing, or sticking out her tongue, or hanging upside down from the sofa, or making a beard out of bubbles in her bath. Marta was more often at the edge of the photo, carrying a tray, turning away, fixing Birdy's hair. I looked at them a long time. I stared at the visible corners of our apartment, the little end table piled with books, the shoes in the hall. Only when I looked up did I see my mother standing and watching me, the two cups of coffee in her hands.

41
The Heist

ALL THROUGH LATE WINTER AND into spring, Valentine's days were numbered but he didn't know it. Perhaps Marjorie didn't know it either, but she had already met Grant Bluestein, her future husband, that March-break trip to Whistler. Grant's father was a diplomat and the family had lived in Mexico City, Paris, and somewhere in the Middle East before his father had brought them home so that he could take a lucrative position on a corporate board. Grant was thinking of going to medical school, although it later turned out that he didn't have the marks and had to settle for law. He wasn't really good-looking — his chin was too big, his large feet stuck out duck-like when he walked, and when every other kid had hair down to his collar or a Jewish Afro, he looked as if he'd just got out of the chair of Mayberry's barber shop. But he was arrogant enough to make you think he was, so naturally when he entered Arthur Meighen after the break, Annie and I despised him.

The two of us were witnesses to the blossoming of this secret romance. Annie was, improbably, the chair of the Arthur Meighen Dance Committee, a position she volunteered for, considering it the world's greatest joke. She hadn't counted on being the committee's only member, responsible for organizing the school dance every two months. She dragged me to every one of them and I had to stand against the wall listening to some local rock band covering the greatest hits of April Wine and hope that some teacher-chaperone wouldn't urge me to get the dancing started. In small towns, or so I'd heard, high-school dances were packed, but at Arthur Meighen the crepe-decorated gymnasium looked depressingly empty. There would be maybe three dozen kids, most of them loners, and nobody ever danced.

This night was "Back to the Sock Hop." Annie had dressed in a pink cashmere sweater and a pleated skirt that showed her bare legs above her saddle shoes. The attendance was as dismal as usual, the mirror ball turned disconsolately under the baffled ceiling, and the band played the same songs as always. The only unusual thing was that Grant Bluestein was there, standing uncomfortably by the punch bowl.

I wanted to go home. Annie was pleading and then threatening me to stay when Marjorie walked into the gym. She peered warily into the dimness. Annie stopped and the two of us stared as Grant crossed the gymnasium floor to meet her.

They must have arranged to meet, or perhaps Grant had mentioned that he was thinking of coming. He asked her to dance. She shook her head no, fought him off playfully, and let herself be pulled under the hanging mirror ball. It was a slow number and he put his hands around her waist and his chin over her shoulder. Annie and I were mesmerized. As if by signal, other boys went up and asked other girls to dance so that soon there were eight or ten couples on the floor.

"Oh God," Annie said into my ear. "Grant actually knows how to dance! He must have taken lessons. How revolting."

They danced for two more songs and then they left. This was early May. Valentine and Marjorie had not been getting along. In fact, Valentine had been so miserable and mopey that they seemed to be doing each other more harm than good. Possibly they were coming to a natural end, and if Marjorie had found an easier way out, their relationship would have become just another wistful memory. But they were kids and didn't understand their own needs. Valentine was terrorizing her with his panic and Grant was her way out.

About the only conversation that Valentine never recounted to me word for word was the one he had with Marjorie that Sunday. I only knew about it because Marjorie came to see me the next morning — the first time she ever came to my house — and asked me to look out for Val. She was worried about him. She said that they had been walking to school and he had banged his head against a tree at the side of the field, hard enough that his forehead started to bleed. But I couldn't help Valentine because for the next three days he wouldn't let me. He didn't come to school, didn't answer the telephone. When I knocked on his door, his exhausted-looking mother said that he wanted to be left alone. That he didn't want an audience for his latest emotional drama worried me more than anything.

And then he reappeared. There he was at his school locker, pulling out the books he needed for his morning classes. Neatly dressed, shaved (he needed to shave every other day, not once a week like me), he looked pale and gaunt. He had a small scab on his forehead. He chatted as if nothing had happened but he had this bright intensity, this almost visible glow around him. He said that we had better get a move on with our presentation for Tillitson's history class if we were going to be ready for next week.

Huh? Where was the weeping, the rending of garments, the refusal to live one more minute? In the lunch room he was unnaturally jovial, his eyes burning. In the middle of a joke that Larry Nussbaum was telling, Val turned to me and said, "What do you say we go to the ROM after school? I can drive us. We'll take a last look at that armour. I can finish my drawing. Then we can work on our presentation after dinner."

"Sure, Val," I said. "That's a good idea."

He turned back in time to laugh at the joke, although I didn't think he'd heard it. After school I had to wait by Valentine's car for him to show up and then he insisted on stopping at the McDonald's on Avenue Road, claiming that he was starving. He consumed two Big Macs and a large fries and went back for a hot apple pie, with the result that we got to the ROM only a half-hour before closing. He was working on his drawing, finishing off the sabaton that covers the knight's foot when the announcement came that the museum was about to close. Valentine smiled at me, said, *Come on,* and I packed up and followed him, but instead of going to the exit he ducked into the men's room. He just stood there, not even using the urinal.

"What are you doing, Val?"

"Waiting."

"For what?"

"For the place to close up. For everybody to leave."

"So you can finish your drawing? We can't do that."

"Sure we can. I saw it in a movie once. Just see."

"I don't want to see. I want to get out of here."

He looked at me hard. "Don't desert me, Huddie."

"I'm not. Come on, Val."

"They've probably already locked the doors. I bet the security guards are checking the rooms. If they find us now we'll be in trouble."

"You're really freaking me out. Let's go."

"Uh-uh."

We went back and forth like this for another couple of minutes, until we heard footsteps. Without a word, Valentine dashed into a stall and climbed onto the toilet seat. I went into the other one, crouching to keep my head from poking over. I heard the door open and someone come in, take an excruciatingly long leak, and then leave without washing his hands. We waited another ten minutes before climbing down again.

"What a putz," Val said. "He didn't even check the stalls. The guy ought to be fired." He opened his knapsack and drew from it a rolled-up duffle bag, the kind that kids use for their stuff when going to overnight camp.

"Take this," he said, tossing it at me.

"Why?"

"You'll see, smarty pants."

He clapped me good naturedly on the shoulders, as if we were on a lark. Only now did he leave the bathroom and walk straight back to the tall glass case holding the armour. He fished a pair of needle-nosed pliers out of his knapsack and dropped the knapsack to the floor. Then he took hold of the small lock on the case door.

"Holy shit, Val, what are you doing?"

"Trying to open this thing."

"Are you nuts? There's got to be an alarm."

"Nah, only the really valuable stuff."

"Well, the lock's too strong."

"Yeah, but look at the metal loop thing. It's held to the door by a couple of nails. It ought to pull right out —"

And it did. Valentine held it up in triumph.

"Oh Jesus. Please stop, Val. Let's just go."

"Are you going to help me or not?"

I did not. I did not help him remove each piece of armour — helmet, throat piece, gorget, epaulière, breastplate, tasse, cuissard, jambeau — or put them into the duffle bag. Instead, I kept up a steady pleading, cajoling, begging, demanding — none of which had the slightest effect on his concentration. When he was done he closed the cabinet door, wiped it with a handkerchief, and heaved up one end of the bag.

"Come on, pick up your end."

"There's no way I'm helping."

"The longer we take, the better the chance of getting caught."

I picked it up. Damn, it was heavy. We half-carried, half-dragged the duffle bag to the elevator and took it down to the basement level, where the theatre and special events rooms were. Now I understood why Val had insisted on illegally parking in the alley behind the museum. To get out we had to push on the emergency exit door and a terrible, clanging alarm began. My heart felt like it would explode. We hefted the duffle bag into the trunk of the Celica. The back wheels sighed a little from the weight. Sprinting for the doors, we were like the Keystone cops, struggling to open them, smacking our own shins, but finally we were inside. Even Val looked scared and he almost dropped the keys. At last the engine roared as he put his foot on the gas.

We headed south on University Avenue, the opposite direction of home, but at least we were away. Valentine hooted with glee, banging an open hand on the wheel. "I'm going to show her," he said, rocking his head. "Yes I am. She's going to know what true love is."

He comically stretched out the word "love." Yeah, yeah, I thought, the adrenaline draining away, leaving me a dish rag. I didn't care what he was going to do; all I wanted was to get home. Valentine hooked back up north, fought the rush-hour traffic, and we finally pulled up in front of my door. I got out without saying goodbye, stumbled into the house and past my startled parents, and threw myself onto my bed.

I didn't see the armour again. Didn't ask about it and didn't see it. Not until a week later.

42
Yellow Shoes

THE TELEPHONE RINGING WOKE ME. It rang and rang — my mother didn't believe in an answering machine — until I finally managed to fumble the receiver to my ear.

"Hello?"

"Hi, Daddy."

"Maggie, sweetheart, it's so good to hear your voice. I've tried phoning but you guys have never been in."

"*Máma* told me to phone. Do you think I can walk to the park by myself? I want to meet Franka there but Máma won't let me. She says she has to walk with me."

"Mom's right. What else is going on?"

"Nothing."

"How's school?"

"Fine."

"Well, tell me about the nothing that's going on."

"Really, Dad, nothing."

"Did you have your sleepover?"

"Yes."

"Was it fun?"

"Yes."

"Did you visit your grandmother?"

"Yesterday. She isn't talking so much. And when she did she talked about some man named Blazek. Máma never heard of him. She thinks maybe he's from a long time ago, when she was young. Birdy laughed but I think it's scary."

"It can seem that way but it isn't really."

"Are you with Bubby?"

"I am. She misses you both."

"I want to see her. Is she going to come back with you?"

"Not right now. But you'll see her soon. Have you made me anything? A picture maybe."

"Dad, I'm too old to make you pictures. Bela has made you about a hundred ..."

She turned from the phone and began speaking Czech to Birdy, telling her it wasn't her turn yet. I could hear them arguing and tried to intervene but nobody was listening. At last Birdy came on.

"Daddy, Daddy, I miss you! Did you buy us anything?"

"What a question. I need a hug. You better send me one."

"Okay, I am. Are you coming back soon?"

"Yes, a few days."

"Are you going to live somewhere else? That's what Máma says."

"Don't worry, we'll figure it all out. No matter what, I'm coming home to you."

"I forgot to tell you, we have a mouse in the apartment. When Máma saw it she screamed. It ran behind the television. She's going to get Mr. Kopecky to put out a trap. But you know what I did? I put a bit of bread behind the television. Also I had a bad dream."

"Can you remember the dream?"

"A man came into my room. He wore yellow shoes and he had a knife."

"That's awful. But it's just a dream, sweetheart. You're always safe in your room. Did you maybe watch something scary on TV?"

"Maybe. Máma wants to talk to you. Don't tell her about the bread. *Miluju tě.*"

"I love you, too."

I heard Marta telling them to wait downstairs for her. "I'm sorry," she said to me, "but we have to go out."

"Listen, I've been thinking. Maybe it would be easier if we moved here. To Toronto. We'd have so much more. I'm even thinking of getting a real job."

"What sort of job?"

"You won't believe me."

"You are afraid to tell me."

"At my uncle's eyeglass shop. He wants me to take it over."

"You would do that? It would kill you."

"Ten years ago it would have, but not now. I'm tired. And ready for some security. I really think we could make a go of it here."

"I don't know, Huddie. I don't feel so sure that we can change, you and me. We lost something. I don't know how to find it. In bed it's not the same. A couple can't make it without that."

"I still think you're beautiful."

She laughed. "I have to go."

"We've got to talk. I have to make some decisions. *We* have to."

"Soon, soon. We are still separated, Huddie. You understand this?"

"Yes, I know."

"I will call. Goodbye, Huddie."
"Marta —"
But she was gone.

43
What Art Lent Knows

HEARING MAGGIE AND BIRDY'S VOICES made my insides shake. It seemed to me that Maggie's lisp was a little more pronounced, or maybe it was just not speaking to her for a few days. We'd talked about getting her a speech therapist but hadn't found an available one in Prague. Surely in Toronto we could find one.

And why had Marta insisted again on us being separated? It wasn't as if I didn't know it. She couldn't already be wanting to see somebody. Unless of course she was. I worried about it but I didn't think so. If anything, she'd want to be alone. Marta knew herself and what she needed. She had had the courage to say we were unhappy when I was afraid to admit it. I could never get over the fear that saying it would make it worse.

I heard my mother downstairs but couldn't face her, and stayed up in my room until she went out. Some time later a horn honked twice and then, after a pause, honked again. I looked out the turret window and saw an aquamarine Jaguar purring in the drive. The meeting with Art Lent had completely flown out of my mind. At this moment I didn't give a damn about the armour but I went out the door.

The Jaguar had California licence plates. It seemed the wrong sort of car for driving across the continent, too low slung and temperamental. Arthur Lent had obviously done well for himself and wanted to show it. As I walked towards the car I became conscious of my running shoes, ragged-ass jeans, and loose shirt with the frayed cuffs. He didn't get out but leaned over to swing open the door. As I lowered myself in I could smell leather and aftershave.

"Huddie Rosen." A deep voice, phlegmy with emotion. He wasn't the person I had thought — that must have been Lenz after all. Art was too tall, well-proportioned, confident. And he didn't look Jewish either, with those cheekbones and that aquiline nose. His leonine hair, silvering, was swept back from his broad forehead. A healthy complexion, if excessively tanned. His age showed in the pouches under the eyes and the beginning of a double chin and the slight hunch of his broad shoulders.

"I can't believe it's you," he said, backing out of the drive. "Good old Huddie."

I tried to cover up my embarrassment at not remembering him. "This is a beautiful car. And you live in California. So you've prospered."

"I own a house that used to belong to Eddie Cantrell," he said. "You ever heard of him?"

"I don't think so."

"Me neither, you have to be a real film nerd. He was in a lot of Laurel and Hardy pictures. A stone face until he blew his top, that was his gimmick. But he made his real money from inventing a special camera lens, made the women look beautiful in soft focus. A ranch house with a big property, like the garden of Eden."

He didn't sound as if he was bragging, more astonished by what he had. I said, "So what is it that you do in California?"

"Old-age homes. We build and manage them. More like country clubs. The market is booming, we have a waiting list for spaces and we're building more. California has a lot of aging rich people."

"And did you really come all the way here for Valentine's memorial?"

"Of course. I wouldn't have missed it. You've come from even farther, after all. From goddamn Prague."

"Well, I really came to see ..."

My voice trailed off. Art had put his large hand on my arm and was squeezing it even as he drove. "That you would come just for our friend Valentine. I'm personally touched. Deep down."

He took his hand back to shift. This was truly strange. Maybe Art had gone to Arthur Meighen the years before I got there and had moved away just as I was arriving. Either that or Art was suffering from some kind of dementia and the sooner I got out of the car the better. He did have a strange light in his eyes, intense and downbeat at the same time.

He pulled the car over. I looked out the window and saw with a start that we were parked in front of Valentine's old house. It was as huge in real life as it had been in my memory, and as gaudy, with its vaguely Aztec architecture. I remembered my father, who rarely disparaged anyone, musing about the ego of a man who would build such a monstrosity. He used to say, "Are you making a visit to Manderley after school?" (It wasn't until years later that I saw the Hitchcock film *Rebecca* and knew what he was talking about.) Marshall Ornitz had told me that Mr. Schwartz was mob-connected and explained that Jews could get pretty high up in the organization but weren't allowed to be full members; information that he got from Mario Puzo novels. I had spent hours and hours in that house, either in Valentine's enormous bedroom, with its own ensuite bathroom, or watching television and eating pizza in the living room, or playing snooker in the panelled basement.

Art Lent was looking at the house too, and clearly experiencing at least as much emotion as I was. To break the silence, I said, "I wonder who lives in it now."

"A family named Chan. Hong Kong money. Their son has the best marks in grade ten at Arthur Meighen and the daughter is the school chess champion."

"How do you know?"

"I keep up. And with you too, Huddie. Listen to this. It kept me company on the drive from the west coast."

He touched a button on the CD player and the Jag was filled with the sound of banjo, guitar, mandolin, fiddle, bass. A live performance of "On the Old Kentucky Shore." Only when the singing started did I feel the shock of recognition.

"Hey, where did you get that?"

"A bootleg. From a gig you played in Düsseldorf."

"There's a bootleg?"

"Here's your solo coming up."

"You must be one hell of a bluegrass fan."

"Not really."

"Then why do you have it?"

"Because I was interested. In you, Huddie. In your career, your music."

He smiled a slightly lopsided grin. God, that grin was familiar. If he was interested in me, he couldn't have left the school before I arrived, a thought that made me increasingly uneasy.

He said, "And in your life, too, Huddie. I know about Marta. And the girls, Margita and Bela."

"Wait a minute," I said, shifting away from him. Instinctively I groped for the door handle. Art just looked at me, still smiling, eyes glistening. Oh Jesus, it couldn't be. It just couldn't. My heart thundered in my chest. That was Valentine's smile. Those were Valentine's eyes. But the face — the nose, the cheekbones — were different.

My voice came out a whisper: "Val?"

"It's going to be all right, Huddie. Everything's going to be all right."

I pressed my fingers to my pounding forehead. It couldn't be. It *couldn't* be. My entire adult life I had thought Valentine was dead. But he wasn't. He was here. In this car. Now. It was impossible.

"I need some air," I said, grasping the door handle. I managed to get it open and stumbled onto the sidewalk. I bent double as bile burned the inside of my mouth.

Art Lent — no, Valentine — got out and came around beside me. "Breathe slowly, Huddie. Deep breaths. I took a first-aid course in California. I figured I'd need it, with all the things that happen to me. Can you stand? You've gone white. Come, let's take a little walk. It'll do you good."

"Yes."

He clicked the remote and the doors locked. As we started down the sidewalk everything looked vivid and unreal to me: the blades of grass along the edge of the sidewalk, the date imprinted in the cement, a circle of ants surrounding a striped candy. I managed to look at Valentine again.

"Do you mind if I ask you some questions? Just to be sure."

"Shoot."

"What did we do during the cross-country run for gym class?"

"We hid in Leon Selznick's garage and then joined up again near the finish."

"What's Valentine's — what's your favourite ice cream?"

"I don't like ice cream."

"Who got the best mark in Tillitson's class for the essay on Canadian identity?"

"Me. I got the only A. I'm still proud of that essay."

I stood where I was. And then I couldn't help it; I had to put my arms around him, something I never would have done when we were teenagers. He hugged me back, lifting me onto my toes. I couldn't help registering the suppleness of the leather jacket he wore, tan-coloured and cut like a blazer, a spring weight. I pulled away again to look at him.

"Your face," I said.

"Surgery. It got pretty smashed up when I fell. I shattered my right cheekbone. Took a couple of sessions under the knife. And I figured that since the nose had to be fixed anyway I might as well choose a new one. I was never too happy with that schnozz. What do you think of this one?"

He grinned and gave me his profile. Granted, his old nose was the only unbeautiful thing about him, but it had given his face character. The new one was film-star perfect and mildly snooty. I said, "How is it we all thought you were dead? Your funeral was supposed to be in New Jersey."

"That was my father. The day after I fell he made special arrangements for us to fly to Newark. I went into a hospital there. A few days later he phoned the school and told them I'd died. He didn't tell me for a couple of weeks, after my first surgery. I was pretty upset but he said it was better, that I needed a fresh start and had to break from everybody I knew. The truth is that he himself needed to get out of Canada, something about charges of tax fraud and maybe some other charges, I never really understood. After he left the police here just dropped it. And maybe — this is what I think now — my dad just wanted to be cruel to me. He was a real prick, you know."

"You couldn't have contacted me? Sent me a letter?"

"I thought about it, but it was just too hard. I mean, I was dead already. I felt humiliated. I just couldn't."

"So what happened to you? I mean, how did things turn out? I can't begin to imagine."

"How is any life, Huddie? I finished school and managed to get a college degree thanks to the work habits you got me into. But I hated the idea of working for somebody else. My dad staked me and I found a good partner. I may be no P.T. Barnum, but I know how to sell. Oh yeah, I've been married three times."

I paused. "Three?" I said. "Actual legal marriages?"

"Each one took me for a lot of money, but let them have it. I've got three kids, two with the first and one with the second, but I only see them on holidays. The last wife I divorced a year ago. You know what the real problem was?"

"I can't begin to guess."

"None of them was Marjorie."

"Oh come on, Val. That was twenty-five years ago. A high-school romance."

"They all looked a little like her. Raven hair. Tall. Slim but built. But none of them was as smart or sweet or good or patient as my Marjorie was. I looked but I never found her again. But you, Huddie Rosen!" He landed his hand on my back the way his father used to. "You were the best friend I ever had. And maybe now we'll be friends again."

"Sure. But we live rather far from each other."

"I can visit. Maybe they need old-age homes in Prague."

"Most people don't have any money."

"Oh, I bet there's more money around than you know. There always is. I've never been able to talk to somebody else the way I could talk to you, Huddie. Letting my guard down, from the heart. And even when you didn't agree with me you were always a loyal friend. Right to the end."

"I don't think you ever gave me much choice."

"I'm an orphan now. My parents are both dead."

"I'm sorry."

"My dad got shot in a restaurant in Albany. It was a mistake — they thought he was some other guy. Ten years ago now. If you want to know the truth, after he was gone, my mom seemed a lot happier. She started taking salsa lessons. I think she had a fling with the instructor. But then she got sick. Just her luck. I don't talk to my sisters. So I'm pretty much on my own. It's a big house to be living in by myself."

We turned around and started to walk back. The houses looked deserted, although there were a few service trucks — duct-cleaning service, chandelier hanging — parked in drives. The underground sprinklers of the house we were passing went on, sending out jets of water and catching our trouser cuffs, which made Valentine swear under his breath. "They're just Ralph Lauren, but still."

As we neared the car I said, "I went to see Madeline Day."

"Who?"

"The curator at the ROM in charge of the armour we stole. Remember? They quoted her in the newspaper the day after we took it."

"Right. She sounded like she wanted to castrate us. I remember it scared the shit out of you."

"I was already scared. She still wants that armour back for the museum."

"So?"

"So do you know where it is?"

The Jaguar doors unlocked. Valentine said, "Have you seen Marjorie?"

I hesitated a moment. "Come on, Val."

"I'm just asking."

"Yes."

"How does she look?"

"Older but still beautiful."

"I mean *inside*. How does she look inside? I know she's still married to Bluestein."

"Well, I don't have X-ray vision, but she doesn't seem too happy."

He grabbed both my arms.

"Ow!"

"What do you mean she's unhappy? What does that son of a bitch do to her?"

"A lot of people find that their marriages are less than paradise after a couple of decades."

"And what does she think of me?"

"She thinks you're dead. You're still eighteen years old to her."

"I have to see her."

"Now that's a bad I idea if I ever heard one. For better or worse she has her own life, Val."

"I don't mean talk to her. She doesn't have to know I'm there. I just want to see her, that's all. After all these years of thinking about her, dreaming about her, I just want to see her one last time before I go back to California. You can arrange to meet her, in a restaurant maybe. You've always come through for me, Huddie. I'll tell you what I know about the armour. I can see that you still feel guilty about taking it. And don't worry, I know it wouldn't do Marjorie any good to know I was alive. I can at least do that for her. Even if Marjorie saw me by accident, she wouldn't recognize me. I'll keep my distance. I'll look and then go."

"It won't do you any —"

"Here's my cellphone. Call her right now. Make a date. For me, Huddie, your old pal Valentine. Do it for me, will you?"

44
Having and Eating

AFTER VALENTINE LET ME OFF in the driveway of my mother's house, I had trouble unlocking the door. I had to use one hand to steady the other. I let myself in and went up to my old room, where I picked up the mandolin from its case, drew the pick from under the strings, and started to play "Billy in the Low Ground." Playing always helped to settle me when I was upset or anxious, but my fingers wouldn't work right, the pick kept missing the strings. I persisted until my hands steadied and my mind descended from the out-of-body place it had wrenched itself up to, settling back closer to my body, if not actually in it.

Valentine hadn't died; he'd merely gone to California. All these years that we had all been mourning his foolish life cut short, Valentine had been living under palm trees, driving expensive cars, marrying or divorcing his latest wife, building another swanky old-age home. And the strangest, most disconcerting aspect of this new information was my not even knowing for certain that I was glad. I was used to Val being dead. It gave my last year in Toronto a certain compact, if gruesome, narrative form, with a tragic and absolute ending. An ending — it occurred to me with a new jolt — that was about to be marked by a memorial ceremony and a statue.

And then there was the actual, living presence of Valentine Schwartz to contend with. Not exactly the Valentine I remembered — thicker-set and with that off-the-rack, movie-star nose and looking like he'd been baked at four hundred degrees — but the essence underneath still unmistakable. I had no idea what to do with him. I had called Marjorie, but only because I couldn't think clearly enough to say no, and we had arranged to meet at the Movenpick to talk about the choice of song for the ceremony. She had sounded a little wary, as if suspecting I might want something from her now that I knew she was vulnerable. Hanging up, I instantly regretted what I'd done. But Valentine was ecstatic. He kissed me on the forehead, holding my ears in his big hands. He swore on his mother's grave that he would keep his distance and just take a last look at her.

The telephone rang. After the third ring I picked it up.

"Huddie, you have to tell me that you are coming back soon."

"Annet. What's wrong?"

"We're falling apart here. I never understood how much you really did to keep the band together. Yesterday we almost missed a booking — the gig at that bar in Cheb. Grisha and Lukáš got in such a fight about it I thought they were going to hit each other. We arrived a half-hour late and left behind our best microphone. And the mandolin player, he forgot the words to "Tennessee Stud." All his breaks sound the same. The owner was so mad he paid us only half. He said if we mess up one more time he's going to replace us with a Dolly Parton cover band from Budapest."

Great. This wasn't what I needed right now. I said, "I'm very sorry, Annet. It sounds pretty rough. But it's bound to get better once people start dividing up the responsibilities. Put Saburo in charge of the schedule and Lukáš the equipment. Maybe you should look for another mandolin player for the next gig. There's that young guy with the braids, I forget his name. Lukáš knows him."

I heard her take a breath. "Okay. I needed to get it out. You are right. And we will manage somehow until you get back. Before I go, I want to know if there is any news of the girls."

"I talked to them. They sound all right."

"And Marta?"

"She sounds ... I don't know how she sounds."

"And is there any —"

"I don't think I have anything to say about it right now. Enough about me, Annet. What about you? It's time for something terrific to happen. You deserve it."

"Ha ha, that is very funny. It doesn't work that way, Huddie. Right now I have a rash all over my chest that is very unattractive. My banjo needs new frets and I don't have the money. Probably something worse will happen. I'm going to get off the phone and have a good weep for the girls and then get on the job of finding that mandolin player. Goodbye, Huddie."

"Annet —"

But she was gone. It felt as if a wet sack was pressed against my lungs. I hadn't yet taken my hand off the phone when it rang again. I had a premonition and snatched it up.

"Marta?"

"Ah, no. Is that Huddie?"

"Who is this?"

"It's Felix. Felix Roth. I was hoping that you might have some time to get together with me today and talk about Valentine. For the novel I want to write. I particularly have some questions about the day he died. I'm wondering whether you believe he fell by accident or deliberately jumped. Naturally, that's crucial. This is what I'm thinking: my character plans to commit suicide as a kind of exhibitionistic, narcissistic display of his love. At the last minute he's overcome by a sudden desire to live — he realizes that death isn't some game, that he won't get to see everybody mourning for him the way he imagines it — but the weight of the armour as he's lurching around causes him to lose his balance. He topples over. Having my cake and eating it too, you might say. But I want to know your take on what happened."

"This isn't a good time for me, Felix."

"How about tomorrow then? I can — oh, shit. The dog just peed on the stereo. I'll meet you wherever you want."

"Some other time."

I hung up. No, I did not want to talk to Felix Roth so that he could write a novel about an idiot who fell off a roof and killed himself. Especially if the idiot wasn't really dead.

45
Seurat in Needlepoint

A THUNDERSTORM IN THE LATE evening, and then a downpour of rain. Something that Felix might have conjured up for his novel. Pathetic fallacy — that was the term we'd learned in English class. I stood in the dark basement and watched my mother sitting by the glow of the computer screen, her knuckles a little swollen with arthritis, working at the keyboard. It hadn't occurred to me before that typing must be painful for her. The records kept sailing out and there were only a couple dozen left on a shelf. What had taken my father fifteen years or more to collect needed only three months to disperse.

Watching her, a memory came to me of the time that my father's boss at AmericaInk made a surprise visit to the Toronto plant. My father came home from work exhausted and stressed from Elsdon Neebe's bullying, from his demands that the presses be halted, the account books opened, pressmen and typesetters and platemakers privately interviewed. My father had come home just to change; Elsdon Neebe wanted to be taken out to a steak house for dinner and then have a tour of the Yonge Street strip clubs. My father didn't come back until three in the morning. I knew because I woke to the sound of him retching into the toilet. When he finished he didn't go to bed but went downstairs to listen to his records with his earphones on.

"I've been talking to a tax lawyer," my mother said.

"Why?"

"To protect this money, of course. The more you get for a house, for the girls, the better. Well, I'm about done for the night. We'll check the new sales in the morning. Always a little thrill, seeing the bids that have come in."

We went upstairs and sat in the living room without speaking much. My mother got out her canvas bag and pulled out the needlepoint of *A Sunday Afternoon on the Island of La Grande Jatte*, which would be a pillow for the big armchair. She'd been working on it for three or four years as she was only able to work for short periods. When she couldn't do needlepoint anymore, she had once told me on the phone, that was when she'd get her knuckles replaced.

I didn't mind the silence after the kind of day it had been, but after a time my mother said, "So Howie, why don't you play something for your old Grandma Moses."

"You don't really want to hear. That's okay, Mom."

"I'm not going to say pretty please, if that's what you want."

"It's just that you've never asked me before."

"Before it always took you away from me."

"All right."

I fetched the mandolin from upstairs. With the rain falling it seemed a good evening for the Stanley Brothers. "The Angels Are Singing (In Heaven Tonight)." "Too Late to Cry." "Let's Part the Best of Friends." Simple, old-timey songs with a melancholy feel. My mother didn't say anything, didn't look up, but I noticed one of her slippered feet gently tapping on the carpet.

46
Bottled Water

VALENTINE PICKED ME UP AT my mother's house and drove us to the Movenpick. He was dressed in the most beautiful silk jacket I had ever seen, a shimmering teal, with a soft white open-necked shirt that revealed greying curls, trousers with narrow cuffs, no socks, Italian loafers. But his face looked raw, as if he had scrubbed it with pumice after shaving too carefully. His high state of nerves came out in an endless stream of disjointed sentences. What I could take in was that he had not slept for a minute, had been drinking too much coffee since six that morning, and had been ignoring a growing pile of faxes from his partner in regard to the deadline for an impending land deal just outside of Santa Barbara. He drove too fast.

At the restaurant, I chose the same table where Marjorie had waited for our first meeting, beside the stucco wall that, I noticed this time, had a shadow painted across it to give the effect of late afternoon. Valentine hid at a table on the other side of the artificial plane tree. I picked up a stray newspaper from the next table to read the headlines while I sat like a piece of bait on a hook, the hunter hiding at a table behind the imitation tree.

I was trying to make sense of what I was reading when I felt the presence of someone and looked up.

"Are you sure she's coming? It's already ten after."

"Go away!" I hissed. "She'll see you! You promised to stay hidden. I'm going to leave if you don't stick to the plan."

"All right, all right. God, I can't endure this. I can't *endure* this."

He moved back to his place. I had a very bad feeling. Maybe I ought to run outside and head Marjorie off. But as soon as I turned my gaze from Valentine I saw her coming in through the doors. She paused a moment to scan the restaurant, saw me, and, without smiling, marched efficiently forward, swinging a canvas bag on her arm. She wore a short red-leather jacket, very tight jeans, and black high heels. I thought of how spectacular she and Valentine would look together. I started to rise from my chair but she waved me down as she took her seat, a cellphone starting to ring in her bag.

"Sorry, Huddie, I have to take this." She spoke into the phone. "Nettie? What's with this message that you're serving farm-raised salmon instead of wild? You promised me wild. Yes, I do think people can tell the difference."

She snapped the phone shut and dropped it back in her bag. "It's being catered?" I said. "If you don't mind my asking, Marjorie, who's paying for all this? It can't be the school."

"That's a good joke. I'll be lucky if Annie asks the janitors to scrape the gum off the seats. I'm paying for it. Well, Grant really. He doesn't know it yet but what can he possibly say? That's the one plus in having a husband who — oh, I can't talk about it. I'm already running late, Huddie, so if you need to talk, let's talk. It isn't your fault but my tolerance meter is almost at zero."

No more vulnerable Marjorie on display, that was clear. I realized the mistake of not quite figuring out what I was going to say. "It's ... it's about the song. I thought you might want to hear it first."

"I trust you, Huddie. The caterer I don't trust. But fine, if you want to play it for me, go ahead."

"I didn't actually bring my mandolin to the Movenpick."

She looked at me as if I were the pin-headed boy at the circus sideshow. "Then what am I doing here?"

"Actually," I said, changing tactics. "It's about Grace. I mean, about the song and Grace."

"I don't get it."

"Has she mentioned that she came to see me?"

"No, she hasn't. But then I'm the Wicked Witch of the West."

"We played some music together. Most kids her age wouldn't even want to listen to the stuff I play, so she gets credit for having an open mind. But I think she's struggling with a lot of things right now."

"I know. I just wish she'd talk to someone about it."

"I had this idea that maybe she could play at the memorial with me, rhythm backup on her guitar. It might be a good experience for her."

"At Val's memorial? My own daughter? I'm all for music therapy or whatever, but that would be a little weird."

"Frankly, Marjorie, the whole thing is weird. I think it would add a nice touch, the new generation of students mingling with the old. And it might give her a little confidence boost. If she's willing, that is."

"All right I guess, if you think so. But you have to talk to her because if it comes from me it's not going to happen. And now I've really got to go —"

"Hello, Marjorie."

Damn it, damn it, damn it. I should have known that Valentine wouldn't keep his promise. There he was, standing beside the table, leaning slightly over us but looking only at Marjorie, his mouth twisted, eyes wild with hope, desire, terror. The sound of his voice made Marjorie's own face change; it softened into puzzlement as she looked up with unnatural slowness. As soon as her eyes reached his face she started to scream.

For a moment I was paralyzed. Then the restaurant staff came running, thinking she was being molested or robbed, or perhaps having some kind of fit. I turned to assure them while Valentine got down on his knees to soothe her and stroke her hand. When Marjorie was able to get up from her chair, Valentine and I each took one of her arms to lead her outside. Her legs buckled. She trembled as if in a feverish chill and twice I saw her eyes roll up so that only the whites showed. Outside on the plaza sidewalk we held her against a lamppost, where she gagged for several seconds before catching her breath again. Valentine said, "I'll take her to my car," and he was in the midst of scooping her up to carry her, bride-like, when I put my arm on him. Instead, we walked her slowly across the lot. Valentine unlocked the Jag and we eased her into the passenger seat. The two of us stood by the open door.

"I'll talk to her alone."

"I don't know if she can handle it. She's in serious distress, Val."

"I'll be careful what I say."

"That doesn't change the fact of your being alive."

Murmuring came from below us. I motioned to Valentine and then leaned down to Marjorie. She managed to look at me, her eyes blinking rapidly. "I need water. Can you get me some bottled water, Huddie?"

"I don't think I should leave."

"Please."

"All right."

I had to agree, not having a better idea. I started to walk back to the plaza, turning to see Valentine close the passenger door and then go around to the other side of the Jag. I couldn't face going back into the Movenpick, so I went into the Dominion store instead. I stood in the aisle debating whether to buy San Pellegrino or Perrier before I realized what I was doing. I waited in line at the checkout and when I came outside again and approached the car I saw Valentine being anything but careful, sitting behind the wheel as he spoke urgently, his face close to Marjorie's. She was staring out the front window, tears streaming down her cheeks. I realized the bottle was too big to drink from easily but Valentine opened the window, took it from my hand, and closed the window again. I walked back to the sidewalk and, just to do something, went back into the Dominion and tried to browse through the magazines on the rack, but I was too acutely aware of Valentine and Marjorie in the Jaguar, and too busy condemning myself for being such an idiot, to concentrate. When I'd looked through everything from *Vegetarian Times* to *Knitting Fashion* I went out again and stood under the plaza overhang. After another ten minutes Marjorie got out of the car, swinging the door closed and almost running to her own Lexus. She got in and drove slowly out of the parking lot, rolling through the stop sign and onto the street. I waited a moment to give Valentine a chance to compose himself and then came around the Jag and got into the warm seat just vacated.

Valentine turned the key, making the engine purr.

"Are you all right?" I asked.

"I love her. I've never stopped loving her."

"Val —"

"And she loves me too."

"Did she say that? Did she actually say that, Val?"

"I know she does. She doesn't have to say it. I know."

I wanted only to get back to my mother's house but Valentine begged me to keep him company. He was afraid to be alone right away, and what could I do, seeing as I felt partially responsible, but to go along? He was staying at the Inn on the Park, a four-star hotel perched on a rise across from one of the city's ravine parks and just down from a stretch of corporate offices. He must have chosen it for nostalgic reasons, as it was just a ten-minute drive from school. Val, Marjorie, and Annie and I used to go there for dessert after a movie. Annie used to say that she and I were like the sidekicks in some forties Hollywood movie, the comic relief to set off the more beautiful but less amusing romantic leads.

Now I followed him as he paced down the hotel halls, from the restaurant to the magazine shop to the front desk and back around the outdoor pool, talking all the while with the vehemence of one who had reached exhaustion but kept on going. He told me about their first kiss twenty-five years ago, about the day she gave him her photograph, even their first time, in the room of a motel in Etobicoke owned by someone who was in debt to his father. How his hands shook as he tried to get her narrow bra strap unfastened. All details that he had in gentlemanly fashion refrained from telling me back when I might have actually wanted to hear them. If it wasn't before, it was now the greatest love story of all time. Now I heard him trying to write a new ending by force of his own desire. I let him talk because I was concerned about what might happen if he didn't.

But when the walking had begun to make me dizzy, when my head throbbed from the sound of Valentine's relentless voice, I finally said that I had to leave. To my surprise he readily accepted. It turned out that the time was coming up when Marjorie had promised to call him.

"What if she doesn't call?" It was a mean question but a serious one. I was worried that he might lay siege to her house.

"I believe she'll call," he answered, not arrogantly, but with soft assurance. "I know she loves me and I know she'll call. But I don't know what she'll say." He stood very close and looked at me with wounded but hopeful eyes and damp lips. He might have kissed me the way one sister kisses another if I hadn't turned and fled.

47
A Favour

BACK AT THE HOUSE, I thought the top of my head was going to come off. Despite the hours I had just spent with him, the barrage of words I'd endured, I couldn't get used to the idea of Valentine being alive. And if it was hard for me, I couldn't imagine how it was for Marjorie.

I stripped down to my boxers and leapt into the pool. Held my breath for as long as I could and came up again, gasping. Nothing seemed to make sense — the roses blooming on the bushes along the fence, the still leaves of the trees, the sun lowering on the roofs of the houses. I went upstairs, showered and changed, and came down to the kitchen, where I found a note from my mother under a plate in the fridge. The plate held a whole-wheat pita stuffed with tuna and bean sprouts, and the note said that she was going to see the new Michael Caine movie. *The one movie a season they make for us old people. I knew you wouldn't want to go and I'm used to seeing movies by myself.* I read the words again, hearing the unspoken reproach.

The telephone rang. I resisted answering it for the first three rings, knowing how unlikely that it was Marta or the kids again, but before the fourth had finished I swiped up the receiver.

"Huddie, it's Marjorie."

Shit. "You sound awful," I said. "You must have just got off the phone with Val."

"What am I supposed to do?"

How the hell should I know, I wanted to say, but her voice was raw and panicky. "Do you have to do anything?" I asked.

"He wants me to divorce Grant and move to California with my kids and live in his house. Or he'll move here if I want to stay. He says he loves me even more than he did twenty-five years ago. How can that be?" She started to cry.

"I don't know, Marjorie. Do you think it makes sense? If it's not impossible, it certainly is extraordinary. It must be hard for you to know how you feel."

"I thought he was dead! All these years thinking I loved him and that I'd made a terrible mistake. But it was a long time ago. We were kids. Even if I did make a mistake in marrying Grant, it doesn't mean I should have married Valentine. I mean, most people don't marry their first high-school boyfriend. He's so much the same, Huddie. In all the ways that endeared him to me and that also drove me crazy."

"You need time."

"I do, I do, but he's so sure. And it does something to me when he says that he loves me. I don't know when Grant stopped being in love with me, but it was years ago. Living so long like this has done something awful to me ..."

Her voice trailed off. "It's clear you haven't been happy, Marjorie. If Valentine coming back forces you to do something about it, then at the very least he's doing you some good."

"Yes, he *is* doing me good."

"Take the time you need. Don't let anyone rush you. Think

about yourself and also your kids. And be straight with everyone. Don't lead Valentine on. Don't tell him something you're not sure of. He'll just have to give you a chance to take all this in."

"Yes, you're right."

We hung on the line for a long minute. It wasn't like Marjorie to waste time with me, but now she seemed reluctant to let go. I said, "I guess you've got to call off the memorial."

"What? Oh, shit. Shit, shit, shit! It went completely out of my head."

"I can't see us putting up a statue to a forty-two-year-old man."

"We can't call it off. Then everyone will know. Grant will know."

"Shouldn't you be straight with him too?"

"Yes, but not now. I can't possibly deal with Grant at this moment. And besides, Valentine made me promise not to tell anyone until everything is settled."

"Leave it then. You can cancel at the last second."

"This is too much to think about. My heart is going to explode."

"You need to calm down. You need to be careful."

"Huddie, I have to ask for a favour."

"Sure."

"Let me send Grace over there this evening."

"Okay. But why?"

"I told Valentine he could come over and we'd talk some more. Grant's in New York overnight. My son is sleeping at a friend's. I mean, half the time I don't know where Grace is, but the last thing I need is her walking in while Val is here. I've got to know for sure she's staying away."

"Is this a good idea?"

"We're just going to talk. He's so insistent. And I did hurt him, I hurt him so much." She started crying again.

"Okay." I said. "I don't know if Grace will come. It didn't end so well last time. But go ahead and try."

"Thank you, Huddie. I wasn't really that nice to you in high school."

"It's a long time ago."

"I'm so terrified, but I feel something else too. Something I haven't felt in a long time."

She didn't say goodbye, but gently hung up the phone.

48
Private Showing

MARJORIE DROVE GRACE TO THE house but didn't get out of the car. I could see them arguing, and although the windows were closed and I couldn't hear what they were saying, it was not hard to guess that Grace was less than thrilled at being dropped off like a kid at the babysitter's. Finally she got out of the car, slamming the door and not looking back. Her hair was straighter; she'd done something to make it go limp. Dark purple lipstick, beat-up leather jacket, shorts made from cut-off army pants, storm-trooper boots. Marjorie stewed in the car a moment before reversing over the curb and bouncing back into the street.

I met Grace at the door. "Your mom looked a tad upset."

"She's not upset. She's psychotic."

"I've got your guitar here. No damage, at least."

"Yeah, like I was up all night worrying."

"I was hoping you'd practise a song with me."

"I'm not staying. I've got somewhere else to go."

"Your mother thinks you're going to be here."

"As if she ever knows where I am."

"Anyway, come in for a bit. You want a Coke?"

"No, but I'll take a beer."

"There just happens to be a new stock in the fridge. Can't see that one would hurt."

"Yeah, since my limit's like five."

In the kitchen I pulled out the beers. It was good of my mother to get them — Molson Export, my father's old brand. I handed one to Grace and she used the end of her shirt to twist off the cap. We went into the living room, where she slumped on the sofa, throwing her boots up onto the coffee table but being careful, I noticed, to land them on a copy of the *Canadian Jewish News*.

"Do you do any babysitting?" I asked, although I wasn't sure whether I'd leave a dog with her, never mind kids.

"I used to."

"I've got two daughters, six and nine."

"I don't babysit anymore. I've got a weekend job at Yorkdale. In the Eden store."

"What do you sell?"

"Cheap jewellery. And I do ear-piercing. It's totally gross, I have to close my eyes when I do it. Naturally my mom wants me to quit and concentrate on school. But I'm not going to university, so what's the difference?"

"Just going to get by on looks and talent, are you?"

Dumb thing to say. Her look said: *Fuck off*. Just then a car horn started to blare outside. "Oh, great," Grace said, slumping deeper into the sofa.

"Friend of yours?"

"*Pleeease*."

"Well, we can't have all that honking. This is a respectable neighbourhood."

I got up and went to the door. A spanking-new Ford pickup truck with oversized tires hulked in the drive. The guy behind the wheel had one of those triangles of fuzz under his bottom lip. When he saw me he stopped honking.

"Excuse me," I said loudly, "would you mind going away."

He called through the window: "Tell Grace to come out."

"I asked you to leave."

"Her cellphone's off. Tell her to come out."

"If you don't —"

But I didn't get to finish because Grace came up behind me and started shouting. "I told you to go to hell!"

I put my hand to my ear. "I think I've gone deaf." Grace pushed in front of me and stepped defiantly onto the drive.

"Come on, Grace," the guy said. "We'll talk."

"You don't actually know how to talk. You know how to grunt. You know how to belch. But talking is just something you pretend to do. Forget it, Jacob."

This kid didn't look anything like a Jacob to me. Jacobs took violin lessons and tutored kids in math.

"I miss you," he said.

"And I trusted you. You understand? I don't give that to anybody. I thought you were different. I thought you had a mind of your own. But you're just a fucking pack animal like the rest of them. I hate you and I hate your stupid friends."

"Okay, I was stupid. But I'll make it up. I mean it."

She started to walk over to the truck. "Don't go, Grace," I said, but she waved me off, going around to the passenger side and opening the door. I was surprised at the disappointment I felt. But she just reached into the cab and pulled something from inside. A knapsack. Then she kicked the door shut with her boot. Walking away, she held one finger in the air. I noticed that her knapsack was covered in animal-rights buttons from PETA, the organization that likes to throw fake blood on people with fur coats. Jacob sat in his truck, his face fallen, but then something in him changed, as if he was filling up with anger. He pushed open the other door of the truck and got down. It looked as if some of the Jewish boys were spending more time at the gym than the library these days; his upper arms had bulges the size of mangos.

By now Grace was back beside me. Jacob strode up to us and put his hand on her shoulder. "Come with me," he said, not as a request but an order. I was steeling myself to physically remove him, preparing for him to swing at me, when Grace herself shrugged him off.

"Let me say it more clearly, Jacob. Do please go fuck yourself."

He raised his hand again but I intercepted it, only to have him shove me backwards. All I could think was, thank God my mother wasn't home. I was stepping forward again when another blare of honking made us all turn. A little red Honda was stopped at the curb.

Annie got out.

"Jacob Kapinsky," she said, coming towards us. "Didn't I just see you in my office yesterday?"

Jacob Kapinsky looked down at his feet. "I guess so, Ms. Lynch."

"Go home, Jacob."

"But, Ms. Lynch —"

"Right this minute. Get into your car and drive away. You see my phone? I'm one number away from calling the police. And then it won't be a matter of after-school detentions."

He looked up, sniffed loudly as if to show he didn't care, but walked to his truck. We watched him back out and drive away.

"I'm impressed," I said.

"Some of us are born to be principals. Am I wrong, Grace, or weren't you going out with Jessie Howe?"

"He was stoned all the time. I got tired of it."

"Enough said. Is anybody hungry?"

"I'm starved," Grace said.

"I've got Thai food in the car. Huddie, you put out the plates."

Grace and I set the table in the kitchen while Annie fetched the bag from her car. So these were the kinds of problems I would have with my own daughters, if I was lucky enough to be with them. I hadn't expected Annie to show up but I sure was glad, and she'd brought enough food for six people. The three of us heaped our plates with pad Thai and mango salad and spicy rice, the warm food putting us into a good mood. Grace clearly got a kick from hanging out with the head of her school, and she and Annie started telling stories about the place, laughing as only insiders could. Then Grace asked about Valentine Schwartz. Had her mom really been "hot and heavy" with him? Was he really always injuring himself, jumping into empty pools, walking into fire hydrants, banging himself in the head? We assured her on all counts.

"Sounds like he was kind of dumb," Grace said.

"Well, it's not anybody's smartest period of life," I said.

"Are you referring to me?"

"If the boot fits," Annie said and then ducked as Grace swatted her.

After we cleaned up I told Grace that I wanted her to play with me at the memorial. Her first response was to laugh, her second to say "no fucking way," and her third was to agree to try the song with me. I got our instruments and showed her the chord sequence and how to end a phrase with the Lester Flatt

G-run. We ran through the song a couple of times and I decided it was best to leave it at that. We turned on the television and found *Casablanca* halfway through. Grace said she'd never heard of it, making Annie and me groan in disbelief. My mother came home and joined us on the sofa, remembering how she saw it as a kid at a Saturday matinee — two movies, three shorts, and a set of dishes given away. Annie, my mother, and I all said the "hill of beans" speech along with Humphrey Bogart while Grace looked at us as if we were the most pathetic losers she'd ever met.

"Okay," Grace said. "It was party central here but I'm a bit tired. Maybe somebody could drive me home?"

I'd promised not to bring Grace back until at least eleven. "Oh come on, you can't bail out now. We're just getting started. Right, Annie? Mom?"

The two of them looked at me. "Is he quite all right?" my mother asked.

"Musicians." Annie rolled her eyes.

"I know," I said. "Annie, nobody but you has seen the statue of Valentine. Why not show it to us now?"

"I don't think you mean it."

"Cool. I want to see it before anyone else," Grace said.

"It's already past my bedtime," my mother said.

"You've got to come too. Annie needs our opinion."

"Oh why not," Annie said, getting up. "Let's break into the school after dark. After all, I am the principal."

"Exactly," said Grace. "I mean, what's power for?"

"Let me put on my walking shoes." My mother smiled. "They don't make any noise."

Annie drove. It took about two minutes for us to get to the school parking lot. We emerged from the dark into the floodlit circle before the front entrance and Annie used her key to let us in. It might look suspicious if a lot of lights suddenly went on so we walked through the dark halls to the shop class at the rear of the school. "This is *so* freaky," Grace said. "Nobody's going to believe it when I tell them."

"Another reason why you're *not* going to tell them," Annie said.

"Well, I'm going to tell the girls at bridge and you can't stop me," my mother said.

"I wouldn't even try, Mrs. Rosen."

"Call me Fran, for goodness sake. Times have changed, you know."

We reached the shop door, but it was locked too. Annie had to get the key from her office to let us in. In the dark the power tools hulked like sleeping beasts. "It's back here," she said, leading us to the far corner. The statue was covered by two tarps. Annie and I had to stand on chairs to pull them off. Only then did she turn on the light. We blinked from the brightness and stared at what stood before us.

"It's ... it's very nice," my mother said.

"It is so *not* nice," Grace said and laughed sharply.

The statue must have been eight feet tall. It was a knight in armour all right, made of discarded scrap metal — car fenders, hubcaps, small oil drums, a radiator. A hibachi grill was a visor on the helmet, which also had what appeared to be the blades of an electrical fan on top. But what really stood out, or rather up, was the lance, grasped between the legs by two hands made from hockey gloves painted silver. The lance, a discarded outdoor lamppost, thrust upwards from the body, the metal shade forming a bulbous end.

"That's the most juvenile thing I've ever seen in my life," I said. "Nobody but teenage boys would find that funny."

"Bingo," said Annie.

"I don't believe Valentine was holding a lance."

"No he wasn't, Mom."

"Oh, now I see. It's like a, well, like an erect penis, isn't it?"

"Yes it is, Mom."

"I asked them to remove it, but the kids refused. And the teacher supported them. He's mad at me for not funding shop more."

"Maybe you should call in the school board."

"I considered it. But who am I to advocate censorship? There's no way I'm going to be that kind of principal."

"I can see why you haven't let Marjorie in," I said. We all looked at it in silence. I wished that I could tell Annie the ceremony was going to be called off anyway, but I couldn't break my word to Valentine. Which meant that I was lying to Annie instead, but I didn't see what else I could do.

"We can hang Christmas decorations on it in December," said Grace.

"Mistletoe right on the end there," my mother said.

Annie drove Grace home first, now that it was late enough for Marjorie's assignation to be over. Then she drove us home. I told my mother I'd follow in a moment and Annie and I sat in the car as we watched her go into the house.

"Well," I said. "I haven't had that much fun since grade twelve."

"You said it. So listen, Huddie. Not that I'm an interested party or anything, but this separation from your wife —"

"Marta."

"Yes, Marta. What do you think is the real reason?"

"I've thought about it so much I think I know less now than when I started. A lot of the time I blame her — that she's too demanding, that she won't just let things be. But at the moment I guess I see things differently. I think when we first met — do you really want to hear this crap?"

"Uh-huh."

"All right. When we first met I think she wanted to give me everything that she had. Herself. Her family. Her country. I think she would have made love with me on the Charles Bridge. To make it all a part of me, I guess is what I mean. To have no reservations. And I think that gradually, over time, I've disappointed her."

"Disappointed her how?"

"I don't know. By not accepting everything she wanted to give. By not giving as much in return. It's as if all this time she's been lying on the bridge waiting for me and I've been standing there with my socks still on, saying, well, maybe it's too cold on the bridge, and it doesn't look very comfortable. Holding back this part of me. Retreating a little further. Not letting her in all the way."

I stopped talking but Annie didn't say anything, just held onto the steering wheel and looked straight ahead. "This," I said, trying to sound light, "is where you tell me that it's really all her fault."

"I just feel sad for you both."

"Then I've accomplished my goal for the night. Sorry."

"I better go." She leaned over and kissed my cheek. "Goodnight, Huddie."

I left the car and walked up the drive. I wanted to turn around but I walked to the door, opened it, and went inside.

49
Eggs

FROM THE LIVING-ROOM WINDOW I could see my mother doing exercises in the shallow end of the pool using a large plastic ball. I got on the phone and made a Monday appointment with an immigration lawyer at a firm with the unlikely name of Huckabone, Mawhinny, and Inch. I'd gotten the name from Larry. Then another call to reserve my return flight to Prague on Tuesday.

I was glad to make breakfast for myself, just a couple of pieces of toast. In Prague I had enjoyed letting Marta sleep in on Sunday mornings while I made eggs for the kids on the tiny stove in our tiny kitchen. Maggie liked hers extra-well done, with cheese sprinkled on them, while Birdy loved hers loose and runny so that she could dip her toast into the mess. "Gross," Maggie would say in English when she saw Birdy's plate. That, in a nutshell, was the difference between them. Like the way Maggie would discreetly slip her hand into mine as we walked up Petřín Hill, and how Birdy would wait for me on the sidewalk and then fling herself into my arms. Or how Maggie would never get overtly angry but would brood for days, reluctant to give up her dark mood, while Birdy would ignite with fury, scratching and biting like a cat, only to be happy again minutes later.

I made myself breathe. I took a bite of toast.

50
Inner Beauty

WHEN I OPENED THE DOOR of the teachers' lounge, a student I didn't recognize from the earlier meeting was standing at the head of the table. He was a string bean of a kid in a Che Guevara T-shirt and a fuzzy upper lip overdue for its first shave, and he was holding a sheet of paper in a trembling hand.

"You're just in time," Annie said. "Matthew has written a poem that he would like to read at the memorial."

"Isn't it enough that you publish a poem in every issue of the newspaper?" This from Krista, student president.

"Let the poor kid read it before he faints," Larry Nussbaum said, giving me a thumbs up.

"Yes, go ahead, Matthew," Annie said.

The boy began to recite his poem, or rather to chant it —

> *Down you went, down, down*
> *like some wannabe Achilles.*
> *Only your weak spot?*
> *Not your heel, man, but your head.*
> *Bashed.*

Still, you also rose
to Arthur Meighen immortality ...

— but I stopped listening because I was staring at Marjorie. She looked stricken. Her skin had turned practically translucent. I could see the finest veins in her neck and around her nose. Her lips looked raw. Her eyes stared at a cracked water pitcher on the end table beside her, as if into the deepest spot in the ocean.

As soon as the boy finished his poem, Krista lit into him. "Who do you think you are, Allen Ginsberg? Your poem sucks."

The boy looked crestfallen. "It doesn't suck," he said, but not as if he believed it.

"I like it," Larry Nussbaum said. "It's catchy."

"Matthew," Annie said. "The service is already running a little long. I'm glad you read the poem for us, but can't you give it to the newspaper? There must be an issue coming out soon."

"It's coming out tomorrow," Matthew said. "The poem's already in it."

"Because you're the poetry editor," Krista said.

"Well, there you go." Annie smiled. "Your poem is going to live forever in the back issues of *Arthur's Rag*."

At this moment Marjorie burst into sobs. It was the awful sound of a person who has no weeping left in her but still can't stop.

"Marjorie?" Larry said. "It's all getting to you, eh? Have a drink." He poured half a glass of water from the pitcher and tried to hand it to her but her fingers didn't grasp it and the glass dropped to the floor. Stuart, the other student rep, who'd appeared asleep until now, fetched paper towels from beside the coffee machine.

"I'm so sorry," Marjorie managed to say. She was the only one who hadn't moved. Annie looked at me, as if to say, *What now?* Aloud she said, "I don't think we need any more meetings. Or to extend this one. The ceremony is tomorrow. The arrangements are all made. Everyone knows their job."

"Sounds good to me," Larry said, heading for the door. "I'm already late to pick up a client." Looking at me, he said, "Hey, bluegrass boychik. Come for dinner tonight. Bring your mom."

Annie had another meeting, and everyone else filed quickly from the room, leaving me alone with Marjorie. I wanted to go too but didn't see how I could just desert her, so I came over and said without conviction, "I'm sure everything will work out."

Marjorie said, "I had sex with Valentine."

"You don't need to tell me everything."

"I didn't mean for it to happen. He wanted me so badly and I felt so terrible for everything that happened and how I was responsible for him dying."

"He didn't die, remember?"

"It was like sleeping with a ghost. Except he's real, flesh and blood. And it was good. I haven't felt that in so long. That's why I'm crying too, because it was good. And now I'm afraid Grant will find out and do something terrible. Oh God, what time is it?"

I looked at the school clock on the wall. "After eleven. What do you mean by terrible?"

"Come with me," she said. "I have to eat something. I haven't eaten in twenty-four hours."

"All right, I guess. But Marjorie, maybe you need some professional help. I'm in over my head here."

She was already at the door. I followed her out of the school to the parking lot and we got into her Lexus. "Where are we going?" I said.

"I don't know. The Pickle Barrel."

"You're serious?"

"I'm comfortable there. And it's close."

She took a pair of designer sunglasses from the glove compartment and put them on, looking a little like Jackie Onassis. She drove fast but well and seemed to calm down. We got to the plaza and she pulled up in front of the restaurant, parking illegally by the curb.

It wasn't quite noon but the place was almost as busy as when I'd come with Uncle Norman, mostly older couples and groups of teens who were probably skipping classes. We got a table by a ficus plant in the back and Marjorie ordered a coffee and the all-day breakfast special. I ordered a coffee and a toasted bagel with lox. If she was going to keep forcing me to advise her, she might as well feed me too. "Marjorie," I said. "I think you need to back off everything. Take a week away from this craziness, maybe even go away by yourself. Have some time to think —"

"I love him, Huddie."

I leaned my forehead on my hand. "Oh, swell."

"I made a mistake in high school. I was swayed by superficial things. Grant seemed glamorous to me — handsome and smart, even a good dresser. Val didn't get very good marks, even with your help, and I couldn't see what he was going to do with his life. He had no ambition. He wasn't even thinking of a professional career. Most girls that age lose their heads to romance, but I was practical. I lost sight of what made Valentine so special. His inner beauty. And he still has it, it's never left him."

VALENTINE'S FALL

I let the phrase hover over a picture of Valentine with his new nose and middle-aged thickness and manic insistence. Perhaps it took the right person to see someone else's inner beauty. I said, "You've only known him again for two days. Don't misunderstand me, I don't have the slightest idea what you should do. But you're in an unhappy situation with Grant that until now you haven't been able to deal with. Maybe you can save your marriage, maybe you shouldn't try. Maybe Val is what they call a 'crowbar,' someone to help you get free. People who leave their marriages for somebody else don't usually end up staying with that person. My point is there's a lot to think through. It would be foolish to make a decision now."

"You were always Val's friend," she said. "After I dumped him you came to my house, remember? You stood in the doorway — it was pouring rain but I wouldn't let you in. You told me how miserable he was."

"Only because his mother begged me to."

"I understand you want me to be careful. You're protecting us both. But I know what's in my heart. I feel it. I don't care how many years have gone by, it might as well have been a day or an hour or a minute. I love Valentine with body and soul and I don't want to lose him again. I'm leaving Grant. I'm going to divorce him and marry Val. It'll be hard on the kids at first but I know they can handle it. And they know their father is a shit to me. They love him, but they know."

"Have you told Valentine?"

"This morning. He cried on my shoulder like a baby. He said it was like waking up and finding that your dream was true. I love Val so much, I'll go anywhere with him." She reached across the table and grasped my hands in hers. "Thank you, Huddie, thank you so much."

"There isn't anything to thank me for."

"You've brought him to me. And Val says that you've given him the courage because you never stopped believing in him. We owe you everything."

It wasn't true. I didn't want it to be true. But there was no point in saying anything. "I assume you're calling off the memorial tomorrow. A relief really."

"No, no, we can't. We have to go through with it. I can't be ready to leave for a couple of weeks. I've got an appointment with a lawyer on Monday. There's the kids. I've got to make sure my own assets are safe from Grant. He'll suck me dry if he has a chance. He's got an ugly temper and he's already suspicious. The memorial will work to our advantage. And afterwards, who cares what people think? We'll be living in beautiful California."

"So we're going to keep on pretending that Val is dead. I don't know if I can do that."

"All you have to do is play your song. That can't be so hard. Don't look down, Huddie. Look at me. Say you'll do it."

She reached out and grabbed my chin as if I were a child, turning my face to her own. Her eyes were dark, sleepless, but also frighteningly intense. "I *love* Valentine," she said. "I *need* him. I'm getting a chance to live my life over again. Who ever gets that, Huddie? It's a miracle. And I'm going to take it."

51
Not Enough

I WOULD HAVE TAKEN A lift with Marjorie if she hadn't announced an urgent need to be somewhere and then abruptly left the restaurant, leaving me to wait for the bill. Counting out the tip, I thought about how careful I'd had to be with money all these years. We'd owned nothing that wasn't essential — no car, no microwave, no computer, only a TV and a CD player. My kids had less than other kids, although I stretched as much as I could for them. It was only last Christmas that Maggie had pleaded with tears in her eyes for some American toy, a talking fairy doll with wings that changed colour. It had taken me three weeks to scrounge up the money, by which time they were all gone from the Prague stores. Maggie was so angry and disappointed; she said she hated me about a hundred times until finally I yelled and sent her to her room. These are the times you'd prefer to forget when you're separated from your kids.

I paid the waitress and made my way towards the front of the restaurant. Diners were ordering enormous platters of smoked meat and barbecued chicken wings. As I passed a table I felt a hard yank on my sleeve and turned to see Uncle Norman. "What, you're pretending you don't know me?" He was sitting with a man of about the same age but with hollowed cheeks, and eyes sunk deep in their sockets, corpse-like. A well-dressed corpse, however, in a black Armani shirt and with a gold chain around his neck.

"Irv, it's my nephew, Howie. Howie, you remember Irving Gould."

"Sure I do," I said. My uncle was still holding onto my shirt. "How are you doing, Mr. Gould?"

"How do I look like I'm doing? I weigh less than I did when I was sixteen. I look like I've been French-kissed by the goddamn Grim Reaper."

"Heart transplant," Uncle Norman whispered loudly.

"You're not serious."

"You want to see the scar?" Mr. Gould put his hand on his shirt, as if to pull the buttons open. "It looks like I've got a trap door. The heart belonged to a thirty-two-year-old Filipino woman, if you can believe it. She cleaned people's houses for a living. She had a crappy life, got hit by a bus, and now her heart ends up in me. Not much compensation for her. Actually, I gained two pounds this month. I've always been a fighter, haven't I, Norm?"

"Since the Spadina days," my uncle nodded. "Howie's a musician in Europe."

"What, with a symphony?"

"No, more like folk music." I hoped we could move the conversation on.

"You mean like that Jewish kid, Bobby Dylan? That's okay, nothing wrong with it. My son David — you remember him? — now he's a Buddhist. There are probably Jewish matadors and Jewish sumo wrestlers. Say, weren't you friends with that kid who took a fall off the school? David got an email about a memorial but he's at some monastery in Switzerland if you can believe it."

"Yes, he was my friend."

"I never liked his father, there was something fishy about the way he made his money. Still, it was a terrible thing, that boy dying. I didn't know what to say to David so I didn't say anything. Nowadays, some kid's kitten dies and they send in grief counsellors, therapists, they hold hands in a circle, they write poems, they leave flowers. When we were kids, if somebody got hurt, your father would slap you on the side of the head and say, 'See? You kids should smarten up.' It worked, didn't it, Norm? Now the whole world's gone *meshuggenah*. Hey, Howie, while you're here, tell your uncle to stop overcharging for glasses."

"What are you saying? I'm the cheapest in town. Listen, Howie, join us. Have a little salad, a sandwich maybe."

"Thanks, Uncle Norman, I already ate. But I would like to talk to you a minute. About, well, you know."

"No, I don't know."

"You *know*," I said more insistently.

"If I knew I wouldn't ask. Irv is the big joker, not me, aren't you Irv?"

"I was always the class clown."

"The shop, Uncle Norman. I want to talk to you about the shop."

"Oh that." He frowned. Was he having second thoughts about asking me, or did he just not like to think about retiring? "Let me tell you what's important," he said. "The customer. And let me tell you what else is important. The customer. And the third important thing? The customer. He has to feel special. You have to take time, make him feel good, you understand? You're not just selling glasses, you're selling a whole package, a look, an identity. How a person feels about himself. The most important moment is the first look in the mirror. It's like seeing yourself as a stranger, from the outside. Do you look interesting, mysterious, attractive, sexy? It's fraught with anxiety. You've got to help things along."

"I'm sure there's a lot you would have to —"

"But it isn't just about sales. It's about running the business properly. Keeping costs down, overhead. All that my sons are going to care about is that you pay your rent on time. They're not like me, easygoing, all they care about is money. You'll have to negotiate hard with suppliers, keep the right amount of stock, make sure the accountant, the cleaners, the lens company aren't taking you for a ride."

"I can do that," I said.

Uncle Norman stared up at me through his own thick lenses. "I don't like to mix lunch and business. Call me at work."

"Sure," I said. "Keep well, Mr. Gould." My uncle's friend shook my hand, squeezing my fingers until they hurt. His grip said: not bad for a guy with a new ticker. The conversation did not leave me with a good feeling. I reached the front bar of the restaurant with its display of pickle jars and salamis when a voice called out.

"Huddie!"

Jesus, did I know more people here than in Prague? I turned to see Felix Roth, perched on a bar stool with a large bowl before him. "Huddie," he called again, motioning with his spoon. "Pull up a stool."

"I've only got a minute, Felix. What are you eating, matzo-ball soup?"

"It reminds me of New York."

"I was thinking that you might have gone home."

"Are you kidding? I wouldn't miss the memorial tomorrow for the world. I'm considering using it as the opening scene and then moving back to the start. Though I am concerned that it's an overused device, too movie-of-the-week. But I'll tell you what I think the real key to the novel is. Figuring out who the narrator is. Who's going to tell the story? I need someone closer to the action than I was. Someone with more at stake."

"I don't get it. Are you writing fiction or the truth?"

"Good question. Most writers like to say they use fiction to tell the truth. I think there's a bit of BS in that. They use fiction to tell a more compelling story. We steal from real life what works and whatever else we need we make up. Deciding on the narrator isn't just a matter of perspective. It's the tone. And from the tone comes the meaning, if I can find any. I could write it as a kind of satire, but I don't want to be condescending. I want sympathy. The reader has to love the characters to want to understand them."

"You've got your work cut out for you. I'm glad I'm no writer. Anyway, I've really got to go," I said, sliding off the stool. 'I'm sorry that I'm not being of any help."

"Oh, everything's a help," Felix said, giving me a smile and then turning back to his soup. I left the restaurant. Outside I saw the rheumy-eyed pooch that he was taking care of, sprawled beside a sign post to which his leash was tied. When I reached down to pat its head, the dog barely raised its tail.

I'm Going to Get Up Now

WALKING BACK HOME TO MY mother's house, I asked myself whether I really wanted this new life dangling before me. There had been more times than I could remember when I'd thought about doing something other than music, when I was tired of yet another gig in a crummy drinking joint. When I felt sick of playing, sick of my bandmates, and most especially, sick of the lousy paycheques. But I'd burned my bridges long ago — there wasn't anything else I *could* do. And now this had come up. Maybe the courageous thing wasn't to continue as a musician, but to have the guts to give it up. I tried again to imagine the new life that hovered before me. My mother babysitting on Saturday night so that Marta and I could go to a restaurant or a movie. Larry Nussbaum asking me to a ball game. I would have to find a new identity for myself, something that I could live with. It would be that much harder for Marta. And was it courage or stupidity to enter again into the suffering that had been our marriage this last couple of years?

The telephone was ringing as I let myself in. I rushed to pick it up, thinking that it might be Marta, but it was only a duct-cleaning service. I decided to try to speak to the kids again and began punching in the number, but now the doorbell rang and I put the receiver down.

Outside the kitchen window I saw a car I didn't recognize, a red BMW convertible. I couldn't imagine who was going to appear next, so I just opened the door to a man already stepping inside, eyes enraged, fist cocked back. A moment later searing pain blossomed in my face and something hit my back and then my tailbone and I felt a warm gushing down my lips and tasted blood in my mouth.

Somehow I was on the floor. What was I doing on the floor?

"You son of a bitch. You low-life bastard."

"Aaah ... aah ..." My mouth wasn't working right.

"I'll give you more, you cocksucker, you fucking home wrecker. If you touch my wife again, if you even go near her, I'll kill you. I'll tear your goddamn lungs out."

I touched my fingers to my nose. The blood kept gushing. I tried to stop it with the tail of my shirt, but it wouldn't reach. I couldn't understand what the man was saying to me. When I looked at him, he was all blurry, a bad photograph. I squinted to see him better in case he was going to hit me again.

He wavered into focus. "Grant?" I said. "Grant Bluestein?"

He took a step forward and raised his foot as if to kick me. I whimpered and pulled myself back and he kicked the wall beside me.

"I could kill you."

"Don't hit me again. I need something for my nose. I'm going to get up now. Please don't. I'm just going to go into the kitchen."

My legs wouldn't work right. I managed only to get on one knee and had to gather my strength a moment before hauling myself up all the way. I tilted my head back and felt the blood course down my throat. I couldn't see and had to feel my way into the kitchen and grope for the dishtowel by the sink. I held it under the cold-water tap, balled it up, and pressed it to my nose. Turning back, I saw that Grant had followed me in.

"You think you can breeze into town, screw my wife, promise her the moon, and wreck my life? It's not going to happen."

A pain crawled across my cheekbone as if invisible hands were pulling my skull apart. I closed my eyes; if he was going to hit me again there was no reason to watch. "Grant," I said, breathless. "I'm not screwing your wife. I'm not having an affair with Marjorie. I'm not even interested in her."

"Yeah, right. Every guy is. There's no reason you'd tell me the truth."

"Shit, this hurts." I hoped the sinus cavity hadn't been crushed. The blood was stopping and I let up a little on the towel. It was because of Valentine, that idiot. It was because of him that my head was filled with pain. "If I was seeing her I hope I'd have the courage to admit it."

"You're not sleeping with her?"

"I already said no. Why are you even so sure?"

"I can tell. Nobody knows Marjy like I do. She's all agitated. The last two nights she's been sleeping in the guest room. She turns her head when I try to kiss her. She's being strange, more gentle and more distant at the same time, like she feels guilty. She's stopped asking me where I'm going when I leave the house. There's a million things. Plus I could smell it."

I opened one eye.

"Excuse me?"

"On her panties. I took them from the hamper. I smelled semen."

"Tell me that you didn't actually do that."

"If it's not you, then, ah shit, I don't know who it is."

"Now there's a great apology. How about you leave now."

But he didn't leave. He sank onto a kitchen chair and started to cry. Now I realized why men weren't supposed to cry; it was a disgusting sight. I said, "Maybe you should just ask her straight out. Anyway, from what I understand, you've been pretty much of a shit."

"How do you know?"

"Appears to be common knowledge."

"I'm sure I look like the bad guy. But it's not like that. I'm a human being like everybody else. I have my reasons. Marjorie gave them to me. Sometimes I feel like I'm going to explode. I've tried to be careful and not hurt her. I never promised anybody anything. I never told another woman I loved her. A person has to feel wanted, has to feel that he can give what somebody actually wants. And in every other way I've been good to Marjorie. She's never had to work a day in her life. I've put her on a gold pedestal."

"Maybe that was part of the problem."

"Is that my fault? She couldn't tell me? Fine, I accept the blame. I just don't want to lose her."

"There is the little matter of the other woman. I assume there is currently one."

I had no idea why I was giving Grant Bluestein advice. He said, "She's gone. I'll fire her tomorrow."

"Nice."

"I'll give her a big severance package and a recommendation. I'll help her get a new job. I've got to save my marriage. I've got to hang on to Marjorie. You know what I think has driven her into another man's arms?"

What an expression: *another man's arms*. But I said, "No, what?"

"That pathetic memorial ceremony. It's unhinged her. Brought up old emotions. I'm sure none of this would have happened if she hadn't got the idea into her head. She's just projecting some fantasy of that guy, Valentine Schwartz, onto whoever she's screwing. God, I've got to get her back. But what do I do?"

He held his head in his hands and rocked back and forth. "Maybe you can start by apologizing. And being open to some real change." I gingerly pulled away the towel. No blood came but my face felt like a melon.

"Yes, yes, I'll apologize. And I'll show her I really mean things to be different." He got up now and moved towards the door. I gladly followed, wanting to encourage him to leave. In the doorway he pulled out his wallet and grabbed a few hundred dollar bills. He put them on the little table. "You'll need a new shirt." And went out the door. I shouldn't have accepted the money; I should have thrown it after him. But I picked the bills up with my fingertips, trying not to smear blood on them.

53
Dumb Luck

I WOULD HAVE PREFERRED MY mother not to come home and find me lying on the sofa with an ice pack on my face. The side of my nose and one cheek had swelled, turning the colour of a blooming rose, my right eye was half shut, and one nostril was blocked, though it might have just been with blood. Also, I had a pounding head. My mother gasped, pulled herself together, and administered a couple of extra-strength Advils as I told her how I was trying to adjust her little kitchen television when it dropped on my own face. She insisted on taking me to the emergency department of North York General, the same hospital where I'd visited Valentine after his dive from the pool, and where they'd taken his supposedly lifeless body still in its dented shell of armour. It was a quiet day and we had to wait only two hours, and then another hour while the X-ray was developed and the doctor had a moment to look at it. The result of which was that I came home with a new ice pack. As I no longer qualified for Canadian health care, my mother had to write a cheque. For a moment there I thought she was going to take me to the hospital gift shop for being such a good boy.

At home again I took a nap, waking with a worse headache but able to breathe out of both nostrils again. After I assured my mother that I was well enough to go to Larry's, she drove us to his house. At the door we were greeted by the youngest, Nate, who was at first frightened by my face and then fascinated. I had to crouch down so that he could thoroughly examine the damage and then he took my mother's hand and led her upstairs to meet the guinea pigs.

I was glad to find Annie in the kitchen, who turned to greet me and screamed. When she gingerly touched my cheek with her fingertips I winced from the pain. I was sorry to have to repeat the ridiculous television story, but all I could do was stick with it and endure Larry's head-shaking amazement. "Let me get this straight. You pulled it off the shelf towards you and then you *let go*?"

Before dinner, Larry passed out yarmulkes and, after a squabble about whose turn it was to light the Shabbat candles, let Mark put the match to the wicks while he hovered. Then came the prayers over the wine and the bread. That was the last moment of quiet. But the chaos of dinner with kids only made me wish that Maggie and Birdy were here with us. After dinner, the seven of us played Monopoly, Nate teaming up with Annie and the rest of us building our own empires. Larry bragged that his work in real estate gave him an advantage, but the truly ruthless, win-at-all-cost player was his oldest son, Daniel. With no killer instinct of my own, I went bankrupt first, to be followed by my mother, who had taken so long deciding whether or not to buy a property or put up a hotel ("I won't be rushed") that after she was out, the game moved along much faster.

Nate fell asleep on the sofa and Larry, yawning, carried him upstairs. I asked Annie if she wanted to come over and talk for a while, and she agreed, following us in her car. My mother said she was tired and went to her room, leaving the two of us downstairs. I looked in the cupboard and found a dusty bottle of Drambuie — it might well have been there in my dad's time — and poured us drinks. We sat on the living-room sofa.

"You really look terrible," Annie said, touching her glass to mine. "It must hurt."

"I'm being very brave about it."

"So tell me the truth."

"What do you mean?"

"You didn't drop any TV on yourself. I've been working in high school for years. I know the result of a right hook when I see one."

"Ah. I can't pull anything over on you."

"So what happened?"

"I don't want to lie so I'll be honest and say I can't tell you. Except that the punch wasn't really intended for me. I was mistaken for somebody else."

"You lead a very exciting life."

"Not by choice. But I am glad to see you, Annie."

"It makes me happy too." She took my hand, running her fingers over my palm. It didn't take more than that. I leaned over and kissed her. It hurt to kiss.

"Maybe," she said, "you were supposed to come back and find me."

"Do you believe that?"

She shrugged. "Nah. Random chance, dumb luck. That's what I really believe in. But it doesn't always feel that way. And here you are."

She kissed me, slipping her hand under my shirt. "I want a second chance at you," she whispered.

I put my hand on hers, held it still. Took a breath. "I'm trying to get Marta — my wife — to come here. I'm trying to make it work. At least to see if it can work."

"Oh," she said and gave one of those smiles. "Okay. You can be honourable." She squeezed my hand and withdrew hers.

"Am I being honourable? I don't know."

She looked at me. "Well, I'm glad you're back, Huddie Rosen. Shit, lovers are a dime a dozen. It's an old friend that's rare."

"I'm your man." I sat back in the sofa and sighed. I wished that I felt better about what I'd just done. Annie finished her Drambuie and stood up. "Tomorrow's the big day. I'd better get my beauty sleep. Don't move, I can see myself out. Goodnight, Huddie."

"Goodnight, Annie."

54
The PowerSeller

MY MOTHER WOKE ME. NOT gently, the way she had when I was a kid, stroking my forehead and whispering into my ear, but by banging on my door, bursting into the room, and shaking me by the shoulders.

Confused, the first thing I thought was: where are my children? The second: today was the memorial ceremony for Valentine.

"I've done it, Howie! I've done it! You have to come and see!"

I had to follow her groggily, still in my T-shirt and boxers, down to the basement where the cement floor was, even in May, like ice on the bottom of my feet. What my mother had done was sell the very last of my father's old blues records, a Memphis Minnie and Kansas Joe duet of "She Wouldn't Give Me None." And some time in the night she had become an eBay PowerSeller, which meant that her selling name would be accompanied by a special symbol. I didn't see why this would matter since she had already sold off my father's entire collection, but she said that now that she had the eBay bug there was no reason she should stop. There were all kinds of things stuffing the closets that she could sell, and after that she could start hunting the garage sales or maybe buying cheap goods in lots and breaking them up the way others did.

"We've got your down payment, or most of it anyway," she said. "Oh look, SuperGal103 is in the chat room. I've just got to tell her I'm a PowerSeller."

I left my mother at the computer and dressed for this day of the dead. While I was eating a bowl of granola at the counter, I heard a knock on the window. Oh great, did Grant want to take a swing at my other eye? But it wasn't Grant, it was Felix Roth, holding the leash of his rented dog while peering in.

I wasn't terribly pleased to see him but went out the side door, taking my bowl of granola with me. "What's up, Felix?" I said.

"Jesus, what happened to your face?"

"Hazards of being a musician. Do you want to come in?"

"It's beautiful outside, why don't you bring your bowl? That looks like it hurts."

The two of us walked around to the back of the house and Felix let go of the leash so the dog could sniff around. We pulled up chairs near the pool.

"I'm suddenly remembering all those high-school pool parties," Felix said. "What a crazy way to grow up."

"I never actually got invited to one."

"Better for you, maybe. Lovely day for a memorial, don't you think? It's funny but somehow I feel unnerved by it. Maybe it's just being dragged back to that time of life. I think I'll be glad when it's over."

"I suspect more than a few people feel the same way."

"Mind you, I'm hoping it'll be a good scene. I need the material."

"If you're looking for material, here's my advice. When they do the unveiling, don't look at the statue. Save that for later. Keep your eyes on the audience instead. That ought to give you something."

Felix looked sideways at me. "You've got some inside knowledge. Will do. So there's a rumour going around that you're moving back to Toronto."

"Maybe."

"I think it would be a good place to raise kids. Not in the suburbs maybe, but in the city. Easier than New York. Hey, do you want to hear my Valentine story?"

"I wonder if everyone has one. Sure, why not."

"My locker was three down from his."

"I remember."

"One day, maybe in February, he turned to me as I was getting my dreaded gym bag. I mean he just stared at me. Finally he said, 'Felix.' I said, 'Yeah?' He said, 'Did you change lockers?' I said no, I'd had the locker since September. He said, 'That's funny, I never even noticed.' Then he banged his locker shut and left."

"I hate to tell you, but that's a lesser Valentine Schwartz story."

"You don't get it. I was stunned. To Valentine I was invisible. I mean, how insignificant can you get?"

"But it was Valentine. You can't — couldn't — judge his remarks the way you judge other people's."

"Maybe so, but I brooded on it for days. I would look at myself in the mirror to see if there was an actual image reflecting back. I was thinking about being a writer even then, but somehow Valentine tipped it for me. It seemed like a good job for an invisible man. Or maybe it would be a way to make myself visible, to paint myself with words. I don't know if I should thank him or curse him for it, but there it is."

I looked at him and then tipped the last of the milk from the bowl into my mouth. "You know what you sound like to me? Like you're working yourself into your book. Figuring how you fit in."

Felix laughed. "Hey, did you see this?" He pulled a few printed pages out of his back pocket. "The latest edition of *Arthur's Rag*. I picked it up at the school office first thing this morning. There's a poem for Valentine in it, quite a piece of work."

"Well, I guess if I'm going to play at this ceremony I better warm up."

"I get the hint," Felix said. He picked up the dog's leash and we walked together to his Taurus parked in the drive. "Go on, Regret, get in," he said, helping the dog into the back seat by lifting its rump. He got in and rolled down the window.

"Hey," I said, "did they print Valentine's essay on Canadian identity?"

"It's here on the first page. I forgot what a good job I did. Want to read it?"

"I know it off by heart. What do you mean by good job? Oh no, you didn't. Did you?"

Felix shrugged. "He paid me twenty bucks. It was the first time I ever wrote for money." He slowly backed up the car, offering me a mock salute as he pulled into the road.

55
Get in the Car

BACK IN THE HOUSE, I went up to my room, wiped the mandolin with a soft cloth kept in the little compartment in the case, tuned up, sat on my old desk chair, and played some arpeggios. Looking up, I caught a piece of my reflection in the small mirror on the desk. For a moment I had the impression that my teenage self was looking back at me, seeing the adult he was to become.

When my hands felt loose I packed up and left my room. My mother was in her own room with the door open, buttoning her blouse. A glimpse of practical white bra, wrinkled skin. She caught sight of me and turned around.

"I'm not used to having to close my door. What do you think of this blouse?"

"It's fine, Mom. I wouldn't be too worried about it."

"Proper clothes show respect. Are you really going in those jeans?"

"I don't have anything else."

"I want to get a good seat. Weddings, funerals, I like to sit up close. Do you want a drive over?"

"You know, I think I'll walk. I could use a stretch."

"All right, I'll save you a seat."

I came downstairs and saw my mother to the door. She kissed my cheek. "My musician," she said. I heard the automatic garage door go up and watched her drive away. Then I went to the phone and called the apartment in Prague.

The line rang and rang. Maybe Marta had taken the girls and disappeared. I knew it couldn't be true but a wave of panic washed through me. I was about to hang up when somebody picked up the phone and I heard Marta's voice.

"It's me," I said. "I've been trying to get you."

"Huddie, this isn't a good time."

"But I've got to know something, Marta. What you're thinking at least. I can't be on my own here."

Silence. A sigh. "Fine. I'll tell you. It's not going to work, Huddie."

"What do you mean?"

"I'm sorry. I don't know what else to say."

"But what about starting over here, in Toronto?"

"I can't," she said softly. "I live here, Huddie. In this place. My mother is here and has nobody else."

"But the kids would have so much."

"So much what, Huddie? Material things? That isn't any more important to you than to me. Yes, it might be easier, but is that always better? If you want to stay in Canada I don't know what to say. We will have to work something out. Visits. Holidays."

"What are you talking about? Holidays? They're my kids. Jesus, Marta, this isn't fair. You can't just dictate the way things are going to be."

"I'm not trying to. But the kids live here, that's just the truth. We will work things out. We will talk. All I know is that the marriage, it has to be over. I think you know it too. I'm sorry. More sorry than I can tell you."

"You're breaking my heart, Marta."

"I have to go. Goodbye, Huddie."

I hung up the telephone and then went to the sink and opened the tap over a glass. I drank the water, picked up the mandolin case, went out the door, locked it. Outside, the sun was directly overhead. I hadn't noticed before how large the trees had grown. Their leaves wavered in the slight breeze. I started walking, down the drive, onto the sidewalk. I couldn't feel the pavement under my feet, the handle of the case in my hand. Past a fake Tudor, then Spanish, then English cottage, then Tudor again. Maybe I would just keep walking, down one crescent and another, walking until the kids straggled home from school, and the fathers pulled their cars in the drive, and the lights went on, and shapes appeared behind the curtains showing families at the dinner table, and the televisions glowed blue, and the lights went out for sleep.

I realized that a car had pulled up and was inching along beside me. I ignored it. I didn't care who it was. I didn't care if it was Bill Monroe himself.

The window powered down.

"Get in the car, Huddie."

I kept walking.

"Get in."

"Leave me alone, Valentine."

"If you don't get into this car, I'm going to hit the gas and drive it straight into the front window of the next house. I'm going to kill myself and anyone in my way."

I stopped. The car stopped. I turned and looked at Val. "I want to be left alone, Valentine."

"Please, Huddie. I need you."

He popped the door open and I got in, holding the mandolin case between my knees. In the back seat of the Jaguar, Valentine had thrown his suitcase. Also his leather toiletries kit, which had spilled its contents. He hadn't noticed my swollen face. "I don't have much patience, Val. What is it? Shouldn't you be getting ready for your dream come true?"

"It's off. Everything's off."

"I don't know what you mean."

"Marjorie changed her mind."

I looked at him. Dark skin sagged beneath his eyes. The rest of his face was almost jaundiced. "I don't see how that can be," I said. "She told me herself that she loved you."

"That's what she said. But last night she told me that she changed her mind. Somehow Grant found out that something was going on. He talked to somebody, he didn't say who, but he said that it straightened him out. Marjorie told me that Grant promised never to have another affair. He even said he'd go to a marriage counsellor, like that's some miracle cure. He booked a holiday for next week without even asking her — a trip to Bermuda for all of them. He promised her a new start."

"And she believes it?"

"I guess so. Maybe she wants to. Maybe it's just easier after all these years. Maybe she's scared. But she told me that it's over. She said she can't ever see or talk to me again. She was bawling her eyes out, but she said it."

"That's a tough break, Val."

"I don't know what happened. It was all set. My dream is now my nightmare. My worst nightmare. And you know what else? She said that since I'm going back to California anyway and really nobody knew I was alive, would I mind if the memorial went ahead? She doesn't want anyone else to know she slept with me. She doesn't want Grant to know that I was the one. She wants everyone to think I'm dead."

"And what did you say?"

"What could I say? I said sure. Go ahead, bury me. I was too stunned. Marjorie used me to fix her marriage. What an idiot I am."

"That wasn't her intention."

"I'm the one who showed her that life could be better. And that asshole Bluestein gets the benefit. All the excitement is probably goosing their sex life. He's probably giving it to her right now."

"That isn't necessary. You tried your best."

"What the fuck is that supposed to mean?"

"You tried and you failed, Val. Now you get on with things."

He stared at me malevolently. "That's all you can say? That's all you can suggest? Not how I can get her back? How I can turn this around? I thought you were my friend. I thought you were on my side, looking out for me."

"You know what, Val? I have my own life. And to be honest, I've had enough of yours. Go back to California. Build yourself another pyramid for rich old people. Marry another Marjorie look-alike. Do whatever you want."

His jaw shifted around, as if he were chewing a piece of leather. He stared at the steering wheel, which he still clenched with his large hands. "Get out of my car."

"Get some perspective, Valentine. You're just one person in what, six billion? And so am I. And we're not starving, we're not in a war zone, we've got all our limbs. We're so damn privileged we think our own little dramas are important."

"I said, get out of my car."

So I did. And watched him hit the gas and squeal his tires as he took off, disappearing around the next corner. And felt no remorse for what I'd said. Felt, in fact, that I'd said the first right thing in days.

56
Unveiling

I MADE MY WAY TO the main road and walked until I reached the school. The Canadian flag, flapping in the breeze, had been set at half-mast. A dozen rows of folding chairs had been set out on the grass by the statue, which was still covered by the grey tarps. The statue's shape underneath looked just as large in the open air, a good couple of feet higher than life-size. A folding table laden with food covered in plastic wrap was being watched over by a sour-looking waitress in a black uniform. A wooden platform had been set up, on which stood a microphone, whose wire trailed to an amplifier and speaker at the side, and with an electrical cord running along the grass and through the open window of the nearest classroom.

People were already seated: Larry Nussbaum, who waved at me; Anita Gornkoff, wearing a blue suit and a hat as if she were going to synagogue for the high holidays. People I didn't recognize. My mother sat in the first row, her purse on the next seat. As I was coming up to her I heard a car and turned to see Felix Roth parking his Taurus in front of the school.

I came over to my mother and took the seat beside her,

slipping the mandolin case underneath. She looked at me. "What's happened? Something's wrong. Is it the girls?"

"I can't talk about it right now." I took my mother's hand. "I should have brought the kids here. To see you. I'm sorry, for what it's worth."

Her lip started to tremble. But she said, "I used to be very fond of Valentine. Do you remember how he used to call me Mrs. R? 'Do you have any of that cold chicken in the fridge, Mrs. R?' 'I do love your apple cake, Mrs. R.' The poor boy, I don't think his mother ever cooked."

Annie came out through the front doors of the school. She had made a concession to the event, putting on a long skirt. She smiled at us all before the custodian asked her to check the sound system. Meanwhile the seats were filling up. Even though they hadn't been explicitly invited, there was a sprinkling of students, including the poet Matthew, the student-council president Krista, and the representative Stuart, who was eating from a bag of popcorn as if he were about to see a double feature. I noticed someone with a heavy gait crossing the grass and recognized Madeline Day, the curator from the museum. I couldn't imagine what she hoped to get out of coming. As she got closer I could see a line of perspiration on her forehead.

Next came Marjorie, walking from the school parking lot. Her husband, Grant, held her arm. Grace wasn't with them, which meant she wouldn't be playing the song with me, but I couldn't blame her for not showing up. Seeing Grant made me touch my face with my fingers.

Annie tapped on the microphone. "Ladies and gentlemen, students of Arthur Meighen. Before I start, would you kids smoking in the pit please scram? That's right, you. Friends, we are here to celebrate the life of Valentine Schwartz, a former student of this school, a once promising young man whose life was cut short. A dear friend to many of us."

Back in high school, Annie had kidded Valentine mercilessly, but half the time he didn't understand her digs. Now as she spoke I could hear a genuine affection in her words, and if I hadn't known that Val was at this moment driving recklessly on the highway, making his way back to another fortune in California, I might have shed a tear along with several people in the audience, including my mother. Annie concluded by reading aloud Val's essay, "My Canadian Identity." I'd thought that Marjorie was supposed to read it, but apparently there had been a change in plans. I could not resist turning to see Felix Roth, alert with interest as he listened to his own words.

Annie stepped down and Krista came up. She looked completely at ease in front of the mic; she even took it off the stand and held it, like a stand-up comic. "I guess," she said, "it's ironic that we are here on such a beautiful day. A day that reminds us of anything but death. Of course I never knew Valentine Schwartz. But I'm seventeen years old, the same age he was when he died. I can't imagine my life ending now, when it feels as if it's just beginning. I go to the same school, I walk the same halls, I sit in the same classrooms. My locker is only twenty-three lockers away from where his used to be. And the last couple of weeks it has felt to me like a ghost is walking the halls of Arthur Meighen. There's a saying that I found, I think it's from some ancient Greek. *Whom the gods love die young.* Valentine, you died young, but when I'm in school it feels as if you are watching over me. Like you are a guardian angel, making sure everything is all right. I feel your spirit, Valentine, and I'm glad you're here with me."

She had closed her eyes, bringing the mic so close to her mouth that she might have been kissing it. Now she put it back on the stand and stepped down, smiling.

Next to come up was a man with a bulbous forehead and a full moustache. He'd never been mentioned at the committee meetings and turned out to be the shop teacher. He wanted to make it clear that the statue about to be unveiled was the accomplishment of his students and that he'd had no hand in its design or execution. He said it three times, and then he stepped down again.

Nobody rose immediately to take his place and I realized that Marjorie was not going to speak. That was one wise decision anyway, I thought, watching Annie take the stand again.

"It's now time," she said into the microphone, "to unveil the statue. This permanent memorial to Valentine Schwartz will, I'm sure, be an enduring inspiration for the students of Arthur Meighen. I would like to ask Ellen and Andy Chung, members of the shop class, to come forward."

Two identical kids with bangs and round glasses rose from their seats and took up the two ropes attached to the tarpaulin. Annie came down and took the empty seat on the other side of my mother. "Go on," she whispered across to me. "Play nice." I took the mandolin out of its case, put the strap around my head, and pulled the pick out from under the strings.

"Stand up," my mother said. "Let everyone see you."

"Okay, okay." I stood up and began to play in an old-timey tremolo. Although I played it as an instrumental, I could hear the words in my head.

> O bury me beneath the willow,
> Under the weeping willow tree.

> *When she hears that I am sleeping*
> *Then perhaps she'll think of me.*

The Chung twins pulled at the ropes. I took another quick glance at Felix, and sure enough, he was watching the audience instead of the statue. Then I turned back to watch as the two tarps, held together by Velcro, pulled away from each other and fell to the grass. There was absolute silence and then someone — it may have been Madeline Day — laughed sharply. With that protruding lance, the thing could have been used as a giant sundial. People started to whisper and the students to giggle, so I played louder.

> *She told me that she dearly loved me.*
> *How could I believe it untrue?*
> *Until an angel softly whispered*
> *She will prove to you untrue.*

> *Place on my grave a snow white lily*
> *To prove my love for her was true.*
> *To show the world I died of grieving*
> *For her love I could not win.*

I was just doing a final flourish when someone — it was Krista — screamed. She was pointing upwards and I followed the line of her finger to the roof.

Where I saw Valentine.

I couldn't actually tell it was Valentine since he was wearing the suit of armour and the visor was over his face, but I knew it was him. He was standing bowlegged at the corner of the roof, wobbling a little and gesturing with one metal-clad hand as if trying to tell us something. The armour shone gloriously in the sunshine, the details not visible from this distance but the gilt lines reflecting brilliantly along the shoulder plates, the breastplate, the knee guards.

The shouting and commotion grew. The audience rose from their seats, including Annie, her hand shielding her eyes so she could see better. "This isn't funny," she said. "Whoever's playing this prank is going to be in deep shit." She cupped her hands around her mouth and shouted, "All right, you. Get down from there *this instant*. And get into my office."

"It's Valentine," I said.

"What?"

"He's not dead."

"*What?*"

But another voice was shouting even louder. "Give me back my armour!" It was Madeline Day, standing up and shaking her fist. Right after that Marjorie screamed, as if in delayed reaction. She fainted and fell backwards. Grant barely had time to catch her.

Valentine took a step closer to the roof's edge, making the people on the ground gasp. My own heart leapt to my mouth. "Move back, Val!" I shouted. He opened both his arms and clanked forward, wailing something that I couldn't understand; the visor distorted his words. He took a half-step forward, wavered a moment, and then lunged or tripped, his arms shooting outwards. He toppled headfirst, the edge of the helmet dinging on the edge of the roof as he went over. He hit the ground with a metallic crunch, a little bloom of dust rising up.

Val was alive when we rushed to him on the ground. He lay on his back, not his front like the first time, and we could hear him moaning behind the visor. Larry Nussbaum was already on his cellphone trying to explain to the 911 operator why we needed an ambulance. Annie, who had taken a lifesaving course, instructed us not to move him. But she did push the visor up so that Valentine would be able to breathe more easily. His eyes were open and blinking rapidly, but he struggled with each breath and there was blood in his mouth and nose.

"Back away, everyone," Annie said. "Let him have some air." But as soon as we did Marjorie pushed past us and threw herself onto Valentine. She kissed his face even as she pulled at his armour, trying to get it off. I moved in to restrain her and received a slap to the side of my face, flaring the pain from Grant's punch. Grant himself just watched as Annie and I pulled her off and held her while she shrieked at us and then dissolved into violent shaking and tears.

The ambulance arrived, the siren dying as it pulled up behind Felix Roth's car. The paramedics brought out a stretcher and a red metal box, like a large fishing tackle kit. When they reached us they stood for several seconds, deciding what to do.

"Maybe you need to cut him out with the jaws of life," the student named Stuart said. But since Val was breathing they decided to leave the armour on and enlisted a couple of the larger boys to help lift him onto the stretcher. Larry worried that the stretcher would break but one of the paramedics assured us that it was constructed to carry obese men and would hold.

We followed them to the ambulance, the paramedics and the boys panting with the effort. They slid Valentine into the back. When one of the paramedics asked if anyone would ride with him, Marjorie broke from us and climbed inside. Grant took a step towards her but then just let her go and stood with the rest of us watching as the doors swung shut and the ambulance pulled away.

57
I've Got

... THOSE BLUE RIDGE MOUNTAIN BLUES, the Mississippi blues, the Tennessee blues, I bid farewell to old Kentucky, the places I have loved, the road looks rough and rocky, I don't know why I left so free, I'm lost and I'll never find the way, I got two dollar shoes they hurt my feet, it's a highway of sorrow, blue days black nights, I have no friends to help me now, they knew not my name and I knew not their faces.

58
Vending Machine

VALENTINE DIDN'T DIE THIS TIME either. He suffered a concussion, three broken ribs, a broken leg, a compound fracture in his arm, bruised vertebrae, and assorted other minor injuries. I heard the report from Annie on the phone, who followed the ambulance to the hospital and stayed the night. Only after she had recounted the details did she give me a tongue-lashing for not having told her about Valentine in the first place.

I stayed away from the hospital for three days but finally I went. By the time I got myself to go, visiting hours were almost over. Just as well, since I didn't want to run into anyone I knew. I went past the nurse's station and found the room at the end of the corridor. The door was open and I could see the small bathroom on the right, and ahead the curtain partly pulled around the hospital bed, with the light from the window casting a silhouette of a raised leg onto it. Gently I knocked on the door frame.

"Come in," came the drowsy voice.

I stepped towards him. Valentine's eyes shifted to me but his expression didn't change. "Hey, Huddie," he said.

"Hi, Val. How are you feeling?"

"Not so bad. It's the painkillers."

"And I hear you'll live."

"Yeah. They had to put a pin in my leg. The alarm's going to go off every time I walk into a clothing store. The worst is the cracked ribs. It hurts when I breathe."

"So don't breathe."

"Funny. I'm trying to get out of here tomorrow. Flying back to California. I've got this uncle in New Jersey, my only living relative. He's coming in today and will help me get back. I've got a special seat on the plane, a private nurse to get me to the airport and another when I land. It's costing me a fortune."

"What do you mean, trying? The hospital might not let you go?"

"Not the hospital. The cops."

"Oh, right."

"They've been here four times. First, I had to convince them and the doctors that I wasn't going to be a danger to anyone, including myself. They got this shrink in yesterday to talk to me. Then there's the little matter of the armour. Stolen property. That Madeline Day, she's a piece of work. Insisting that they press charges. I'm going to have to post bail and promise to come back for sentencing after my convalescence, as my lawyer puts it. Oh yeah, I've got the lawyer to pay too. But don't worry, I kept your name out of it this time. It's the least I could do."

"They wouldn't actually make you do jail time, would they?"

"Probably not, but it isn't a sure thing."

I shook my head and took the chair by the bed. I noticed one vase of roses on the window sill but I didn't ask who they were from. "You sound all right, Val. Considering everything that's gone on. But what were you thinking? I mean, the first time you were an adolescent, that's a crazy time. But now?"

"The heart doesn't grow old."

"What was your intention? Did you want to fall?"

"It's over, Huddie. I don't want to think about it anymore."

"All right."

We sat silently for a long stretch. I remembered coming all those years ago and finding Val watching cartoons on the television. Now he closed his eyes for a while; he might have been sleeping. Another stretch went by before he opened them.

"Marjorie's gone," he said. "She left this morning for that holiday with Grant and the kids. For a moment there, in the ambulance, I thought I had her back. Hey, Huddie, how about you come out to California some time? You can stay as long as you like, I've got lots of space. We'll tour some vineyards, drive to San Francisco. What do you say?"

"It sounds good, Val, but I don't know. Let's see, all right?"

"Sure. You've got other things to do with your time."

From the doorway came the sound of noisy throat clearing. A small man came into the room — hunchbacked, an elf-like face, wearing a yarmulke. Val said, "Uncle Shmuel. You made it."

"I don't like flying," the man said. "It isn't natural. Being in a car, that's natural. A train, okay. Who's this?"

"An old friend. Huddie Rosen."

"Your old friends you need like a hole in the head. You made sure my hotel room is non-smoking, didn't you?"

"Yes, I did. Where's your luggage."

"I left it with the nurses, not that they were very co-operative. In my day, a nurse used to look like something. Now? Never mind. I'm going to get a cup of tea. I like hospital cafeterias. You want something?"

"Nothing, thanks."

The man went out again. He had an energetic hobble. Valentine and I seemed to have run out of things to say. He talked about some business project in California, but I didn't listen very closely. Finally I got up and shook his left hand. "So tell me," I said, "where did you hide the armour all these years?"

"You know what I think?" he said. "You should start your own record company. Make your own CDs. It's the only way you'll really get somewhere. I could back you."

In the hall I found Valentine's uncle returning with his Styrofoam cup of tea. He squinted up at me. "His father always needed to be the big shot," Uncle Shmuel said. "Nobody could be bigger than him. To me, better you shouldn't be noticed. Who has it better, the tiger or the fly that buzzes around his tail? They only had orange pekoe. I prefer Earl Grey."

I nodded and went past him, past the nurses who weren't good-looking enough these days, past the gift shop, and out the doors into the sunshine.

59
Tin Cans

I TOOK A LONG WALK through the old neighbourhood. Along Sunshine Crescent and Verdant Way, past the modest houses like our own and then across the main street to the palaces on the other side. The streets were as quiet as they had been in my day, but the people I did pass were not quite the same. I saw Asian and East Indian and even some black families loading into their vans or playing ball hockey on driveways. It had always seemed to me like a lousy place to grow up, the neighbours rarely seen, no shopping street to walk to but only malls and plazas, but maybe these new kids got around more, and had more experience to draw on, and were just smarter and more worldly than we had been.

I walked back to my mother's house. There was the silver Taurus in the drive, and as I got closer I saw Felix Roth leaning in the doorway. He was reading a book and didn't notice me until I was close enough to see a grainy picture of New York on the cover.

"Hey, Felix," I said. "Reading the competition?"

"In a way. A writer I once knew. He's dead now. That's the thing, I'm not just competing with my peers. I've got the whole of literature breathing down my neck. On the other hand, I do have the advantage of being alive. That's got to be worth something. So I hear you're going back to Prague."

"Tomorrow. And what about you?"

"My flight to New York is tonight. It's been pretty interesting coming back, but I can't wait to get home and start writing again."

"You sound excited."

"I am. It's amazing how that just keeps being there. Anyway, I did want to say goodbye."

"I appreciate it. I was just over at Sunnybrook, visiting Valentine. Have you been?"

An oddly embarrassed look came over him. "I tried. Got as far as the parking lot. But then I didn't go in. This is going to sound awful, but I know that my book needs a different ending. Valentine's fall — he can't survive a second time. That would be ludicrous and I need tragedy."

"So you're going to kill him off?"

"I just couldn't visit him. I need him to be dead in my imagination too."

"It's a cruel trade you've got there."

"Sometimes," he nodded. "Listen, if you're ever in New York, look me up. I'll take you for dinner."

"Likewise if you're in Prague."

"I'd like to see Prague, even if that other Roth has already written about it."

Felix held out his hand and we shook. "Oh, wait, I've got something for you. He went into his car and came out with a copy of *Rattsmann*. "A bit of a narcissistic gift, I know, but I thought you might like to read it."

"I would, thanks."

He got in the car and drove away. I turned around and went into the house, where I found my mother making *verenikas* by hand, stuffing the mixture of cheese and potato into the little dumplings, her palms white with flour. "Mom, I can't believe you're going to the trouble."

"It isn't any trouble. I'm supposed to tell you that your glasses are ready at the shop. Uncle Norman wants you to come in and have them adjusted. I'll drive you. I've got shopping to do anyway. How is Valentine?"

"Not bad, considering. A relative came in to help. He's going back to California."

"You missed quite a scene this morning."

"What scene?"

"I was on my walk at six this morning. A bulldozer knocked down the statue in front of the school. Mashed it up under the treads like a bunch of tin cans and then scooped up the remains and dropped them in a dump truck. You'd hardly know it was there."

"That was quick."

"Better that way. Okay, I'll fry these up later. I know you like them with the edges crisp."

She wiped her hands on her apron and picked up her keys. We didn't talk much in the car. I tried to tell her that we weren't going to move to Toronto, that Marta and I weren't getting back together, but I couldn't get the words out. She told me that Annie Lynch had phoned a couple of times, worried that she would miss me before I left, and that I ought to phone that "nice girl" back, but I knew that I wouldn't be able to.

The car pulled up in the strip plaza and my mother let me off, promising to be back in twenty minutes. I went up the stairs where Mrs. Nathanson put down her copy of *Entertainment*

Weekly to usher me into the examination room, closing the door after me.

The room was dark and for a moment I couldn't see anything. "Uncle Norman?" I said aloud. There was a stirring and I saw my uncle sit up in the examination chair, which had been tilted back all the way. He rubbed his face and groped for the light switch.

"Howie, it's about time you got here. I was just checking the equipment. Here, change places, I warmed up the seat for you. I've got your glasses right here. We need to make sure they sit right on your schnozzola."

I did as I was told and Norman slipped the glasses onto my face, his hands trembling a little. He took them off again, dipped one temple in what looked like sand, bent the temple, and put them on me again.

"One more little tweak and we'll have it. Good. How do they feel?"

"Just right, I'd say."

"Here, try this magazine. See if it's easier to read."

I took the magazine and the words became immediately clear without my having to move it closer or farther. "It's a miracle, Uncle Norman."

"I'll take a twenty percent tip. Which is twenty percent of nothing. Wear them in good health."

"Listen, Norman." I got out of the chair. My uncle looked at me with his mouth half open. "I want to thank you for your offer of the business. It was very generous, but it's not going to work out."

"You're sure?"

"I'm afraid so."

"Your mother will be disappointed."

"I know."

"My kids, on the other hand, will be thrilled. Greenbaum wants to buy the business from me. It's hard to give up work, you know. Forty-one years I've been here. This hole in the wall has been my little kingdom. And now I give it up to wander in the wilderness. Meaning Florida. Here's the case, and a spray for cleaning them, and a cloth. Don't use tissues or toilet paper. You might as well use sandpaper. Understand?"

He opened the door to the waiting room and put a hand on my shoulder. "At least come back once in a while. Don't be such a bad son."

"I'll try not to be."

"Mrs. Nathanson, we have another satisfied customer. At this rate we'll go bankrupt. Show him the door before he asks for an extra pair."

Tartufo

I ASKED MY MOTHER IF I could take her out for dinner so that she wouldn't have to cook. On the way we stopped at Larry Nussbaum's house so that I could say goodbye and give the kids yo-yos that I'd picked up at the plaza. They had little lights in them that flashed as the yo-yos went up and down. Larry gave me a bear hug, and as he pulled away he had tears in his eyes.

My mother didn't want to drive downtown, so the number of options for dinner was limited. We settled for an old-fashioned Italian place on Yonge Street that my father had liked. Iceberg lettuce salads, lasagna, glasses of cheap Chianti. It was quiet and candle-lit and we talked of small things, trips to the beach when I was small, visits to my father's relatives in Chicago. To my mild surprise, my mother finished her first small glass of wine and ordered another.

I said, "I've been kind of hard on you. About Dad. And his work."

"So we're going to have that kind of conversation, are we? All right. I don't think we had an unhappy marriage. He didn't love his work, but you know what, Howie? Most people don't. You're one of the lucky ones. He was glad to make a steady living and to be good at what he was paid to do. And he got a lot of pleasure out of his collection. It gave him something to daydream about, finding this record or that. He was still young when he died. We never got a chance to see what the second half of life was going to be like for us, the time after you were grown and on your own. We talked about doing a lot of things."

"What sort of things?"

"Travel mostly. Your father wanted to get one of those camper vans and drive down through the southern United States, Tennessee, Mississippi, Louisiana, to Memphis and New Orleans, places where the musicians came from. He used to joke that he was going to take me to joints where we'd be the only white people and have to drink homemade liquor. And I said all right, I wasn't afraid, as long as he came along with me to Spain."

"Spain? I didn't know you wanted to go to Spain."

"You didn't know I have a pool."

"Okay, fine. Why Spain particularly?"

"I don't know, I guess it seems a little more out of the way than London or Paris. About as adventurous as I can be. Madrid, Barcelona. I want to see the architecture by Gaudi. And feel that warm sun."

I wanted to say that I would go with her if she wanted me to, and maybe take the girls too. But I didn't want to make any promises that I wasn't sure I would keep, since I'd disappointed her enough. Be a good son, I told myself. Take your mother to Spain.

"Let's order dessert," she said. "I remember they have tartufo."

"I like tartufo," I said. "Mom, this idea of us moving back. It's not going to work. Marta and I aren't getting back together and the kids are staying over there, which means I have to be there too."

"I figured as much," she said. "I'm sorry for all of you. I don't understand all this separation and divorce. I worry that it's too easy to solve problems by giving up, but maybe it's better than staying together, I just don't know. But if that's the way it's going, then I just want all of you to be all right. I know you're sad, Howie. I saw it the moment you walked into the kitchen. But at some point you have to think of this as the beginning of a new stage of your life. There's happiness out there for you. You're a lovely man, and I know there is."

"I don't know if I deserve that, but thank you for saying it."

The waiter brought the tartufo. We picked up our spoons and began to eat. It was sweet, rich, and delicious, and I let it melt on my tongue so as to taste all of it.

61
Cups and Straws

BEFORE LEAVING THE HOUSE FOR the airport, I cleaned out my old room. Into a green garbage bag went my essays — on Darwin, on John Diefenbaker, on *The Heart is a Lonely Hunter*. Also clippings from the student newspaper, film-club notices, drawings of teachers. I almost kept a note from Annie that she must have stuffed into my locker or slipped to me in the hall, but I put that in too.

My small suitcase and a larger one that my mother had given me for clothes and toys for the girls were already packed. There wasn't anything left to do, so I went to the backyard and stood looking at the swimming pool for a while. A screen door slamming, a roofer hammering nails. My mother came out to say it was time and I loaded the car, putting the mandolin case in the back seat. I offered to drive, but my mother said she preferred to. On the highway she didn't like to talk, for it took all her concentration to overcome her nerves with the trucks going by. We drove up the ramp to the terminal and pulled over to the curb. I had already insisted that she not go to the trouble of parking. I pulled out the suitcases and then we stood at the curb and I kissed my mother on each cheek.

"The money's there whenever you want it."

"Okay, Mom. Thanks."

"I really, really hate this moment." She hugged me and got in the car crying and drove away. I couldn't move for a moment, but then a porter came up and I had to wave him off. I pulled the two suitcases with the mandolin under my arm and made my way to the check-in counter. Something was wrong with a wheel on my old suitcase and I had to half-drag the thing.

This time I wouldn't let them take the mandolin, but kept it with me, along with the book that Felix had given me. People in the waiting area were speaking German and Czech more than English. We boarded on time and had a smooth takeoff. Then came the drinks cart, the duty-free booklet. I watched the beginning of a bad Czech movie with English subtitles, the equivalent of an American teen movie, and remembered the early days when Marta had taken me to see *The Fireman's Ball* and *Closely Watched Trains*. We had sat in the dark cinema in our winter coats — a lot of places were still inadequately heated back then — and Marta had leaned close to whisper to me what was going on. But now I stopped watching and began to read Felix's book instead.

When turbulence began to shake the plane, I stood up and opened the overhead bin to stuff pillows around the mandolin case until the stewardess made me sit down. I closed my eyes and dozed off to be woken by the arrival of the meal cart. I read Felix's book until we landed at Heathrow, where we were given the London papers. An elderly American couple took the seats next mine, from Salt Lake City but not Mormons, they told me before they were even buckled in. The husband talked with me the entire trip, growing quiet only as we began the descent to Ruzyně Airport.

When the plane banked I could see the northern outskirts of Prague. I felt as if I were seeing the land for the first time. I thought of Valentine and how he had lived for so long inside a dream that he had made for himself, and how through sheer force of desire he had tried to will his dream into becoming. And I wondered if I had been any different, or if I had been living inside my own dream, using my mandolin as a magic lamp, playing it so that a genie might emerge to enchant the air around me and make the real world vanish. How much, I wondered, did you have to want to break from the dream in order to wake at last.

The landing was bumpy. I had already decided to splurge for a taxi to Annet's apartment, where I would crash for a few nights until I could find something on my own. The pilot announced that we would have to sit on the tarmac for thirty minutes. At last the doors opened and we filed out. The customs agent pulled me aside, went through both suitcases, and made me take out the mandolin so that he could peer through the f-holes. I was half-pulling, half-dragging the suitcases along with the stragglers and airport employees, feeling exhausted and with my head throbbing, when I saw Marta.

She stood beside a cigarette stand, wearing the spring jacket that she had bought two years ago. She had already caught sight of me. A man carrying a tower of packages bumped into her as he passed, but she didn't move, only continued to look at me. I came up to her, put down my bags, and we kissed carefully.

"I see you are loaded down," she said. "The kids need some new things."

"I didn't expect to see you here."

"I know. But I wanted to come. Where are you going to stay?"

"Annet's. I'll start looking for a place tomorrow."

Her mouth trembled and she looked down. "I am trying to be strong," she said. "It's hard. If you want to come home ..."

"No, no. It's all right. Don't worry."

"Will you have dinner with us? I know the girls would like that."

"Sure, that would be nice. I can't wait to see them, that's for sure."

"They're here."

"You brought them? Really? So late?"

"They need to see you. Over there —"

She pointed to a coffee stand farther ahead. Maggie and Birdy were sitting at a little table with paper cups and straws in front of them. They weren't talking. I felt my heart beat fast. Maggie seemed to sense me looking at her because she turned her head. When she saw me, her face changed. She said something quickly to Birdy, who looked too and then they were out of their chairs and running down the hall. I got down and suddenly I could hardly see, but I opened my arms and waited for them.

Acknowledgements

MARC CÔTÉ AND I HAVE talked about working together for years, and at last we've done it. Many thanks for his keen editorial judgment. Bernard Kelly and Rebecca Comay both provided detailed responses that were immensely helpful. Thanks also to Bethany Gibson for her pithy remarks. And to Rebecca, again, for the days in Prague, and for every day.

On the music side, much gratitude to Andrew Collins for his brilliant mandolin playing and for his instruction, enthusiasm, and conversations about life and music. Thanks to him and his bandmates in the Foggy Hogtown Boys and Crazy Strings for so many hours of great bluegrass in Toronto. Also thanks to: my jamming friends, collectively known as the Hollers, for five years (and counting) of Wednesday night pickin'; Oliver Apitius, for showing me his mandolin-building workshop; Nashcamp in Cumberland Furnace, Tennessee; Mandolin Camp North in Groton, Massachusetts; the Tottenham Bluegrass Festival in Tottenham, Ontario; Rockygrass in Lyons, Colorado; the website mandolincafe.com; Timothy Josiah Morris Pertz for sending me his thesis, *The Jewgrass Boys: Bluegrass Music's Emergence in New York City's Washington Square*

ACKNOWLEDGEMENTS

Park 1946–1961. And to Rachel and Sophie and Emilio and Yoyo for putting up with all that "hick" music.

A final thank you to the Ontario Arts Council for providing financial assistance.